Singled Out

Single Dads of Dragonfly Lake

Amy Knupp

In memory of my dad, Richard Stumbo
1935-2024

He taught me the appreciation of a correctly placed comma and so much more.

Chapter One

Max

Sometimes life could sack a guy out of nowhere, leaving him stunned stupid, wondering what the hell had just hit him, trying to figure out how to get back on his feet.

Sometimes that sack was literal and sometimes figurative.

I'd experienced both.

The literal sacking had happened thirteen years ago and ended my short but promising NFL career. I'd gotten through that trying time eventually. Switched to a plan B.

The figurative knocked-on-my-ass incident had happened a little over a year ago, and most days I still felt dazed and stupid, as if I had no hope of ever being on solid ground again.

Instant parenthood could do that to a guy.

I had the men's room at the Marks Hotel to myself, thank God, because I needed to breathe.

I needed to get my mental shit together, paste on my public-Max smile, and get this night over with.

After washing my hands, I checked my phone one more time for a text from my mom.

Nothing.

Ty Bishop, the basketball coach and my colleague at the high school, burst through the door, interrupting my anxious thoughts.

"You ready for this, Dawson?" he asked, heading for the urinal.

"Hell no." I said it with a smile, a tone of brotherhood. Then I exited and headed down the hall toward the backstage fray.

In the past, I would've embraced an event like tonight's bachelor auction wholeheartedly. I knew what the people of my hometown of Dragonfly Lake, Tennessee, expected from me. They saw me as the smart, athletic, good-looking guy who could handle anything. The guy who'd suffered a devastating setback and come out unscathed. The guy who had it all.

Privately, I was none of that, but I'd usually done my best to play the role.

These days it was harder to hide private Max, with all his fears, doubts, and anxiety.

And now I was minutes away from having to walk up on a stage, stand under a spotlight, and wait for someone to bid on a date with me.

I'd have to stand there and smile, act like the fun-loving guy who had it all, while in reality, I was worried as hell about my little boy at home with a fever and a cough.

"Hey, Max."

I turned at the sound of my sister Dakota's voice, relieved it was someone I didn't need to fake it so hard for.

"Hey, shorty," I said as we side hugged. I pressed a kiss to the top of her head. "You going to buy yourself a date tonight?"

She made a *pfft* sound and waved away the idea. "As if. I've got better things to spend my cash on."

That worked for me. The fewer guys she dated, the fewer guys I had to give that stern, big-brother glare to keep them in check where my sister was concerned. She turned plenty of heads on a normal day. Tonight she was dolled up in a too-short black dress, crazy-high heels that made her closer to my six-one height, and enough smoky eye makeup to choke a horse. Her blond locks were up in an intricate style.

Ignoring the opportunity to give her some low-key hell, I asked, "Have you talked to Mom?"

Her expression turned sympathetic. "I'm sure Daniel's okay, Max. He has a cold. Mom knows what she's doing. She'd call you if he got worse."

The rational side of me knew that was true, but the worried father side of me was having a hard time embracing it.

"Do you know how many kids have had colds before?" she asked, her tone dripping with smart-ass.

"Do you know how many of *my* kids have had colds before?"

"I guess that would depend on how many secret babies you have running around in the world."

Normally that would make me laugh, but tonight it caused a shudder. I held in a growl, closed my eyes, and shook my head.

"Max." My sister's tone was suddenly serious. "This is supposed to be a fun night out for you, but look at you. You're a stressy mess. Daniel's in good hands."

I nodded, knowing she was right and wishing I could snap out of it. "Yeah. Okay. I need to get in there. I think I hear them rounding up the cattle."

"I think bulls is a better word here," Dakota

said. "Work on that smile so you aren't the lowest bid of the evening."

Hell. I hadn't had a chance to worry about superficial shit like that. "You think I'll go for less than Sergio Vega?"

My sister scoffed. "Shut up, golden boy." With a roll of her eyes and a smile, she pivoted and clacked off in her ridiculous heels toward the ladies' room.

Nothing left to do but get in there and get this over with so I could go check on my boy.

I smoothed the front of my button-down shirt and braced myself as I opened the door to the noisy holding area backstage.

"Hell, I was hoping you'd gone home," Kemp Essex said, clapping me on the back as I joined him, Cade McNamara, and Anton White in one of the multiple clusters of men decked out in a mix of dressy-casual and casual clothes. "Thin out the competition."

"Isn't it supposed to be more bachelors, more money for the cause?" I asked dryly.

"Sure, but I'd prefer to get the highest bid," Kemp said.

"Wouldn't happen even if Max stepped aside," Cade said.

"Sure wouldn't be you either, bro," Anton said.

"I guess we'll see what the ladies think," Kemp

said as Talia Latimer, one of the organizers, whistled for everyone's attention.

She went over the same info she'd given us earlier, about the cause, about what we were supposed to do when it was our turn on stage, what was appropriate and what was inappropriate. Stuff she shouldn't have to go over, but with this group, it was a good idea.

The cause was one I was happy to support—art in education. As a math teacher myself, I valued education to the highest degree. Our small town had suffered multiple cuts to non-STEM programs like art and music.

What was more, I couldn't help but wonder if people like my sister would be more productive and successful in life if our high school had an art department. Dakota had drifted through school, uninterested in all of it. As a full-time bartender at Henry's, she did okay, but I couldn't help but wonder when she'd start wanting more for herself. For fun, Dakota created hand-thrown mugs and other ceramics. She turned out some impressive pieces. If she'd found her art interest sooner, where would she be today?

Most importantly, though, I was a parent now. I had a kid who would grow up in the Dragonfly Lake school system. I sure as hell wanted him to have every opportunity in the world to explore his interests and become a well-rounded human.

At the thought of Daniel, that general pang of worry twisted my gut, so I pulled out my phone. Nothing from my mom. Fuck it. I typed in a message.

Her reply came right away.

> Danny's sleeping soundly. Cough medicine is doing its job, and his fever went down with Tylenol. I've got this, Max. Relax and have fun! That's an order.

Easier said than done.

I thanked my mom yet again for being there for my boy, then put my phone away and tried to do what she'd suggested.

As Talia sent the first of the twenty bachelors, Elijah Watt, toward the stage like a prime piece of twenty-two-year-old meat, I wasn't really feeling it, but I was determined not to let it show. Time for public Max to do his thing.

Chapter Two

Harper

I stepped away from the bar with my vodka cranberry and took in the room at large.

The ballroom of the Marks Hotel was decorated elegantly with colored fairy lights against a midnight blue backdrop, silver accents that picked up the array of colors, and centerpieces made of unique-shaped bottles with more fairy lights inside, arranged on a splash of silver confetti. The sum of it all illustrated the "Art Lights Up Lives" theme perfectly.

The townspeople of Dragonfly Lake had embraced the event and sold out the three-hundred-ticket fundraiser to benefit arts in education.

They'd shown up in summery cocktail dresses for the women, a wide range of attire for the men, and good spirits. I'd finally settled on a short sequined fuchsia dress with a halter-style neckline, because I couldn't wear a boring black dress to an event celebrating color.

Naomi would love the hell out of this. It was exactly as she would have wanted it.

I felt the familiar, raw pang of grief in my chest at the thought of her. Instead of shoving it down deep as I often did, I took a full breath, picturing my friend and mentor with her beautiful smile. Just for a second.

"Cheers, Naomi," I whispered, the corners of my eyes damp. I lifted my cocktail slightly, then took a drink.

I made my way back to my table, dabbing at my eyes, glad for the low light, smiling at people as I walked by.

Dessert had been served while I was in line for my drink, I noticed as I retook my seat next to Loretta Lawson, the town's sixty-something gossip queen with a mostly good heart.

"Harper, hon, I didn't know if you wanted dessert, so I just told them to give you some. Dakota too," Loretta said. "If you don't want it, I'll sacrifice my figure and eat it for you."

Laughing, I eyed the picture-perfect slice of

lemon meringue pie. It was Naomi's favorite, as I'd told the event planners when they'd asked. "I prefer to drink my dessert tonight," I told Loretta, pushing the plate toward her.

"Bless your heart," she said. "That cocktail looks almost as pretty as pie." Her smile faded a little as she looked closer at my eyes, probably still damp. "You were close to Naomi Finley, weren't you, dear?"

Ahh, shit. The sympathy in her voice caught me off guard, and my throat clogged with emotion. I nodded and took a drink to wash it away. "Yeah," I managed with a faint smile as I set my glass down. I dabbed at the corner of one eye again and said, "Dammit," then laughed. "Everything about tonight is so Naomi. It's as if she's still here."

She had, in fact, been in on the initial planning. The fundraiser was her baby, her idea. Her life motto had been "Art for everyone," and she'd been an untiring advocate particularly in funding art programs in schools throughout the state of Tennessee.

"Are you planning to bid on a bachelor?" Loretta asked as she dug into the second slice of lemon meringue.

"That's what I want to know," Dakota Dawson, who I'd come with, said as she sat to my left. She and I had become close over the past year as we both spent a lot of time at Naomi's studio.

"You never know," I said, not trying to be mysterious. I just hadn't made up my mind yet.

Though I was a server at the Dragonfly Diner and perpetually low on funds, tonight I had money to spend. Dakota was the only one who knew my secret. Naomi had left me in charge of appropriating what she called her petty cash fund, money she'd set aside expressly to donate to her causes. I knew she wouldn't care if I used it for the silent auction or to bid on a bachelor or just made a lump donation. She only insisted it went to the cause tonight. I had just over five K to donate.

As plates were cleared and two organizers appeared on the stage, gearing up to start the bachelor auction, Dakota leaned closer. "For real though, are you going to buy some man meat?"

"When you put it like that, how can I resist?" I grinned and sipped more pink vodka.

Loretta had turned back to discuss the meringue in great detail with Nancy Solon, her fellow Dragonfly Diamond, enabling me to confess to Dakota without being heard.

"Nothing at the silent auction really spoke to me."

"Not the getaway weekend here at the Marks?" Dakota asked.

I shook my head.

Her grin widened. "Man meat it is then." She

leaned over so she was right next to my ear. "I think you should bid on Max."

"Your brother?" I asked in surprise.

"I dare you."

My brows went up as I considered the idea. Max Dawson was...well, good-looking, loved by everyone, and about ten years older than me.

"He works for my dad," I pointed out.

"Yeah, so?" Dakota's smile was full of trouble, and that did nothing to turn me away. If anything, it egged me on. I'd never been one to shy away from trouble. "He'd be good arm candy for the gala."

"A handsome-as-hell former-NFL player as my date would fit the bill, yes." I frowned. "Why do you want me to bid on your brother though?" I asked, suspicious.

"Someone's going to win him. Might as well be you," she said flippantly.

"Sure, okay. What's the real reason?"

Her smile disappeared, and she eyed the other eight people at the table. No one was paying attention to us. The four older ladies—Loretta, Nancy, Dotty, and Darlene—were wrapped up in dessert talk, something about the proper amount of butter. On the other side of Dakota, two of the Henry brothers, Seth and Knox, and their better halves were also deep in discussion.

Dakota leaned closer. "I'm worried about him.

He doesn't have fun anymore. Doesn't go out. Hasn't dated since he took Danny in. I know becoming a single dad is a huge thing, but he's not himself."

"What do you think *I* could do about that?" I asked in disbelief.

"You'll show him a good time," she said matter-of-factly.

"Well, yes. I'd like to think so. How much of a good time do you want him to have?" Innuendo was heavy in my voice, and I couldn't help grinning.

"As much of a good time as you want," she said, "but if it's *too* good, I *don't* want to hear about it."

I didn't allow myself to think about too good of a time with Coach Dawson. I definitely didn't need to tangle with him that much, but I was open to bidding on him. Maybe.

"You said it yourself. He's going to get bids no matter what. Why do you want me to steal him away from some poor girl who's probably pining away for him?"

"That's just it. Half the women here"—she gestured to the room—"are pining away for him. They want to *land* him, ensnare him, marry him. That's the last thing my struggling brother needs. You'll get him out of the house for a night of fun, but you won't want more than that."

"Truth."

"You're the last person looking to settle down."

"Also true."

"So you're perfect."

I considered the idea. Showing up to the art foundation's gala in Nashville with a former-NFL player would outshine being the mourning girl accepting an award in her dead friend's stead.

"Good evening, ladies and gentlemen." Mayor Constantine's voice boomed through the speakers. "Welcome to the pinnacle of tonight's event—the bachelor auction."

The crowd responded noisily, telling me this was going to get lively.

"You all know the proceeds of the evening will go to a very important cause. This town hasn't had a proper art department at the high school level since our own Berwin Jepp was the starting quarterback."

Collective laughter rang out because Berwin was nearing sixty.

"He took the team to state his senior year," the mayor continued, "but regardless, I think we can all agree that's too long for our education system to be lacking in any way. We need art in our schools. Creativity is as vital as the ability to calculate what MC squared equals. So I'm asking you all to open your wallets as wide as you can. Get yourself a date with a Dragonfly Lake dreamboat."

There was laughter again, though judging by the names and profiles listed on the town app, the Tattler, he wasn't exaggerating about dreamboats. The guys they'd recruited to go on the auction block were some of the best-looking ones our town had to offer.

While the mayor explained how the auction would work, Dakota sought eye contact with me.

"Well?" she asked.

"Maybe," I said noncommittally. I'd never been accused of being a planner. I'd do what I did with everything—I'd go with my gut.

First up was Elijah Watt. Dakota worked with him. He was good-looking but too young, barely of legal drinking age. Taking him to a black-tie event in the city...no.

Next up was Anton White. Midthirties. Decent looking. I wasn't feeling him either.

Sergio Vega, age seventy-two and proud of it, was third. Our table exploded in cheers when Nancy timidly bid on him and won him for six hundred fifty dollars. One of the Diamonds, the card-playing mostly over-sixty ladies' group, she was adorable. She even blushed when her victory was announced.

I watched, unmoved to bid, as Luke Durham, Pablo Benitez, and Gideon Webb, who graduated the same year as me, were offered up. Luke, a quiet, muscular farmer, got the highest bid yet at nineteen hundred.

Jake Bergman, whose family had owned the hardware store for longer than I'd been alive, was up next. Not gonna lie, he looked good, but I wasn't sure he was black-tie material. Plus he was forty. It turned out it was just as well I wasn't interested, as Darlene Lionetti, who was twenty years his senior at least, drove the bid up to nearly thirteen hundred to win him, much to the audience's delight. Her fellow Diamonds hooted and hollered as if she'd made the score of a lifetime, and as the longtime Country Market clerk, maybe she had. I would've hated to rain on her parade.

A while later, I'd just finished my drink and was thinking about another one when Mayor Constantine introduced Max, the younger of the two Dawson brothers and, in my opinion, the better looking. Both were in the auction, and either would be a catch if you were looking for that sort of thing. I stayed put, gauging the room. Collective interest was tangible in the air.

There was no debating Dakota's brother was delectable. With dark hair that was a little shaggy, an olive complexion, and a warm smile that took his face from handsome to enticing, he was celebrity-level hot. He had the lean, muscled body of a quarterback even though a lot of time had passed since he'd played pro football. He somehow oozed confidence and charm without crossing into egotistical. My eyes were locked on him.

Bidding had started at fifty dollars for most of the guys, but for Max, Mayor Constantine went straight to three hundred. Within thirty seconds, it was up to a grand, and I had yet to jump in. Isabel Ballantine, Rissa Raymond, and Lucy Whitmore were raising each other by fifty dollars at a time.

I felt Dakota eyeing me from the side, so I looked at her, keeping my expression blank. She widened her eyes, as if to say, *Do it!* I shrugged.

I turned back to watch Max on the stage. Most people's eyes were ping-ponging between the three women bidding on him instead of the stage. From where I sat, though, I could see his chest rise with a slow, deep breath, and he subtly tapped the side of his leg as if he was uncomfortable and couldn't wait for this to be over.

Lucy dropped out when the bidding reached fifteen hundred. I glanced around, wondering if anyone else was playing my game.

"I've got sixteen hundred dollars to spend an evening with Coach," Mayor Constantine said. "Can I get seventeen?"

Rissa raised her paddle, and Max made something between a grimace and a smile. Possibly a grimace covered by a smile.

As the mayor continued trying to get fifty extra bucks at a time, I glanced at Dakota, who sent me a questioning look.

I tried to stifle my smile. Then I raised my paddle and called out, "Five thousand dollars."

Chapter Three

Max

I never saw Harper Ellison coming.

Not her bid. Not her interest. Not the amount she'd spent for an evening with me.

Isabel hadn't surprised me. She'd made no secret in the past about her interest, nor had Rissa. But Harper was out of nowhere.

As I walked off the stage, more than a little stunned at the preemptive bid, and made my way to the cocktail area where we were supposed to mingle with the crowd and connect with our auction winners, my mind spun.

Harper was attractive with her dark, glossy hair, big brown eyes, and engaging smile. But I'd never looked at her as a woman, as a potential date, for a couple of reasons. One, she was young. A year younger than my baby sister, if I wasn't mistaken, which put her around ten years my junior. I wasn't a cradle robber.

More importantly, she was my boss's daughter.

Bob Ellison had been the principal at Dragonfly Lake High School since I was a student myself. He'd hired me eleven years ago.

I was sure Harper was an interesting girl, but I wasn't willing to endanger my job. I genuinely liked both teaching math and coaching football. If I lost this job, it wasn't like I could get another position doing the same thing on the other side of town. Dragonfly Lake High was it unless I wanted to move, and I didn't. This was the town where I wanted to raise Danny, the town where my roots dug deep.

"If it isn't the auction king himself," Chance Cordova called out as soon as I hit the cocktail room. He was standing with Luke and Knox. All three of them were in the single dads' group, even though Knox was no longer single. We gave him a hard time for opting out of the *single* part, but we kept him around in spite of his engagement to Quincy. "Big news travels fast."

"What's up, peasants?" I joked as I joined their huddle. When a server hovered nearby with a tray of waters, I grabbed one. I intended to get out of here at the first opportunity so I could check on my son.

"Seems like you got lucky with your bidder," Knox said.

"I guess that depends on your definition of lucky." *Lucky* was not the word I'd use, but I'd cut him some slack. He was a relative newcomer. Maybe he didn't immediately understand my conundrum. "Aren't you supposed to be in there with your better half?"

"Quincy wanted me to call my father to check on June Bug. He and Faye are keeping her tonight. She's probably having the time of her life with Mimi and Papa. So you're not happy about your over-the-top bid?" Knox asked.

"The bid itself is great," I said. And a date with Harper would probably be fun for a lot of guys, just not me.

"Harper *is* the gender you tend to be attracted to," Luke said. "That's a good start."

"Hey, Linc's a decent guy," Chance said.

My brows went up. "Linc? As in Switzer?"

"That's the one," Luke said. "He's okay. I just hope he isn't expecting a good-night kiss."

"Open that mind," Chance said. "Maybe the right person for you isn't what you thought."

"Who got you, Chance?" I asked.

Knox covered his mouth as if to hide a grin, but he didn't quite do it fast enough.

"Helen Wainsworth," Chance said. His tone dared me to comment, but I had no intention of saying anything about Helen. She might be close to eighty years old, but she was a sweet, spirited lady who attended every home football game. I was a big fan of hers. "Eighteen hundred dollars."

"I wonder where she wants you to take her," Luke said, sounding genuinely curious.

"I guess we'll find out soon enough." Chance glanced toward the doors to the ballroom, where the auction was still going on. "Maybe we'll hit the season opener together."

"Be sure to come say hello," I teased.

"So Harper Ellison," Knox said to me. "I don't really know her, but she seems age-appropriate and attractive."

I laughed. "Says the guy who's marrying someone a decade and a half younger than him."

"Quincy's only fourteen years younger," he said, grinning that damn grin he always got when he talked about his nanny turned fiancée.

"Harper's my boss's daughter," I told Knox, because the others already knew.

Anyone who'd gone to Dragonfly Lake High in the past twenty years knew. Which, come to think of it, probably made dating challenging for Harper.

Bob Ellison was a personable guy, but that didn't mean messing with his daughter, whether you were a student at his school back when she was or one of his employees at any time, would be a good idea. I couldn't remember ever hearing about her having a long-term relationship. It had never mattered to me, but now I wondered.

"Ahh, dicey territory then," Knox said.

"Dicey's a good word for it." I glanced at my watch. "How many more do they have to go?" I gestured toward the ballroom as another round of applause sounded.

"There were only about five left after you, right?" Chance glanced around the room, full of stand-up cocktail tables. A few other people besides the prey, er, bachelors were already out here, mingling and drinking. The doors opened, and a cluster of four women came out, animatedly discussing one of the recent auctions. "Looks like it'll be soon."

At that moment, both sets of double doors opened, and people streamed out, noisily talking about the bachelors as well as the silent auction of goods donated by residents and businesses. The service staff stood up straighter and busied themselves taking orders for cocktails and distributing water.

Knox headed toward Quincy and his brother and Everly. Chance put on his charmer smile and went to meet Helen as she appeared in the doorway.

"I think I need one more drink," Luke said. "Can I get you one?"

I shook my head. I could relate to his uneasiness, but I didn't intend to be here long enough to finish one.

I watched for Harper Ellison, wanting to take care of our date details quickly so I could leave.

When I turned to look the other direction, though, instead of Harper, I came face-to-face with her father. There was nothing of his usual friendly openness on his face.

"Coach," he said.

"Good evening, sir."

"Do you have something to tell me about my daughter?"

I let out what I hoped was an innocent-sounding, reassuring chuckle. "No, sir. I'm as mystified as you by what happened."

He studied me for a few seconds. Took a swallow of his wine. "You don't have anything going on with her?"

"I don't really know your daughter personally. I was shocked by her bid."

"Where'd she get that kind of money?" he asked.

"I have no idea about that either."

He eyed me for another while. "My first thought was that you'd fronted her the money."

"You can't be serious," I said. There was no hiding that I was financially comfortable from my NFL days, but my boss sure as shit should know me better.

His shoulders lowered slightly, and his demeanor became more relaxed. "I don't suppose I am. It just doesn't make sense. But then a lot of things that girl does don't make sense. Her name's on every last gray hair on my head." His tone had lightened up a bit, conspiratorial instead of accusatory. "She's got some explaining to do."

I tended to agree, but I'd prefer to get a separate explanation. As much as I wasn't interested in dating my boss's daughter, I also didn't care to be lumped in with her father as an older guy. Although I was older, I wasn't old enough to be her father. I wasn't sure why that mattered, but it did. Maybe it was ego or maybe just that nobody wanted to feel old, particularly in the eyes of a beautiful woman.

I shoved those thoughts out of my head.

"I can assure you, Bob, your daughter will get nothing but respect from me," I said.

He met my gaze again, sized me up, nodded once. "I'll hold you to that, Max."

I held up a hand in surrender. "You can trust me, sir."

"I don't trust anyone with my daughter." He frowned. "I suppose someday I'll have to." He muttered it more to himself than me, then pierced me with his gaze again. "I'll see you Monday, Max."

"Have a good weekend, Bob."

I took a swallow of water, wishing it were something stronger as I again glanced around for Harper. I felt an arm come around me from behind.

"My brother, always the star of the show." Dakota stretched up and placed a loud kiss on my cheek. "You probably know my friend Harper. Wait, were you her teacher?" Scandal rang through her voice, and I couldn't quite tell if the question was sarcastic or real.

"No," I said solidly. Thank Christ.

My first students were now the same age as Quincy, Knox's fiancée. Fully adults, nearing thirty. And yet I hadn't and wouldn't date anyone who'd been a student in my classroom.

As Harper stepped up to us, I took in her appearance with a quick glance. Her magenta dress stood out among all the little black dresses, the sparkle of it seeming appropriate for her personality somehow. The hem ended high on her thighs, and the neckline showed off tanned, delicate shoulders. She wore heels nearly as tall as my sister's and accessorized with a thick silver bracelet with a large stone the color of her dress and silver rings on several fingers. The dress draped rather than fit her closely. I had the fleeting thought that I wanted a better view of her curves.

Or I would if she were someone else.

"Hi, Max." Harper's voice was melodious and confident.

"Harper." I extended my hand formally as my public-Max smile surfaced. "Thanks for bidding on me. You made me look good up there."

"Anytime. You would've gone for the highest amount even without me though."

"I'll let you two get acquainted without me," Dakota said. "Olivia and Emerson are waving at me. Take your time."

I knew Harper and Dakota had come together. I'd seen them sitting together for dinner. Harper was the type who drew attention even when you weren't specifically interested in her. She was the kind of woman who was hard *not* to notice.

"I've never gone out with one of my sister's friends," I said once we were alone. "Kind of forbidden territory."

She moved in closer, and I caught her feminine scent. It had a hint of spice to it, the opposite of light and floral, in an appealing way that, like the sparkle in her dress, fit her. A long strand of her hair fell onto my lapel, and I had to clench my fists against the urge to brush it back.

"Dakota dared me to bid on you," she confessed just above a whisper.

My mouth fell open as I let that sink in.

She hadn't dropped the biggest bid of the evening on me because of any desire to go out with me.

She'd been dared.

By my sister.

I couldn't decide whether I was more annoyed at my sister or relieved at Harper's motivation.

Or insulted that Harper *wasn't* actually interested in me.

Relieved. I was going with relieved. That meant I could relax during our night out and not worry about whether she was plotting to get me to the altar. As the small-town guy with a brief stint in the NFL, I'd had it happen before with women I barely knew. I hadn't been looking for marriage then, and I sure as hell wasn't now that I had a son to put all my time and energy into raising.

"That's a lot of money to spend on someone you're not interested in," I said.

"The money's a story for a different day," she said, backing off and putting more space between us now that she was speaking at a normal volume.

"Yeah, your dad has questions about that. Just to warn you."

"You talked to my dad?"

"He talked to me."

She shook her head, her mouth curving into a partial smile. "He's all bark. You know that, right?"

I wasn't sure that was true when it came to someone dating his daughter, but I wasn't going to date her.

"Did you have something in mind for our evening out?" I asked.

She made a face like she was worried I'd hate whatever she was planning.

"I do. Naomi Finley, who was responsible for this whole fundraiser, was my friend and mentor, so when the Arts in Education Foundation in Nashville decided to honor her with their Art Ambassador of the Year award, they asked me to accept on her behalf." She frowned. "I hope you don't have a game that conflicts."

"When is it?"

"Two weeks from today."

"I don't have a game," I confirmed. Saturdays were when my single dads' group got together, but I could miss that. "Season opens the night before."

"I could go alone but"—her gaze flickered downward for a barely noticeable instant—"it might be a little rough. I thought it'd be good to have a date."

"Sure," I said. "I'd be happy to go with you."

"It's black tie."

"I can do black tie." I'd have to dig my tux out of the back of my closet and hope it still fit.

We exchanged phone numbers. I found her easy to like, despite my current agitated state, which...

Hell.

I was less agitated about my son because I'd gotten distracted.

Harper had taken my mind off Danny for five minutes, made me forget my hurry to get home to him. And that was exactly why I hadn't dated for over a year.

It was a damn good thing we were only spending one simple evening together.

Chapter Four

Harper

Two days before the gala in Nashville, my head was threatening to be all kinds of a mess. I was doing whatever it took to ignore it.

I'd finished an early microwave dinner, and now I was alone in the studio, hand cutting glass sheets—a dark plum color—into small pieces to be used for mosaics or whatever else people wanted to use them for.

My hair was up, my safety glasses were in place, and I'd taped my fingers for protection as I used my nipper to break...*crack*...the hell...*crack*...out of the glass.

Crack.

It was therapeutic.

Painful, rhythmic, requiring just enough attention to keep my mind from going to difficult places.

I had a steady rhythm going and tears in my eyes.

Damn, I hoped someone, *anyone*, showed up for open-studio time soon.

I still lived in Naomi's house, as I had been for the past three years. It wasn't a long-term plan, but I wasn't good at long-term plans. I'd temporarily taken on keeping her studio open for all the people who needed a place to do their art. No one knew what would become of this place—or my living arrangements, for that matter—when and if Naomi's brother surfaced. I mostly tried not to think about it too much.

I'd met Naomi about four years ago. I'd seen an ad for a pottery class on the town's Tattler app, offered at a private studio on a small farmstead halfway between Dragonfly Lake and Runner. On a whim, the same way I did most things, I'd signed up. I'd come out of the class with my first lopsided, definitely one-of-a-kind mug.

After that, I'd taken Naomi's oil painting class, then cycled through her other offerings—metalworking, mosaics, watercolors, jewelry, woodworking. If she taught it, I'd taken it.

I approached art the way I approached life, much to my dad's annoyance—with the firm belief that variety was the spice of everything. I switched between the many mediums, unwilling to commit to just one.

Naomi and I had clicked during that first class in spite of our nine-year age difference. She'd been impossible not to like, exuding warmth and so much life. Her passion for art and her dedication to exposing the multitudes to it were awe-inspiring.

Within weeks, I'd felt as if we'd known each other for years. She'd been part older sister, part friend, part mentor, and then, when I'd been trying to find a way to move out of my dad's house, she'd invited me to move into hers, charging me less rent than I'd pay anywhere else in Dragonfly Lake.

I put the bucket of plum glass back on its shelf, grabbed the next few sheets of glass, which happened to be a turquoise-and-white swirl, and pulled out the appropriate bucket. Back at the worktable, I flexed my hand—it was going to be sore for days after this—scored the first sheet, then set about crack, crack, cracking away again.

Naomi always said cutting glass was the worst part of mosaics, but I didn't mind it at times like this, when I needed distraction and couldn't settle down enough to commit to a particular project.

I sniffled as I remembered my dear red-haired

friend bringing me more sheets and corresponding buckets when I got on a glass-breaking kick, saying the more I cut, the less she had to. Cutting glass was one of the only things I'd heard her complain about.

She'd been one of the good ones, for sure. One of the best.

She and her brother, Ian, had inherited this farm when her grandfather died a few years before I'd met her. Her brother, who I'd never met, worked for some international company and had zero interest in any of it, so Naomi had the run of the place. She'd never talked about Ian, and I'd suspected they weren't close. That had been confirmed with an exclamation point when she died. Even now, nearly two months later, he'd never returned their aunt's numerous phone calls about Naomi's death, the funeral, or their shared property.

I found myself in a shaky position, where just about every aspect of my life except my job as a server—my home, the studio where I spent my spare time, my closest friendships—depended on a man to whom it was getting harder and harder to give the benefit of the doubt. What possible reason could he have for not responding to such devastating news?

Since farming wasn't Naomi's thing—and the surrounding land had gradually been sold off over the years, leaving her with thirty acres that were no longer worked—she'd created the art mecca of her dreams.

In addition to classes and her frequent projects to bring art to underfunded schools around the state, she'd opened the studio as a shared maker space for anyone who needed one, offering daily rates and monthly memberships. Her mission in life had been to make art available to everyone. She'd managed to expose hundreds of kids to art, maybe thousands. That involvement with schools had earned her the recognition of the Arts in Education Foundation.

The thought had my gut tightening. Saturday would be a tough evening.

When a woman from the foundation had asked me to accept the award for Naomi, I'd said yes without thought, honored to have a part in this final, much-deserved recognition of my dear friend. Now reality was settling in. I'd have to speak on behalf of Naomi and in tribute to her, and that was no small task. The woman had suggested no more than one or two minutes, so I didn't need to write a long speech, but I definitely had to get my thoughts straight beforehand.

I still believed a date would be helpful so I wouldn't be flying solo, wouldn't be driving to and from by myself. Now that I'd had a few days to think about it, though, I wasn't sure Max had been my best idea. On some level, he rattled me, and I wasn't in the habit of letting men rattle me.

It was set though. I wasn't going to chicken out now.

"Hey, Harper."

I startled as Dakota came through the door behind me. I pushed the googles on top of my head and swiped at my cheeks again before turning around and forcing a smile. "Hey, you. I was wondering if you'd come out tonight."

"Here's me. I get to unload the kiln tonight."

"Ooh, I can't wait to see your pretties," I said.

As we walked to the kiln room, she frowned. "You okay?"

I sniffled one more time. "I'm good. You got here just in time to save me from my thoughts."

Dakota made a face. "Those can be nasty. I can see why you're breaking glass."

"Let's unload your masterpieces," I said, ecstatic to have a distraction. There was always an element of surprise when we unloaded the kiln. We never knew what the heat would do to each type of glaze and each piece of pottery.

She opened the kiln, which had been cooling for a couple of days now, and began taking the pieces out and setting them on the worktable.

"Beautiful. I love the way the colors bleed into each other," I said.

"They came out even better than I hoped. Want one?"

"Maybe I'll wait till you put them on your online store, and I'll buy one."

She grinned. "You know how much I suck at getting stuff online."

"I was trying to give you incentive. People like to pay you for your work. You should quit giving everything as gifts. And yes, I'm saying that as someone lucky enough to get those gifts."

"And someone who gifts her own art more than sells it."

"You got me there," I said, grinning.

"Maybe someday I'll get better about selling it. It's a lot."

"It's scary," I acknowledged.

I'd had people say the same to me about my creations. I liked the idea of making money on my artwork, but the reality was harder—the organization required, the business side, the commitment... None of these were my strong points. I was skilled at creating in different mediums, combining colors, adding whimsy.

"Hey, pretty girls." Shawna Jenkins peeked in from the main room, her dark hair pulled up on her head, her art bag on her shoulder. "What's going on?"

"We're admiring Dakota's new pretties."

"Oooh," Shawna said as she reached the table. "Those are gorgeous. Put me down for one of these blue-and-white ones. I'll pay you good money."

I laughed, and Dakota put on an exasperated act, though she was smiling. "I hear you girls."

"I was just saying she needed to sell more, gift less," I explained.

"For real. You've got your shop online. Why not use it? And you." She peered at me. "We can set you up a store."

I made a sound of overwhelm, shook my head, and said, "Maybe. Eventually. What are you working on tonight?"

My question worked exactly like the distraction I hoped it would. "I took a picture of the lake at sunset the other day. It was spellbinding."

"So you're going to paint it," I said.

"Damn right I am."

She showed us the photos. The trees and the hills were in silhouette. The sky was a vibrant orange swirled with the dusky purple of the clouds, and it made the water look like lava.

"I can't wait to see what you do with that," I said.

"It's gorgeous," Dakota said. "I was working at Henry's that night and caught a glimpse of the colors from the bar."

After a peek inside the kiln at the rest of Dakota's work, I went with Shawna to the main room. Shawna set her supplies down next to her favorite easel. I went back to my glass mess as she mixed colors on her palette.

We worked without talking for a while, me making racket with my glass cracking and Shawna deep in concentration. Piper Elliott, who owned Oopsie Daisies, came in to work on the wooden signs she sold in her shop.

There were about thirty studio regulars, all ages, both men and women. Tonight's group was smaller than usual, but the August weather today was a treat, a little cooler than our usual swelter, so people were probably taking advantage of that. I was just relieved to have company. These girls who'd shown up happened to be the ones I was closest to.

After another hour or so of cracking glass, my hand was screaming, so I put those supplies away and pulled out my sketch pad. There was a piece of polished jade in my stone collection that was begging to be turned into a ring. I sketched some setting ideas.

"You're a painting machine tonight," I said to Piper. I'd situated myself between her and Shawna. Dakota had come back in and was unwrapping earlier pieces that had been drying.

"I'm working on my fall inventory," Piper said.

"People will be all about everything fall in another two or three weeks. I want to be ready."

"You're so smart," I said, meaning it.

Piper laughed. "I don't know about that. I learned the hard way last year when I didn't have enough fall merchandise ready. I could've sold so much more."

"We were talking earlier about making money off our art," Dakota said. "How did you get started?"

"I borrowed from a bank. Still paying that off, but I'm making progress. Variety helps. Flowers bring people in initially, but I'm getting traffic for all kinds of decor."

"Your signs are popular," Shawna said. "I see them all over."

"They're easy enough to make." Piper pointed her paintbrush at her current project, which read "Sweater weather" in a scripty, swoopy font. "I don't get to come out here often enough because of all the business stuff, but when I do, I like to crank out a bunch."

"I'd noticed we hadn't seen you for a while. Not since Naomi died."

"Yeah." Piper looked thoughtful for a second. "It's weird, isn't it? Without her here? Maybe you're more used to it though."

"It's definitely weird," I said.

"You're doing awesome with everything, Harper," Shawna said, "but I hate that she's not here."

I blew out a breath. "Me too, sister."

Dakota wiped her eyes. "Dammit, y'all."

We all laughed, which helped to lighten the moment.

"Have you heard anything lately? From the brother or the aunt?" Shawna asked, also swiping at her eyes with her arm.

"Not a word," I said. "Last time I spoke to Sharon was two or three weeks ago. Her advice was to keep on keeping on here. She said if I didn't want to 'mess with' the studio, I didn't have to. But I told her again I love it as much as Naomi did, and so many people rely on it. I'm fine opening it whenever I can."

Sharon Finley was Naomi and Ian's only living relative. When Naomi had died, Sharon had flown in from Oregon and taken care of funeral arrangements.

"I can't even with her brother," Dakota said. "He has to be a real shithead."

"That's all I can guess."

I didn't expect him to reach out to me—he likely wasn't aware Naomi had a roommate—but the old house did have a landline because reception out here in the country was crappy on a good day. Naomi had insisted on keeping it in case of an emergency in the maker space—with the various saws and the kiln and other dangerous equipment, anything could happen. It was ironic that a non-life-threatening injury had been what had ultimately taken Naomi's life.

"Are you still living here in the house?" Shawna asked.

"Yeah. I know I should try harder to find something."

"You should. You don't want to be caught by surprise if this guy suddenly puts the house on the market from afar," Shawna said.

"I've had that thought," I said. "I know you're right. It'll be tough to find something in my budget. Naomi's house is paid for, so she didn't charge me a lot."

"Roommates," Piper said.

If I was honest, I hadn't put very much thought into moving yet. I'd let myself slip into denial because of the unknown factor of Naomi's brother, but that was being stupid. All it took was for someone to say it out loud.

"Dakota, are you tired of living at home?" I said, keeping my voice light, noncommittal.

"Every single day," she said, her gaze focused on her work. She looked up at me. "How much would rent be?"

"It depends. If you're interested, I could look

for a place." The more I thought about it, the more I liked the idea. I could totally live with Dakota. I'd never considered it before because I'd not needed a roommate or a place to live for three years.

"I'm open to it. My mom leaves me alone, and I have the whole basement to myself, but it's probably past time to get a place of my own."

"You think?" Shawna teased.

"She hasn't given me any reason to get out," Dakota said. "I think she likes having me there. But I'm twenty-seven."

"Time to jump, my friend," Piper said.

"I know you're right." Dakota became animated. "This could be fun."

"I'll start looking on Monday, once I get this gala out of the way."

"The gala," Piper said. "Where Naomi's being recognized? Are the rumors true? Are you taking Coach Dawson?"

"All true," I said.

"And you're okay with that?" Shawna asked Dakota. "Ooh, your future roommate and your brother. If that's not a romance trope, I don't know what is."

Dakota laughed. "I'm fine with it. As far as I know, there's no romance." She eyed me hard, and I shook my head.

"No romance. Dakota made me do it," I insisted.

"I did dare her," Dakota admitted.

Shawna tilted her head. "What's the story there?"

Dakota shrugged. "My brother needs to get out for a night, away from town, a break from Danny."

"He's out every Friday night at games, isn't he?" Shawna asked.

"I mean not for work. A date."

"But no romance?" Piper asked.

"I don't think he's in the right place for that," Dakota said. "But he hasn't been on a date since our cousin died and Danny became his responsibility. Harper's safe. She doesn't want anything from him, unlike all the women who are itching to go out with him. None of them even try to get to know him. They just want to land Max Dawson, former-NFL player."

I could see how that might be true. I wondered if it bothered Max or if he even noticed it. I couldn't remember ever hearing about him being in a relationship. Maybe he was like me and didn't want one.

"You don't want to land Max Dawson?" Shawna asked me, grinning.

"I don't," I said. "I don't want to land anybody. I

was going to bid on someone to take to this gala anyway, just so I don't have to go alone because..."

"It might be hard," Piper said with an empathetic look.

"It might be hard," I repeated. Understatement.

"Sounds like a good arrangement then," Shawna said. "He gets out of the house. You don't have to go to the gala alone. And it's no big deal to either one of you."

"Exactly."

I didn't confess that I was nervous, and it wasn't just about speaking in front of a large group on behalf of Naomi.

Max was incredibly good-looking and had this engaging, likeable quality about him that made it easy to forget he wasn't still a star athlete. There were good reasons women went all a-flutter about him.

I wasn't blind, and when I thought too hard about Saturday night, I got butterflies in my gut. That alone told me it might be a bigger deal than I was admitting to anyone, including myself.

Chapter Five

Max

Over a year in, I still had no idea how single parents did it.

I put my dress shoes on and caught myself frowning. The last thing I wanted to do tonight was go to some fancy gala in Nashville with a girl ten years younger than me. A girl I barely knew, who was taking me because my sister dared her.

The guilt over leaving Danny for the second night in a row ate away at me as it did most Saturdays when the single dads got together. Friday night football games couldn't be helped. They were my job. And ultimately I could acknowledge the dads' nights were essential to my mental health—we were all dealing with a lot of the same issues. They were like a support group where we didn't have to talk.

Tonight? A date? To an event I had no interest in, with a near stranger I had no desire to get involved with?

"Bad decision, man," I said to my reflection as I straightened my bow tie. "Should've never agreed to the auction in the first place."

I had, so I would see it through, but damn, I hoped to be back home with my son long before midnight.

After a final glance in the mirror to make sure my tux looked okay, I headed to the kitchen.

"Woo, look at your dressed-up daddy, Danny," Dakota said.

"Dada," Daniel said around the messy little fingers in his mouth.

I walked to the high chair, bent over, and kissed his blond head, catching his messy hand before it hit my jacket.

"I need my hug, little guy," I said, my gut knotting like it always did when I left him.

Maybe it was ridiculous that I had separation anxiety worse than my eighteen-month-old son, but I did my best to hide it from him and the world. Better me than him, I always reminded myself.

Rationally I knew the likelihood was strong that

I'd be back home with him soon, and all would be well. But life had fucked with my ability to put logic over anxiety, particularly when it came to Danny.

"Here," Dakota said, handing me a damp paper towel to wipe off his hands. "He got *into* his dinner tonight."

As I cleaned Danny's fingers, I tried to figure out what was all over them. It didn't look like the chicken and green beans I'd prepared before my shower.

"What did he eat?" I asked my sister.

"Animal crackers," she said. "A camel and an elephant, right, bud?"

"Ephant." Danny gazed up at me with those irresistible, always curious blue eyes and a happy grin.

I tapped him on the nose affectionately, reining in my annoyance with my sister as I looked around for his purple toddler plate and spotted it—with minibites of chicken breast still on it—on the counter by the sink.

"Dakota," I bit out quietly, "you know he only gets sugar on special occasions."

"We decided Saturday night with Aunt Dakota is a special occasion."

"He didn't even finish his dinner."

"He ate all his green beans," my sister said. "Those got him extra credit."

"That's not how this works," I said. "Show me your other hand, Daniel."

On his own schedule, my son slowly held up his other cookie-sogged hand, and I had to grin in spite of my irritation with my sister.

"Dinner is a two-handed, full-contact sport, huh, bud?" I said as I scrubbed his fingers. Once he was clean, I removed his soiled bib and lifted him from the high chair. "Come here."

Danny stretched his arms out to me and puckered his lips to give me a kiss. Just like always, that got to me like nothing else on the planet could.

I kissed him, then squeezed him to me and gave him a growly hug, eliciting that giggle I loved.

"You be a good boy for Aunt Dakota," I said. "Or maybe I should be telling you to keep *her* in line."

"Funny man," my sister said.

"I'm not even joking. Bye-bye, Danny." I kissed my boy's forehead and set him on the floor.

"Bye!" He took off toward the toy box in the living room.

"Please get him to bed by eight." There was a pleading tone to my voice, completely justified with my free-spirited sister.

"We'll do our best."

"Dakota—"

"Max, relax," she said lightly. "It's so easy to get

you ruffled." She walked up to me and adjusted my bow tie even though I just had. "This isn't my first rodeo with this little cowboy. He'll be fine. Promise."

I growled but tried to relax a degree because I knew what she said was true. I was being a dick, and it had nothing to do with my sister and everything to do with the nervousness that had plagued me every day for more than a year.

The truth was, I wouldn't be able to function without my supportive family. My mom took care of Daniel full-time while I was at work. Dakota and Levi, my older brother, pitched in whenever I needed extra help. All of them loved Danny as much as I did and were dedicated to giving him a secure, love-filled childhood.

"I'm sorry," I said to my sister. "I know you're fully capable." I grabbed my keys and headed toward the garage.

"Max," Dakota said, following me. At the door, I stopped and turned. "Try to have fun tonight. Do you remember how to do that?"

I clenched my jaw, holding in a snappy reply. I was learning that nothing good came out of my mouth in the heart of an anxious moment.

"Harper is fun, friendly, funny," she continued. "I think you'll like her if you give her a chance."

"The last thing I need right now is to get involved with someone."

"Not involved," she insisted. "She doesn't want that either." My sister laughed. "Harper absolutely does *not* want to be tied down. She dates, but I don't know if she's ever had a lasting relationship."

At least we had one thing in common.

"It's safe to go out for one night with her, enjoy good food, have a drink or two, dance a little," my sister continued. "Unlike the football groupies, she won't be angling for more."

I didn't have groupies, but I knew what she meant. Women who were interested because I'd played football in a different lifetime and had the bank account to prove it. Maybe some locals who were interested in the spotlight that came with being the high school coach. They wanted a piece of what they thought public Max could provide and didn't bother even wondering who I really was, let alone getting to know me.

I'd never found someone worth the energy of letting them get to know me. I'd always figured it would happen someday eventually, but now that I was responsible for Daniel's well-being and happiness, I wasn't interested. I intended to give Daniel whatever he needed—time, energy, love. Security. It was the least I could do after fate had taken his parents. I loved that kid so much. I just wanted to give him every fucking thing.

The sound of Danny giggling as a ball clunked and rolled down his ball tower had me walking back to the family room. I bent over him and pressed a loud kiss to the top of his head, which made him laugh more. "Love you, Danny boy."

He giggled again and looked up at me.

Dakota waited by the door when I came back through. "Take some flowers," she said.

I stopped in my tracks.

Flowers?

Fuck.

In an attempt to not let on I was so rusty at dating that flowers hadn't crossed my mind, I continued to the door. "Got it handled. Text me if you need anything."

"I won't need anything," she said. "Have *fun*, you grump."

I ignored the insult and said, "Thanks for staying with Danny. See you when I get home."

I got into my SUV, unlocked my phone, and put Harper's address into the map app. I hoped like hell Oopsie Daisies was still open, because my sister was right. Flowers were in order.

As I turned onto Main, I caught a glimpse of Esmerelda the llama making her way toward the back of the shops on this side of the square. To the bakery. I couldn't help grinning at the sight of my friend Ben's pet llama in spite of my alleged—okay, it was a valid accusation—grumpiness.

I could already hear Ben's voice in my head, cussing about the animal. He acted like she was a pain in the ass, and really, she was because she kept escaping her enclosure and heading toward the bakery. Ben was the town veterinarian and loved both his llamas though.

Without pulling over, I called Ben.

"I know," he said instead of a greeting. "Fucking llama. I'm on my way."

"Good luck," I told him. "I have plans; otherwise I'd help you catch her."

"You have a good time with your boss's daughter," he deadpanned, then hung up.

Others would help him. There were plenty of people around at this hour to assist with getting the llama into the van and driving her home. That's what you got for taking in llamas, I thought.

Oopsie Daisies was still open. I parked behind the hardware store, then hurried one block over to the flower shop.

"Hello, Coach Dawson."

"Piper, how you doing?"

"I'm fine. I bet you need flowers for Harper."

Christ. Zero secrets in this town. There was an

upside to that though. "Do you know what she likes?"

"She loves bright colors. You can't go wrong." My former student walked over to the cooler of pre-made arrangements and took out one with large flowers in a range of pinks, from bright to pale. "How about these dahlias?"

"Perfect." I met her at the counter and held out my card. "I appreciate your help. And that you're still open."

"We get our share of people going on dates on Saturdays," Piper said. She wrapped the flowers in a damp cloth, then in kraft paper.

"Nice. Thanks, Piper."

"Have fun tonight, Coach."

"You do the same," public Max said.

Private Max was thinking the odds of tonight being fun were not in my favor.

I hurried to the car, set the bouquet on the seat, then started the map app again. I hadn't realized how far off the beaten path Harper lived and hadn't left myself enough time.

Flying over the country roads, I arrived two minutes after I'd told her I would pick her up. The driveway was long and winding and led to a two-story yellow farmhouse with a big front porch and outbuildings surrounding it. One had a mural that spanned the entire side and a sign that said The Art

Community.

I'd heard about Naomi's studio space, but I'd never been out here. The land was lush and green with lots of trees and flower beds. I made my way from the gravel driveway to the front door.

After ringing the doorbell, I turned to gawk at the porch, full of flowers in whiskey barrels and hanging from crooks. I turned around at the sound of the door opening. Whatever I was prepared to say fell right out of my brain at the sight of Harper.

"Hi, Max," she said, but I barely heard her.

She was dressed in a deep purple asymmetrical gown with a wide strap over one shoulder. My eyes were drawn to the opposite side of the dress, which consisted of cutouts from neckline to hip, with three silver straps holding the fabric together. Her lightly tanned skin was exposed more than covered on that side, and damn, did she make one hell of a vision.

"Are those for me?" she asked, nodding toward the bouquet.

I swung my gaze to her face. "Um..."

I'd never seen this Harper before. Her hair was piled on her head in tousled but controlled waves. Multiple strands hung to her bare shoulders, framing her gorgeous face. Her lips were an understated pink, drawing my attention with their subtle color and sheen.

"Max?"

Fuck, I was an idiot. "Yes. Hello. Sorry. These are for you," I stuttered out.

"They're beautiful. Thank you."

"You're welcome," I said, straightening and getting my shit together just slightly. "You look incredible."

She let out a laugh that sounded nervous around the edges, not like the bold girl who'd bid five big ones for me to go with her tonight. "Thanks. Let me put these in water and then we can go."

"Good idea."

Yep, I was still in half-idiot mode. I stepped inside and waited in the small entry, working to regain my composure, while she went into the kitchen.

I told myself again that tonight was no big deal, but with Harper looking irresistible, with my mind fixating on those lips and the soft-looking skin revealed by that dress...

I swallowed hard, my mouth suddenly dry.

Tonight was going to be an entirely different kind of tricky than I'd expected.

Chapter Six

Harper

Max Dawson in a tuxedo could throw a girl off her game on a good night.

This wasn't a good night, but I was extra determined not to succumb to the swirl of emotions threatening to swoop in at any moment. Distraction was my friend.

Once I'd set the beautiful flowers from Piper's store in their vase on the table, I picked up my evening clutch and rejoined Max. When he met my gaze and smiled, I stopped breathing for a few seconds as I closed the space between us. He held out his arm, and I looped my hand around it, lightly grasping just above his elbow.

The fabric of his tux was smooth beneath my fingers, and I deduced two things. One, this wasn't a rental. Two, it was high quality. Though he didn't flaunt it, Max had money. I knew where he lived; everyone did.

Back when he'd retired from the NFL because of his injury, he'd had a modest home built for his mom and snapped up a prime lakefront lot for himself. His custom-built home wasn't a mansion. From the street, it appeared to be a little prettier and bigger than the average Dragonfly Lake home, but there was nothing about it that screamed former-NFL millionaire. From what little I knew of him personally, that understatedness fit. But there was no question he'd dropped an above-average sum of money on it, probably in cash.

He walked me to the passenger door of his high-end SUV.

"Nice wheels," I said. "I like the way the black sparkles."

"Piper said you like bright colors."

"True. My car is teal. But you get extra points for sparkles."

He opened the door and helped me up into the vehicle with a large hand at my elbow. A quarterback's hand. I might not be wild about the sport, but I could see the appeal in the athlete.

While he walked around to the driver's side, I

closed my eyes and coached myself to ignore the way he looked and—dammit—the way he smelled.

He's Dakota's brother, not some Hollywood star. Just a guy who probably leaves the toilet seat up.

"It's at the Wentworth?" he asked as he slid in. He opened his map app on the dash display.

"Right. It should take us an hour tops, unless we run into traffic."

He typed in the hotel, and we were on our way.

"I heard your team won last night," I said.

"We did, by a hair. Could've gone either way."

"Must've been some decent coaching." I grinned at his handsome profile, and he flicked his gaze at me for a second before returning it to the road.

"That or a defensive line that dug deep and kept the other team from scoring last minute."

"I wonder who inspired them to dig deep," I teased.

"You didn't go to the game?"

"Will you kick me out of the car if I admit I'm not a huge fan?"

He surprised me by laughing. "Not at all. It's refreshing."

That was an interesting response. "I went to games when I was in school, but it was for the social aspect. I don't understand the rules, and I don't like to sit still for that long, particularly once it gets cold."

"If you ever want to understand the rules, I know a guy."

"I'll keep that in mind," I said. He was easier to talk to than I'd expected. Five minutes in and I could tell he was humble and had a good sense of humor. "Everybody knows your football history, but what I'm dying to know is, why math?"

He looked surprised. "I don't think I've ever had a date ask me about math."

"Did you choose to teach math or get stuck with it?" I asked.

"I didn't get stuck with it. I've always loved math."

I raised my brows at this bizarre and too-handsome creature.

"I can tell by your face you don't love math," he said.

"I don't love math. I don't know many who do."

"Math is...neat. It has right answers."

"The problem is finding them," I joked.

"But you *can* find them, and then you can prove them, unlike, say, an analysis of literature."

"I'm with you on that one. I always thought it was presumptuous and pointless to try to figure out what the author meant to say on a deeper level."

"Because who ever knows," Max said.

"Exactly. What's wrong with just enjoying a story because of the plot or the characters?"

"So if you didn't like math and weren't a fan of literature, what classes did you like back in the day?"

"That's such a teacher question."

"It's a getting-to-know-you question."

"You won't like my answer. I didn't like any subject. I didn't like school. Much to my dad's horror, I wasn't a good student."

"We can't all be good at school," he said, surprising me. Again. "That must've caused some friction between you two?"

"We get along. He takes me to dinner every few weeks. I stop by the house to visit. But he doesn't understand me, and I'm pretty sure he hates that I'm a server at the diner."

"He isn't supportive?"

"He comes in and sits in my section. Leaves me bigger-than-average tips. But it drives him crazy that I haven't chosen a 'suitable path' for my life."

"Working at the diner can be a path, right?"

I studied him from the side, looking for a sign of insincerity, because that was not what most teachers would say, at least not in my dad's presence. Max appeared to mean it. What was more, I saw no judgment in his expression.

"It could be, yes," I answered, more intrigued by this man than I wanted to be.

"But?"

"It's not mine. I don't have a path. I don't want a path. The very word itself is limiting, you know?"

"What do you mean?" he asked, and his tone sounded as if he genuinely wanted to understand, not like he was challenging me.

"Take my older sister, for example. She went to school for a thousand years to become a lawyer. But what if she ends up hating that job?"

"Does she?"

"Not that she's admitted to me, but admitting it would be hard after so many years and dollars invested into it."

"A career like that's a big commitment," Max agreed.

I made a face. "I'm allergic to commitment."

He chuckled. "That's not something I hear a lot on a first date."

"*Only* date. No offense. I know you'd never choose to go out with me."

"Says the girl who only bid on me because of a dare."

"Because I know you'd never choose to go out with me," I repeated, keeping my tone light.

"The only reason I wouldn't choose to go out with you is because your dad is my boss."

"And your sister is my friend."

"There's that too."

"And yet here we are, and you're not fired."

"Only warned."

"My dad warned you away from me?"

"Not in so many words."

I bit down on my annoyance because Max didn't need to hear about that.

"He accused me of fronting you the money to bid on me," he said.

I whipped my gaze toward him. "He didn't!"

"To be fair, he was confused that you had so much money to spend on the auction."

"That's sort of justified. I don't normally have five grand lying around."

"At the risk of asking about one of those off-limits first-date topics—"

"*Only* date," I teased.

"I'm starting to get a complex."

"First time for everything, right?"

He let out a full-chested laugh. For some reason, I found that gratifying. I liked making him laugh.

I never would've thought I'd be comfortable teasing Max Dawson on a date, but I was. Whenever I saw him around town or in the hallways back when I was in school, he seemed unapproachable, as if he had a protective shield around him. As if he hid behind a sort of public persona and didn't let people see the real him.

This guy? The one in the seat next to me? I wasn't getting those same vibes. The things this Max said seemed more personable, more...real.

"What off-limits topic were you going to ask about?" I asked.

"The money you used to bid on me..." He hesitated. "You said it was a story for another day. I've been curious ever since."

"Ah." I nodded once and steeled myself. "How well did you know Naomi?"

"I didn't. She didn't go to Dragonfly Lake High, right?"

"She was from Runner. Her whole life was about art and especially sharing it with others. The experience, I mean. She did sell a lot of her paintings and other creations, but the thing that lit her up was getting people involved in art. Especially kids."

"She's responsible for us getting art classes back in the high school," he said. "Even after she died."

I couldn't help but smile at that, even though harder emotions were bubbling up—they'd been threatening all day, getting closer to the surface with every hour as the gala approached.

"She'd be euphoric over that." I sniffled involuntarily, which drew Max's gaze to me. "I'm fine," I reassured him, cringing that I'd let that sniffle escape. "Anyway, she had an envelope where she stashed cash. Her house and land were paid for. She lived frugally and saved whatever she could in her envelope, always with a cause in mind." I stopped for a minute to brace myself further. "When she was in the hospital and the infection was getting worse instead of better, I think she sensed what was coming. She told me where her envelope was, how much was in it, and that she wanted it to go to the Dragonfly Lake fundraiser. She actually put it in writing that that money was a gift for me to donate."

My eyes teared up as I remembered that conversation, remembered insisting she would be okay and that the discussion was a waste of her energy. My breath was shaky, and I dabbed at the corners of my eyes with my finger, hoping to avoid raccoon eyes before I stood up in front of hundreds of people.

Max reached across the console, put his hand on my wrist, and squeezed gently, supportively. "You did what she asked of you, and you added your own bit of Harper flair to it."

I laughed through my tears. "I bought a boy with it. Naomi would absolutely approve."

Max's laugh filled the SUV again. He took his hand away before it could start to feel awkward. "She sounds like a special person."

"She was incredible," I said. "Unselfish. And now we need to talk about something different because I cannot stand up and accept her award and bawl like a baby."

"So let's go back to being allergic to commitment. Is that just with careers or with everything?"

"Everything," I said easily, unapologetically. "There's too much out there to experience, you know? If you saddle yourself down with one thing, you miss all the others."

"Like...what?"

"All the things. Like, what do you like to do in your free time?"

He was quiet for a few seconds, which had me looking over at him again to see if he'd heard me. I still couldn't tell.

"Max?"

"Yeah. Free time. I change diapers, go for romantic jogs in the park...with a stroller, read board books." He shot a grin at me, a little self-conscious but without apology. It seriously jolted me in the chest.

"Your baby," I said.

"Technically he's a toddler now that he's walking, but yes, my son gets all my free time, which isn't nearly enough."

Why was that so...attractive? A man who was so passionate about his son? And if you knew the very basic circumstances of his situation, where the baby was not his biologically but he'd embraced him as his own? I didn't want anything to do with babies or parenthood, but on Max, it was delicious.

Or maybe just Max was delicious in general.

Delicious but not for me.

It would *not* suck, however, to have him by my side tonight.

Call me shallow.

"I can't imagine being a parent," I said. "Particularly all of a sudden."

"Do you want kids?"

"Not specifically. They're kind of commitmenty."

He let out a gasp of amusement. "That they are. So what kind of things do you do in your free time?"

"Lately mostly art." I was dedicated to opening the studio as much as possible, so if I wasn't working, I was there. "But I like stand-up paddleboarding, kayaking, swimming, running, hiking."

"What kind of art do you do?"

"I've tried just about everything."

"What's your favorite?"

The question made me twitchy, and I knew it was because it felt a little like committing to one thing. I also knew that was screwed up, but that was just the way I was.

"I like metalworking and jewelry making and

mixed media. Colored pencils. I did glass-blowing lessons once, and that was fun."

Grinning, he said, "You were serious about not settling into any one thing, weren't you?"

"Hundred percent. There's a little dose of math for your evening."

We were both quiet for a couple of minutes, and I realized we'd reached the outskirts of Nashville. The drive had passed in a blink.

"I'm curious about something," he said eventually.

"What's that?"

"You've been working at the diner for quite a while. That doesn't fit the flitting-from-one-thing-to-the-next way of life. Do you see yourself staying there long-term?"

"I don't really think about the future. I'm more of a one-day-at-a-time girl. Kind of live for the moment."

He nodded. "I've always been the opposite. I'm a planner. I usually have a plan B and probably a plan C too."

"It must have shaken your world up quite a bit to suddenly become a father."

He pressed his lips together, then said, "Yeah. You can't imagine..." His voice went lower, quieter, and I regretted bringing up what was clearly a difficult subject.

Why wouldn't it be? His cousins, the baby's parents, died.

"I'm sorry. I didn't mean to make you sad. That was a careless question."

He shook his head. "No need to apologize. Sometimes life throws us shitty surprises, as you likely know too well."

"For sure." My thoughts turned back to Naomi, and all lightness was sucked out of the vehicle. "I'm sorry for your loss. For your son's loss. From where I'm sitting, it seems like he lucked into the best possible new family though."

"I don't know about that, but I'm grateful as hell to have a lot of support from my mom and my sister and brother."

"Dakota's watching your boy tonight? Daniel, isn't it?"

"That's right. I'll be lucky if she follows a single one of my rules. There's the hotel."

Out the front window, at the other end of the block, stood the historic Wentworth Hotel. I'd seen it in photos, but I'd never been inside it.

"This must be Hale Street," I said. I'd heard plenty about the thriving redeveloped shopping district that was anchored by the century-old hotel but hadn't yet made a trip to check it out. "A mosaic shop!"

A low chuckle came from Max. "I was fixated on the bakery next to it and didn't notice."

The mosaic place, World in Pieces, was small but adorable. "I'll be coming back here soon to shop," I said. "Oh, Henry Interiors. That's Hayden Henry's—North's—place." She was one of ours, or had been. Her brothers owned Henry's Restaurant and the Rusty Anchor Brewing in Dragonfly Lake.

As we reached the end of the block, I turned my attention to our destination at the T intersection.

The evening sun hit the light-colored stone of the Wentworth just right to give it a peach tint. There was a semicircle driveway in front, full of cars and people and activity.

The building itself had giant arched windows big enough you could drive a car through them. They were bordered by double columns and fronted by low stone balusters. The hotel was elegant, majestic, and more than a little intimidating when I let myself think about our reason for going to it.

It hit me at that instant that I was completely out of my element.

I could dress in heels and a gown, pretty myself up with hair and makeup help, and hold my own with accessories, but I'd never been to something as formal as this. The fundraiser at the Marks Hotel didn't hold a candle to it.

My gut knotted as Max drove to the parking garage behind the stunning building.

I'd been so focused on the emotional piece of tonight, on readying myself to stay composed when praises were sung to Naomi, that I hadn't given thought to anything else.

I felt like a small-town girl about to embarrass herself in the big city. In four-inch heels, no less.

I must have made a sound that revealed my sudden nerves, because Max asked, "Are you okay?" as he pulled into a parking spot.

"This is...fancy. Way out of my comfort zone," I said honestly. I was too nervous to try to hide it from him. "I've never been to anything like this."

He turned off the engine. "I'll be with you the whole time. I'll even tell you which fork to use if you need me to."

"Oh, crap. I haven't thought about forks."

"Not worth thinking about. Let's go do this. You're going to do great."

Easy for him to say. I'd bet he'd been to a hundred fancy galas at big, imposing venues.

He came around to my door as I gathered my evening bag and my courage. I slid from the seat with his hand on my arm again. When I glanced up, he met my gaze, and there was a zing through my body at how perfectly handsome he was.

"Thanks," I said, then preceded him out of the narrow space between vehicles.

I peered around for an elevator. Max put his hand at my waist and said, "That way."

Because of the cutouts on that side of my dress, his warm fingers were directly on my skin. I had a hard time not being overly focused on the feel of him, the heat of him, and used it to distract myself from the impending gala.

We walked to the elevator in silence, rode down with an elegantly dressed, obviously well-off couple without speaking, then entered the lobby, Max's reassuring hand still on my side.

The closer we got to the event, though, the less his touch kept my fears at bay. My nervousness ratcheted up as we made our way across the marble floor toward the ballroom. Several dressed-to-the-nines people were entering ahead of us, slowing us down, giving me time to freak the hell out even more.

When we reached the double doors, the main thing that registered with me was the enormity of the room, the multitude of people, and the elegance of...everything.

My heart raced as I took it in. I swallowed, my mind screaming with swear words, then looked up at Max, right by my side. He met my gaze and sent me a reassuring smile. He took his hand from my waist, and before I could panic, his long fingers entwined with mine, his large hand enveloping my smaller one.

"Let's go do this," he said close to my ear. "I think I see someone I know."

As I let him guide me, hand in hand, into the crowd, the thought hit me that, somehow, though my bid on him had been driven by a dare and a winging-it decision, Max Dawson seemed like the exact right person I needed to have with me tonight.

Chapter Seven

Max

Harper Ellison turned out to be nothing at all like what I'd expected when I picked her up earlier this evening.

She might be my wild-child sister's friend who seemed to be drifting through life without a long-term plan, but she'd revealed layers and depths that made it impossible not to like her and maybe even admire her.

In spite of her inexperience with formal galas and her nervousness, she'd appeared to fit in just fine. It didn't hurt that she looked like a million dollars in that classy but sexy-as-hell dress that had nearly been the death of me with all its access to her soft, tempting skin.

That first time I'd touched her, outside of the SUV, had been purely motivated by the urge to comfort her. I'd had to fight to cover the effect her bare skin and the curve of her hip had on me.

I would admit, only to myself, that I'd intentionally found a dozen more opportunities to rest my hand on her side throughout the evening, like a kid who couldn't keep his hand out of the candy dish even though he knew he'd get in trouble for it eventually.

And then the dancing...

Harper had been all about the dancing, saying it was much easier than making conversation with people she didn't know. She'd pointed out the irony of trying to socialize with *education types*, as she'd called them, when she'd barely made it out of high school. So we'd spent plenty of time out on the dance floor.

I'd kept a tight rein on myself, ensuring there was always enough distance between our bodies, even though I'd been aching to pull her into me. Someone was likely to snap photos of us that would undoubtedly get back to Dragonfly Lake for the whole town to see—including her father.

Her acceptance of Naomi's award had done as

much to leave me wanting her as her gracefulness on the dance floor and the alluring feel of her body had. When we'd sat down to dinner and she'd confessed she hadn't prepared a speech or even any notes, my gut had twisted with nerves on her behalf.

You really didn't plan out what to say? I'd asked.

With her brows raised, she'd shaken her head. *That would be a disaster. I'd forget everything.*

I couldn't imagine not writing out remarks word for word and taking a note card to the podium with me, but of course it'd been too late for that. And she didn't want it.

When it was time for her to speak, she'd blown me away and brought the entire ballroom full of people to tears, her voice breaking a couple of times as she talked about the way Naomi had changed Harper's life for the better and inspired everyone she met.

I didn't know how she did it, but Harper rocked the hell out of winging it.

When she'd returned to our table afterward, I'd stood and hugged her, not paying any heed to the flashes going off around us, just wanting to convey without words that she'd done an incredible job of paying tribute to her friend.

No doubt one of those photos would reach my boss, but there was nothing sexual about the moment, and I wouldn't apologize for it.

Even if I'd likely have hot, bothered dreams all night starring Harper.

Midnight had come and gone, and we were almost back to Harper's house. She'd been chattering the whole ride home about inconsequential topics, some recapping the gala, others just random thoughts that seemed to cross her mind out of nowhere. She was either decompressing from the stressful night or avoiding sad thoughts of Naomi or both.

I didn't mind it, and I commented whenever it was appropriate. I was enjoying the peek into her admittedly all-over-the-place mind. She was smart even though she wasn't a fan of school. She was well-rounded and had experienced a lot of things, even if a formal event in a large city wasn't one of them. And she made interesting observations that never would've occurred to me.

When we approached her driveway, she went quiet, as if she was all talked out and ready for the night to end. I turned in and noticed out of the corner of my eye when Harper stiffened in the passenger seat, her attention focused on the house down the half-mile-long driveway.

"What's wrong?" I asked, my gaze following hers.

"I didn't leave any lights on. I never do. I always forget."

The windows in front and on the driveway side were dimly illuminated. I noticed a car by the detached garage that hadn't been there earlier.

"Whose car is that?" I asked as I stopped even with the front walkway.

"I don't know," she said slowly.

"Is the studio open?"

She shook her head. "It shouldn't be. No one has keys except me."

We couldn't see the entire studio from here because the house blocked half of it, but the part we could see was dark.

"I wonder..." she said, her voice trailing off uncertainly. "The only person I can think of is Naomi's brother."

"Are you expecting him?"

She shook her head, her gaze back on the house. "I mean, we kind of expected him to show up for Naomi's funeral, but he never did. No one has heard from him since she died."

I frowned, instantly suspicious. "You think he has the keys to Naomi's house?"

"He's half owner." Harper released her seat belt and picked up her bag.

"How well do you know him?"

"I've never met him. They weren't close."

"I'm coming in with you," I said, all kinds of warnings going off in my head.

When she didn't argue, I knew she was uneasy too. As we walked to the front door, though, she said, "I'm sure I'll be okay. You need to get home to Daniel."

"Dakota's doing just fine." My sister had texted me a selfie of her and Danny at story time, reading *Goodnight, Moon,* and another fuzzy shot taken by the light of the night-light in Danny's room, showing him asleep in his crib. "Keys?" I held my hand out.

Harper handed them over. I unlocked the door and pushed it open, entering before Harper could.

The light came from the room to the left, opposite the kitchen. As soon as we shut the door, I saw a large man sprawled on his stomach on the sofa. He muttered something unintelligible. On the coffee table in front of him was a cocktail glass and a mostly empty bottle of scotch. The guy rose to his elbows and slowly opened his eyes, looking as if he'd been in a fight, his hair a mess, dress shirt untucked and wrinkled, suit pants slightly off-center and also wrinkled.

"Who the hell are you?" he demanded, his words not entirely clear, but I couldn't tell if sleep or alcohol was to blame.

I stepped in front of Harper. "Same question for you."

"I asked you first," he slurred, confirming scotch was the cause.

"Ian?" Harper said, stepping up beside me.

The way his head popped up told me that was his name.

"Pretty," he said quietly, as if to himself.

No way was Harper staying here tonight.

"Mind your manners," I snapped.

"Who the fuck are you?"

"I live here," Harper said. "I'm Naomi's roommate. Was." She frowned.

"My sister never mentioned any roommates." He missed pronouncing the *t* in *roommates*.

"When was the last time you talked to your sister?" I asked.

He stood, swaying a little. "You got a lease?" His tone was cold, angry, as he ignored my question and addressed Harper.

She flicked a glance up at me, and I instantly guessed she and Naomi didn't have a written agreement. "I pay rent every month. You can trace the money that way."

"This's my house now."

"I've been running the studio since Naomi..." Harper said. "A lot of people depend on the art studio to be open."

"Don't give a fuck about any studio." With shaky hands, he emptied the bottle into his glass.

"It was important to your sister," Harper said, but there was no point in reasoning with this asshole.

"You're not staying here," I said to her in a low voice.

"I live here. He doesn't," she said.

"If he owns it..."

Her shoulders fell.

"Naomi's not here," Ian said after downing half his glass. "You need to leave."

"We'll be getting some of her belongings from her room," I told him.

He grunted, then said, "Then get the fuck out. My sister is fucking dead."

"Go pack a bag," I said quietly to Harper. "I'll wait down here." I didn't trust this guy for a minute. He looked likely to pass back out, but I wasn't taking any chances. There was no way in hell I'd let Harper deal with him alone.

Harper stared at him as if she wanted to say more.

"You can stay in my guest room," I told her. "You'll have the whole lower level to yourself."

She met my eyes, looking like she wanted to argue, but then she nodded. "I'll be back in five."

I watched Naomi's brother, but it turned out to be unnecessary as he seemed to forget I was there. He pulled a knitted blanket over himself and passed out again. He was snoring within two minutes.

I heard Harper descending the stairs and met her at the foot of them. She'd changed out of her dress and wore denim cutoffs and a ladies-cut tee. Her kill-a-man heels had been replaced by running shoes. She carried a mini backpack.

Her eyes were wide as she glanced back at her friend's brother, then up at me, looking for a second a lot younger than she was.

"Let's get out of here," I said.

Without a word, she preceded me out the door. I still had her keys, so I locked it behind me. With my arm at her waist again, I had the fleeting thought that I missed the revealing dress and the feel of her bare skin, but I needed to shove that right the hell out of my mind. It was going to be dicey enough having her one floor down in my house when I was sure my brain would hold on to the way she'd looked all night. The way she'd felt.

"Are you okay?" I asked once we were in the SUV with the engine running.

Harper frowned. "Annoyed," was her response, which wasn't at all what I'd expected. "I get that he owns the house, but I've been living there, paying rent, for three years. He can't just kick me out on the street."

"We can take that up with him when he's sober. I wasn't about to leave you alone with him."

"I'm glad you were there."

I had a strange urge to take her hand, but I resisted it.

Ten minutes later, I pulled into my garage, passing Dakota's car in the driveway.

Harper sat up straight. "Dakota's still here?"

I laughed. "Of course. She can be flaky sometimes, but so far she hasn't left Danny alone when she's supposed to be taking care of him."

"Right. Duh. I...don't want her to see me."

"Why not?"

"She'll jump to the wrong idea."

"Probably, knowing her. We don't have anything to hide though."

"I know that, and you know that, but do you think she'd ever believe it?"

"You know my sister pretty well, don't you?"

"Know her and love her, but she can be like a bulldog."

"Wait here. She'll be gone in five minutes, and then you can come to bed."

As her brows shot upward, I realized my error. "Then you can come inside, I'll show you to the guest room, and you can go to bed," I corrected.

And I would go to my own bed, and I would *not*

lie awake for hours thinking about how close she was or wondering what she'd brought to sleep in.

When I slid out of the SUV, I had to adjust my pants and coach my body to calm the fuck down before I could face my sister.

Chapter Eight

Harper

The five minutes in Max's garage before he came back to get me were the longest, quietest of my life.

I'd been fighting off ugly shit in my head since we'd left the gala by chattering about whatever came to mind, trying to keep up a happy front. A bone-deep, suffocating sadness was seeping in, catching me off guard. I'd expected the award acceptance on Naomi's behalf to be hard, but...

I squeezed my eyes shut as I sensed Max reentering the garage. When I opened them, I blinked at the light coming from inside the house. As he reached my door and opened it, offering me his hand, I tried to appear composed.

He'd turned out to be the right partner for this specific evening that could've so easily been hell. Thanks to him, I'd gotten through it intact. When we'd run into several people he knew, he'd included me in their conversations. And since he'd been to dozens of formal events before, he was well versed in the routine and clued me in when I needed it, like with the forks.

What was more, he seemed to be empathetic to my nervousness, not only about speaking in front of people but about managing my sadness. We didn't talk about it; I just sensed he got it, maybe because of his own recent loss.

He'd indulged me by dancing, where I didn't have to make small talk with strangers or think too hard about Naomi. Mostly I had to concentrate on not falling into Max's arms the way I wanted to.

He'd basically been the support I needed to get through the evening. I wasn't sure any other guy would've understood that, let alone gone along with it. So among the many feelings swirling inside of me, there were depths of gratitude.

The other feelings were more confusing, I acknowledged, as he took my backpack from me and put a hand at the small of my back, guiding me into his house.

It was wild to think I was spending the night at Max's, but after that creepy run-in with Naomi's brother...

On the drive into town, after leaving Naomi's, I'd told him I could go to my dad's or a friend's place. The time was nearly one in the morning though, and as he'd pointed out, I didn't want to wake anyone up and worry them.

Before we got to the steps to the house, I stopped and tugged at his tuxedo-clad arm. "In case I forget to say it later, thank you."

His lips caught my attention as they eased upward at the corners. "You already thanked me."

"That was for going to the gala. This is for going inside Naomi's with me and offering a place to stay."

"That guy's not stable. I wouldn't leave you alone there."

He peered down at me, as if to make it clear he meant every word. His eyes were intense. Compassionate. And beyond handsome. My God, I felt that look deep inside of me.

I searched for something to say that would lighten the moment, but I was tired. I couldn't quite get my brain to work enough to be witty.

For three weighted-with-potential seconds, we gazed at each other in the low light.

There was an undeniable physical pull between

us, not just now but all evening. One that, in a different situation, another lifetime, I might pursue for a night or five.

We'd agreed though, one date only, and I fell back on that, relieved the question had been preaddressed and closed. No chance of anything developing between me and Max Dawson.

We broke eye contact, and with a gentle nudge at my back, he guided me up to the door and inside.

"Shh," he whispered into my ear, sending a shiver through me. He pointed to our left as we entered. "Danny's bedroom is right there."

We passed it and entered the kitchen, dimly lit by three pendant lights over an island. The kitchen opened to the living area. The entire exterior wall was windows and French doors I was sure overlooked the lake.

The living room was casual, homey, with a large cream-colored sectional covered in blue, cream, and beige throw pillows, a big, square coffee table, and a stone fireplace flanked by built-in shelves. The ceiling was raised, with exposed beams in warm wood. In the corner, I spotted a blue toy box with a stuffed giraffe hanging halfway out of it.

"Do you want something to eat?" Max asked.

I shook my head. "I'm exhausted." I couldn't wait to collapse in private. If I was lucky, I'd be unconscious in thirty seconds.

"I'll show you to your room."

Still carrying my backpack, Max led me down the stairs, through another family room, and down a hall. At the end was a cozy bedroom with one white ship-lap wall, a plush-looking queen bed, and a restful palette of soft whites and grays with pops of lime. There were windows on two walls, plus a door to the outside.

"Bathroom is there." Max pointed to a door in the hall we'd just walked by, then set my bag on the armchair in the corner. "Help yourself to anything, including the kitchen if you decide you're hungry."

"I won't, but thank you, Max. This looks so peaceful I could live in here."

"For as long as you need to," he said.

"Oh, I didn't mean that for real. It's just...perfect." I cut myself off, hoping to end the conversation faster. Pressure was building in my throat and behind my eyes.

"Good night, Harper."

"Night." I managed a smile and watched him duck out of the room, closing the door after him.

I sank to the bed, inhaling deeply and hearing the shakiness when I exhaled.

I might be alone finally, but I continued to fight off tears. Crying was exhausting. Also, I wasn't sure I'd ever stop if I started.

I hopped back up and dug out the boxers and tank I'd packed to sleep in.

Once I had my pajamas on, I took my toothbrush to the bathroom. It was decorated in navy and lime, I noted, thinking that was a happy color combination. Tonight the colors didn't make me feel happy.

Back in the bedroom, with all the lights off, I crawled under the cool, fluffy bedding, noting the complete silence.

Less than two minutes later, I bolted back up, unable to stand that silence.

I went to the outside door and peeked between the blinds. There was a patio directly outside, then a gentle slope down to the dark lake.

Fresh air.

Water.

Space.

That was what I needed.

I unlocked the door and headed outside.

The properties on this section of the lake were larger, not crammed in so close to each other like they were in other neighborhoods. Here, groves of trees grew from the shore to the house on both sides of Max's property, separating it from the neighbors.

There was a paved path to the water that split the yard down the middle, but I stuck to the cool grass on my way to the shore.

Max owned a boat, because of course he owned a boat. The pontoon was docked under a canopy. Instead of going on the dock, I stuck to the shadows on this side of the boat, noting his land had a small sandy beach.

With my feet bare, I waded into the water, reveling in the cool, refreshing feel of it, standing calf deep and letting the sounds of the outdoors wash over me. Insects. Frogs. The slightest whisper of a breeze in the trees.

I continued a little farther, thigh deep, my feet finding sand and a few smooth stones.

Above me, the vast, black sky was peppered with a million stars. It was a stunning sight. Reassuring at a moment when I was on the verge of being pulled under by doubt.

I'd been burying a suspicion that everything in my life was on shaky, unsure ground for weeks, just trying to make it through the gala. Naomi's award acceptance. It was the last of the obligations I had to see through for my friend. First had been the funeral, then the auction at the Marks for her pet cause. Then tonight's award.

It was all finished now.

My life was my own again, with the exception of the studio, and that was temporary and optional.

I swallowed hard, which seemed to serve as the

valve that'd been holding back my tears, because they now poured down both cheeks.

Yes, my life was my own again, but a thought had been building, gathering steam, that there wasn't really very much *to* my life.

Over the past few years, Naomi had become a large part of my days—my roommate and landlord, my friend, mentor, the person I spent more time with than anyone else. I'd managed to not let myself fixate on her absence because I'd still had those obligations to see through.

Suddenly her loss gaped in front of me. I felt it as a physical pain in my chest.

Her beautiful face, her multitude of copper-tinged braids, her kindhearted blue eyes... I saw her perfectly in my mind's eye, allowing the image in to an extent I hadn't in the weeks since she'd died.

I'd kept myself too busy carrying out her day-to-day responsibilities with the studio and the farmhouse, consulting on the auction when asked about her preferences, the organizers trying to honor her at every step. Then the gala—preparing for it mentally and emotionally, as well as finding the right dress and shoes, choosing from her modest jewelry collection a piece I would wear to have her with me, and spending the day getting prettied up for it—facial, nails, hair, makeup. Coming up with suitable words for the acceptance itself.

By putting all my energy into the details, I'd focused on what alive-and-well Naomi would've wanted. It had kept reality from sinking in—that alive-and-well Naomi was gone forever.

Quivering from the inside out, I choked on a sob and fought to catch my breath.

Once my lungs were filled, I dove underwater, into the welcoming darkness that insulated me from the rest of the world, rushing around me to cradle me and protect me like a loving mother. I kicked, cut my arms through the water, and let out a screech of mourning that only the fish could hear.

I swam farther out, away from the shore, until I ran out of breath and had to surface. I filled my lungs again, panting for oxygen as I treaded water, my tears mixing with lake water.

I checked the darkness around me, making sure there wasn't a silent fishing boat anchored nearby or someone sitting on the edge of a dock. I'd swum beyond the end of Max's dock by a good bit. I didn't sense anyone close enough to see my shoulders shaking with silent sobs.

I stretched one leg downward but didn't hit the lake bottom, so I kept myself afloat by treading water, bobbing my head under frequently to wash away my tears, only to have more pour out the second I resurfaced.

When my muscles wore out, I eased my head

back and drifted into a float with only my head above water.

As I gazed at the stars, I let thoughts of Naomi come, giving them no resistance, just allowing them free rein as I hadn't before. I wondered if she was in the stars. Took comfort in imagining she was. Smiled through my tears knowing that idea would've filled her with joy and inspiration. She probably would've tried to paint it.

The sobs kept coming, pouring out of me. I floated there for I didn't know how long, silently ugly crying, sputtering out lake water, grieving my loss. Missing my friend so much that every cell in my body ached to hug her, longed for the sound of her joyful laugh.

Eventually my breaths evened out, and my shoulders ceased their shuddering, my body thoroughly wrung out. The sliver of a moon was the only measure of how much time had passed, as it had traveled partway across the sky.

Rolling to my stomach, I submerged myself, cleansing my face of my salty tears one more time.

I surfaced again, my body spent, my heart thoroughly wrenched. The night sounds filtered back into my consciousness as I calmed myself, pulling myself out of my head and back into the world around me.

For another few minutes, I floated and gazed at

the sky, appreciating the physical beauty of it instead of pondering whether our loved ones who died were somehow out there in the ether.

Eventually I called on the dregs of my energy, rolled to my side, and started a slow sidestroke back to the shore.

When I reached water that was waist deep, I submerged again to smooth my hair out of my face, then found my footing on the sandy bottom and stood.

I let out a startled gasp when I discerned a shirtless man standing on the dock in the darkness.

Chapter Nine

Max

Coming outside to make sure Harper was okay was a dumb move.

I knew it the second she stood up in water that reached her lower thighs, treating me to one hell of a moonlit view of her soaking-wet shirt clinging to her generous, tempting-as-fuck breasts.

She was obviously fine, and now I'd have that image of her permanently burned into my brain.

And a reaction in my sweatpants that was hard to hide as I stood here on the dock for the world and God to see.

I walked back to the end of the dock, baby monitor in hand, and stepped down to the sand. "What are you doing out here?"

"I could ask you the same thing," she said. Her voice was lower than usual, a little rough.

"I saw someone in the water and had to make sure it wasn't a troublemaker or someone in distress." It'd been drilled into my head at a young age that swimming alone wasn't safe. Swimming alone at night? Bad idea times two.

"I'm not in distress," she said quietly, her usual animation missing from her voice. She folded her arms over her chest as if she'd just noticed the wet shirt effect. "I just needed"—she turned partway around and waved her hand toward the middle of the lake—"this, I guess." Her chest rose and fell with a deep breath, her arms crossed over it again.

Trying to see her face better, I stepped to the edge of the water. "Are you okay?"

"Yeah." She answered too fast, looking down into her chest instead of meeting my gaze.

I knew tonight had been difficult, but she'd seemed okay when I showed her to her room. She didn't seem okay now, regardless of what she said.

Harper walked a few paces toward me. I waited on the sand, anticipating her nearness—and the chance to get a better look into her eyes.

I didn't get that chance, as she stopped several feet out, the water hitting a few inches above her ankles. She turned away and lowered herself to sit on the lake bottom in the shallow water. It felt like a dismissal. I was sure that's how she intended it.

I stared at the back of her head, her dark hair slicked down her back, glistening from the water. If I went back inside now, I was pretty confident she'd be safe. She'd proven she knew how to swim, and I suspected she wouldn't stay out here much longer since she'd been on her way in.

The smart choice would be to go back inside, ignore the pull I felt toward her, and mind my own business.

I glanced at the silent baby monitor. Looked up at my darkened bedroom window. It was no contest between heading up to that quiet, lonely room and sitting out here with Harper, convincing her to talk to me, trying to help her feel better somehow. I was intimately familiar with the heartache of losing someone. I couldn't fix that for Harper, but I could try to be a friend.

After turning up the volume on the monitor so I wouldn't miss a peep from Danny, I strode over and set it on the paved walkway, pointing it in Harper's direction, then slipped off my flip-flops and waded into the water. I sat down next to her, trying not to think about my pants getting soaked. They would dry.

Harper looked at me with a startled expression,

which confirmed she'd thought I'd do anything *but* join her.

Now that I was so close, I could tell her eyes were swollen. With her makeup gone, she looked younger. Sad.

"I'm sorry you had a tough night," I said. "Tough couple of months, probably."

"Thanks. I've kept busy trying to focus on the tasks I had to do to honor her. Everything's done now. It just...hit me hard."

"I get that. More than you know."

"Yeah?"

I let out a self-derisive scoff, thinking back to the early days with Danny. "I was in robot mode for the first few weeks after my cousin and his wife died. I put all my energy into Danny. Figuring out how to take care of an infant. Giving him what he needed."

"Ignoring deep thoughts as much as you could. Because deep thoughts are excruciating." She was hugging her knees to her chest, peering out at the dark lake.

"Exactly." I pulled my soaked knees up to rest my forearms on them. "Everyone kept telling me I needed to grieve, needed to process my feelings, but I couldn't make time for feelings. Not when I had this little guy who needed everything from me."

"I can't imagine what that must've been like. I

wouldn't know the first thing about taking care of a baby."

"I didn't either. Jamie—that's my cousin—and his wife lived in San Diego. I went there to meet Daniel a few days after he was born. I saw him when they came back for a visit, but I'd never even changed his diaper. Didn't know when he napped or what he liked to eat."

"That's a crash course. Way more than I had to figure out with Naomi's studio."

"It sort of saved me." My voice had gone thick with emotion as I remembered those first months after Jamie and Shay died. This was stuff I hadn't talked about to anyone. It seemed like maybe Harper would be able to relate. "I think I needed something to keep me from facing my loss all at once. I don't know if that makes sense. It sounds fucked up when I say it out loud."

A soft, sympathetic laugh came from Harper. "It does sound fucked up, and I can relate to it completely." Her tone went back to serious. "So has the hard stuff hit you yet?"

I nodded, thinking of a single night when all the walls had crumbled, and I couldn't hold my bone-deep grief at bay anymore. "It...was ugly."

"Sounds about right," Harper said.

We both went silent. The insect chorus played on behind us. A fish splashed over by the pilings on the opposite side of the dock. I did my best not to let the details sneak in about that night when I'd been bowled over by grief.

"I underwater ugly cried enough to raise the water level of the lake by at least an inch from all the tears," Harper said a little flippantly. I knew that was to cover her self-consciousness. "Can you beat that?"

"Oh, I think so," I said without hesitation. I did pause before saying more. This story wouldn't paint me in a good light. If it ever got out to anyone else, I'd be mortified. It was the opposite of what this town expected from me. A true example of how much the real Max didn't have his shit together in the least. "I've never told anyone this story."

"I won't breathe a word of it."

I closed my eyes. Was I really going to own up to one of the most shameful, awful moments of my life? Yes, I was. I realized I trusted Harper with it.

"Back in February, I had to go to Nashville for a two-day seminar for math educators. My brother, Levi, was watching Danny at his house." I took a deep breath, feeling the tightening in my chest, the thickening of sadness balling up in my throat. "It was two days before Daniel's first birthday. That was at the top of my mind even though I'd be home in time for it."

Unable to stay still anymore, I stuck my hand in

the water, splashing, swirling it around as I continued. "After the evening session at the end of the first day, I went back to my hotel room. It was quiet, peaceful. Ironically, I'd originally considered driving back that night to stay in my own bed and be home for Danny, but my mom and brother convinced me that getting away would be good for me."

"Not so much, I'm guessing?" Harper asked.

"Not so much. It was so quiet I couldn't escape from my thoughts. It was like all that hard-core shit had just been hovering, waiting for a quiet minute when I didn't have anything else to do, and it all swooped in. Wouldn't let go of me. That was the night when it really sank in that Danny was mine. Forever. He was turning one—a big deal for every child—but his parents wouldn't be there to celebrate it or any other birthdays. I was the one responsible for that now. For birthdays, for sicknesses, for preschool and high school and...everything. His whole life. Boom. Hit me like a boulder fell on my head."

"That's a lot," she said.

"Before that, I don't know, I just...took care of him. Like I was a long-term babysitter or something. I didn't consciously think of it that way, but that night, in the 'peaceful' hotel room, reality bore down, and it was almost like Jamie had just died that day, the way the emotions knocked me on my ass."

Harper reached over and grasped my hand that was still resting on my knee. She squeezed it, silently telling me she understood.

"And?" she asked in a whisper. "What did you do?"

"Well." I sat up straighter, attempting to be as matter-of-fact as possible, trying to disconnect from any emotions it dislodged. "I left and drove home, not for any reason other than I couldn't be in that hotel for another second."

"That's how I felt when I was lying in bed earlier. Nothing against your guest room," she said in a rush. "It wouldn't have mattered where I was. I just needed to get *out*."

I nodded. That was it exactly. "I probably shouldn't have been driving. Definitely not all the way home. I don't really remember the drive, just the pain." I swallowed hard. "When I pulled into my garage, I was a mess. I saw my bicycle. I hadn't touched it for years, but it was in plain view, just sitting there. Jamie and I used to ride bikes together, whenever he came to town to visit, back when we were too young to drive."

Harper squeezed my hand again, as if she sensed the hard part was coming.

"I took a sledgehammer to my bike," I said.

"Just...lost my ever-loving shit and beat the hell out of it until it was mangled and in pieces, and then I hammered it some more. I was out of my mind. I can't explain it or defend it. I was just so fucking upset."

When I thought Harper would've decided I was insane and put distance between us, she leaned her head against my shoulder, still holding on to my hand.

"Then what?" she said.

"Then I drank a bottle of whiskey. I woke up the next afternoon on my kitchen floor. I don't know why I was there instead of bed or what time I finished that bottle. I blacked out. Eventually, I got up, took acetaminophen, tried to shower all the shame and the sadness off me—didn't work, in case you're wondering—and drove out to my brother's that evening as if I'd been at the seminar all day. Never told a soul I wasn't."

For the next few minutes, neither of us spoke. She kept her head resting on me as if what I'd just told her was the most normal thing in the world. I let myself soak up her touch, her support. I wasn't sure what I'd expected, but it wasn't such calm acceptance.

I freed my hand from hers and wrapped my arm around her, pulling her into my side, taking comfort in her companionship. Breathing in her scent.

"You definitely win for drama," she finally said.

I chuckled. "Told you. I'm not proud of any of that. I can't believe I told you."

"I'm glad you did. It's very un-Coach-Dawson-like. It makes you seem almost human."

"I'm so fucking human."

"So after the hangover, did anything get any easier?"

"No."

"Thanks for shattering any hope I had," she said dryly, drawing a smile from me.

"I guess it has gotten a little easier. I haven't felt that horrible rage since then. But I still miss my cousin like crazy. Still worry every minute of the day I'm going to fuck up his kid."

"You're not going to fuck up his kid."

She had no way of knowing that, but I didn't argue. "Do you feel any better after underwater ugly crying?"

"No." She straightened, removing her head from my shoulder, then dipping her hand in the water and trailing it back and forth. "I mean, that physical pressure that builds up in your chest and your throat?"

I nodded, very damn familiar with it.

"That feels less. A lot less. But other yucky thoughts surfaced."

"Like what?" I asked, trying not to miss the weight of her head on my shoulder. Her closeness.

She kept moving her hand back and forth, back and forth. I watched it, mesmerized by the rhythm, the little bubbles that caught the moonlight.

"Naomi was so focused. Dedicated. She had goals and passions, and she was living those out. She literally died from doing something she loved, and though I don't think she wanted to die in her thirties, I think—" Her voice cracked. She took her hand out of the water, pressed her fist to her mouth. "I think she'd not have regrets. She lived a life bursting with purpose, you know?"

"I understood that very well from your acceptance speech tonight."

Harper nodded, her eyes closing. "She did so much. And I've been doing my best to take care of everything she left hanging. The auction. Her studio. The recognition tonight."

"Even though I didn't know her, I feel confident saying you did her proud, Harper."

"I hope so." She pressed her lips together, looking even more troubled. "But it occurred to me that, if I died tomorrow, there'd be nothing for anyone to take care of for me. Not. A. Thing. Because I don't do anything meaningful. I'm just drifting along."

"You can't compare yourself to Naomi."

"No. No one compares to Naomi. But I don't have anything that drives me, that makes me excited to wake up in the morning. Like...coaching or teaching might be for you? Or maybe math?" She made a face.

"I do like all of those. I'm not sure I'd call myself excited to wake up in the morning because of them—"

"You know what I mean. They give you purpose."

"They do."

"If you died tonight, God forbid, someone would have to teach your classes. Someone would have to coach your team. Someone would have to take care of your son."

The last part was like a stab to my chest, but I merely nodded.

"I don't have that. Someone would have to take my shifts at the diner, but anyone could do that." She bit down on her lip, visibly struggling. It was my turn to take her hand. "I've been so adamantly against settling down, but this Naomi thing..." She shook her head. "It's kind of flipping my life on its head."

"Traumatic events can do that."

She whipped her gaze toward me. "This must sound stupid compared to becoming a dad all of a sudden."

"It's not stupid. Maybe less tangible but no less significant. Sometimes less tangible can be even harder to figure out."

"Harder than a baby?" The tips of her lips flirted with a smile. "I don't think so."

"Harder to acknowledge, maybe. But you just acknowledged it." I thought about our conversation in the car, about her refusal to choose a path. I knew better than to use that P-word, but it seemed that's what she was lacking. "Out of all the things you told me you enjoy earlier, which ones do you like best? What could you see getting up in the morning to do every day?"

She peered at me for several seconds, but I couldn't read her expression. I was starting to think I'd pushed too much.

Before I could decide whether I should back down, Harper put her hand on the back of my head and pulled me toward her until our mouths collided in an ungentle kiss.

Her lips pressed against mine. Then, before I could register the taste of her, she pulled back, leaving half an inch of space between us as our gazes met and we took each other in.

I could pull away. I knew I could end this, but I wasn't thinking so much as reacting. I wanted a better taste of her.

I reached for her, ran my hand through her hair

to grasp her head and bring her soft, alluring mouth back to mine. She met me halfway, our breaths mingling as we kissed, our lips lingering, tasting. When our tongues touched, a groan escaped from me. Our connection exploded as our tongues twisted and probed at each other.

My body was all on board in mere seconds, aching for more of her. She ran her hand up my bare chest. All I could think about was more skin-to-skin contact. Our positions were awkward though. Moving would mean breaking contact, and I couldn't get enough of her sweet taste, her confident kiss.

Before I could think past that need, she ended the kiss, ducking her chin, both of us catching our breath.

She took her hand back and faced straight ahead again, not looking at me.

"I don't want to talk about what might drive me," she said quietly, "and I definitely don't want to talk about kissing you."

Harper stood, the water pouring off her lower body. I sat there in the shallow water, my brain still trying to catch up, torn between wanting to follow her to the guest room and knowing damn well it was smarter to let her walk away.

"I'm sorry, Max. I'm going to dry off and try to sleep."

Before I could figure out what to say, she pivoted, waded out of the lake, and headed to her room.

I sat there, my pulse still pounding blood down to my dick, as I tried to figure out what the fuck had just happened.

Chapter Ten

Harper

What had I done?

What the hell had I been thinking?

Why, why, why had I kissed Max? Shirtless, irresistible Max who I was not supposed to kiss?

The questions pounded through me with every step up that hill away from him.

I full well knew the answers, I admitted as I let myself into the guest bedroom.

I'd been thinking, *Distract! Divert attention! Do whatever you can to change the subject!*

I'd changed the subject from what I might want to do for the rest of my life, all right, and I'd screwed myself well and good in the process, because I was not going to forget what it felt like to kiss Max Dawson anytime soon.

I peeled my wet boxers and cami off, patted my body dry with a thick towel from the bathroom, and pulled on the running shorts and cropped tee I'd brought to wear in the morning. As I was towel drying my hair, a distant sound caught my attention. I froze to try to hear it better.

Was that crying?

I opened the bedroom door and stepped into the hall.

It was faint, but I was pretty sure that had to be Danny. My heart lurched in a panic.

I didn't know the first thing about babies or toddlers or kids of any age. The cry didn't have a screaming-bloody-murder tone to it, so I hurried back down the hall, through the guest room, and out the door. Max was still where I'd left him, sitting in the lake, his back to me.

"Max," I said in a whisper-yell as I went down the hill.

He turned when he heard me.

I reached the sand and said, "I think Danny's crying."

He was up in half a heartbeat, rushing to the walkway to a white box I hadn't noticed before.

"Damn battery's dead," he said, taking off for the house in a jog.

I followed him to the family room door and up to the main level.

"Dadaaaa." The cry came from the other side of the kitchen. My heart cracked a little at the sound of fear and need in it.

Max rushed into Danny's room. "Daddy's here, little man. It's okay."

By the light of a night-light, I saw Daniel Dawson up close for the first time. He was standing in his crib, gripping the side of it with one hand, and holding out his other for his beloved daddy. He had dark-blond, shaggy hair hanging over his forehead. His lips quivered as his eyes locked on Max.

"Hey, Danny boy," Max said in a low, soothing voice. "Come here. What's going on, bud?" He picked up the boy. "Ah." He lowered Danny back to stand in the crib but didn't let go of him. "You need a diaper change, huh?"

I stood a few feet back, entranced, as Danny took in a big, shuddering breath. His little fist clung to Max's arm as if he knew everything would be okay as long as his daddy was there.

My heart did a full-on flip.

Witnessing that micromoment, that instant of innate, pure trust between a boy and his father... That packed a punch. I'd thought kissing Max was going to mess me up for a good long while, but this was only going to make it harder to keep the man out of my mind.

"Let's get you changed," Max said in that mesmerizing dad voice. "Harper, could you switch on that lamp?"

I looked where he pointed and saw a lamp on a chest of drawers. I turned it on and noticed it had a rocket at the base and the shade was covered in stars. There were stars painted on the walls too and planets and moons. We were in outer space.

When I turned back to Max, he had Danny lying in the crib and was already stripping him down to change the diaper, which I could now smell. I didn't blame the boy for screaming about that.

I kept my distance but didn't leave, just watched Max, listened to the way he kept up a mostly one-sided conversation with his son.

"Poop happens, doesn't it, little man? Not usually in the middle of the night for you though. Was this from the cookies Aunt Dakota gave you? I bet it was."

Danny had a stuffed yellow dog in his hand, one of the ears in his mouth. A quiet, happy laugh came out, muffled by the dog.

"Your auntie's breaking all the rules, isn't she?"

Max continued, his hands never slowing down with the smelly clean-up and then the new diaper.

When he was done, I was still standing there watching.

"I need to get some dry clothes on. Then we'll rock for a while, okay?" he said to his son.

"Dada." Danny pulled himself up to a stand again, then grabbed Max's forearm.

"I'll be right back. I bet Harper will keep you company for a minute." He pulled Daniel out of the crib, into his arms for a hug, then asked me, "Would you mind?"

"No," I said automatically, trying not to let my awkwardness with kids show. "What do I do?"

He hesitated, as if reconsidering. "Will you let Harper hold you?"

The little boy stared at me with his intense blue eyes but didn't answer.

Max stepped closer, his eyes on Danny. "See if he'll go to you." He handed his son over to me.

I supported the boy with my palm on his pajamaed little bottom, puffy from the diaper, expecting him to protest. His gaze settled on one of my earrings—a small round amethyst from Naomi's collection. It was pretty and purple and apparently pleasing to this little guy because he didn't fuss or complain when I put my other hand on his back to support him.

"I'll be back in two minutes, Danny," Max said, and he left me with his son.

The little guy and I stood there and checked each other out. "Hi, Danny. I'm Harper," I said in what I hoped was a quiet, soothing tone.

He studied me for about five seconds, with me smiling like a dork because I didn't know what else to do or say. Then Danny let out a sigh and rested his head on my shoulder, grasping my T-shirt in his fist.

I melted a little bit.

Maybe more than a little bit.

I didn't have much experience with kids, had never babysat growing up, kept my distance from ankle biters in general because, I'll be honest, they made me uncomfortable. You never knew what they would need from you or what they might say.

That this little guy trusted me, felt comfortable enough to rest his head on me?

"You're trying to steal my heart, aren't you?"

He didn't say a word, just let out another sigh.

I stood there without moving, not wanting to disturb him or do anything that would disrupt this peaceful moment. He smelled like baby shampoo and innocence.

I craned my chin down to see if he was asleep, but his eyes were open, staring back up at me. So he was relaxed but not enough to sleep. That was fair. He'd just met me.

"I'm sure your daddy will be back any second now," I told him, hoping Max would return before I did something to upset his son.

————

Max

Once I was out of Danny's room, I swore under my breath at myself and strode across the family room toward the master.

What the fuck had gotten into me?

How had I let myself lose my damn mind enough to kiss Harper? Because I *had* kissed her, willingly and aggressively. She might've started it, but I'd done the opposite of ending it.

All while my son was inside alone.

I didn't think he'd been crying long, judging by how quickly he'd calmed down, but that wasn't the point.

Who knew when the battery on the monitor had given out? Was it even working when I'd set it down outside? Had I checked, or had I been so distracted by a pretty girl that I just rushed off without a thought to my responsibilities?

I stormed into my bathroom, shedding my

soaked sweats and winging them to the tub. Not wanting to leave Danny longer than necessary, I dragged a towel over my damp skin and tossed it to the tub next to the sweats.

In the connected walk-in, I grabbed the first dry sweats I found, plus a T-shirt, and pulled them on, then headed back toward Danny's room.

None of this would've happened if I hadn't agreed to the damn auction. None of this would've happened if Harper hadn't taken my sister's lame-brained dare to bid on me.

Danny was fine this time, but I couldn't help but think about the many discussions my cousin Jamie and I had over the years about our asshole fathers who never made their kids a priority.

Since Jamie's death, since the day Danny had been entrusted to my care, I'd felt twice the pressure to be and provide everything that sweet boy deserved. For Danny, but also for Jamie.

I had no room in my life for casual dating or women. Not a year ago and not now. Danny deserved as much of my efforts and attention as I could give him around the demands of my career.

When Talia Latimer had asked me to participate in the auction, she'd wisely focused on the fundraising aspect, how the money raised would make a difference in kids' lives. I'd been all in for that. I'd figured I could spare a couple hours on a date for a good cause, then go straight home to my boy and get back to life as usual.

The element I hadn't counted on was Harper Ellison. She'd managed to distract me without even trying.

That was on me, but the sooner I could get her out of here, the better.

When I walked back into Danny's room, I was stunned to find him snuggled up to Harper. I hadn't been sure he'd go to her at all, but I damn sure didn't expect him to relax and accept her so easily.

Understandably, he was hesitant with anyone outside our family. He was used to me, my mom, Levi, and Dakota. I'd never left him in anyone else's care. If my family couldn't stay with him, I canceled my plans.

It appeared my son had as hard a time resisting the allure of Harper as I did.

Any other time, I would've been relieved to see it, but at the moment, it was like rubbing salt into my self-imposed wound.

Biting down on my annoyance, trying to reclaim an ounce of calmness for Danny's sake, I stepped toward her and reached for my son. "Let's get you back to sleep, Danny boy."

I was careful about how I took him back, touching Harper as little as possible, not wanting to catch her scent again. I'd be hard-pressed as it was to get her out of my mind.

Danny came to me as he always did, but he peered back at Harper with interest. She smiled and gave him a little wave.

"Can I do anything else?" she asked.

"You've done enough. Just go to bed so I can get him back to sleep."

I didn't realize how harshly the words came across until I saw Harper stiffen, her mouth open as if she'd been about to say something and then thought better of it.

She pressed her lips together, lowered her chin, and walked out the door without another word.

That was shitty of me and I knew it, but my priority now was getting Danny back to sleep, so I let her go.

Chapter Eleven

Harper

I slept for maybe two hours in Max's guest room and woke up before the sun rose.

I lay there in that luxurious bed, so uncomfortable in my own skin it was as if I'd gotten blackout drunk last night and made irrevocable, bad decisions that would change my life forever. Except I hadn't consumed anything but a couple of weak cocktails at the gala, and I hadn't committed to any decisions, life-changing or otherwise.

I'd merely realized how badly I needed to.

And then there was Max.

Just before six a.m., I stuffed the few things I'd brought with me into my backpack and put it on.

When I snuck out through the guest room's exterior door, the sun was just rising, casting the lake in muted pinks and yellows. In spite of my grouchiness, it was a sight to behold. I couldn't help but wonder what it'd be like to live on the water and start every day with such a view.

I made my way around to the other side of the house, walked through the manicured lawn to the street, and took off in a jog toward home. I knew it had to be seven or eight miles, farther than I usually ran, but I hadn't figured out a better way to get there. I had friends I could call, but I wasn't up for explaining the Max situation to any of them and particularly not to Dakota. I didn't want to talk about Max at all. As far as I was concerned, he could fornicate himself right off after the way he'd acted last night in Danny's room.

Did I screw up by kissing him?

Probably.

Okay, resounding yes.

But there was no justification for him acting like an asshole when I'd only asked if I could help with anything else. I'd take the blame for the kiss but not for his son's dirty diaper or the battery in the baby monitor going dead.

I would need the full eight miles to work off my bad mood.

I headed toward downtown, which was on the

way home, thankful not many people were out and about yet.

I needed to stop thinking of Naomi's house as home since it was clear I was no longer welcome. I wasn't sure how I'd handle her jackass brother when I got there, if he was still there, but I'd figure it out. I hoped everything would be okay now that it was daylight and he'd had a chance to sober up, but I wasn't going to lower my guard.

When I reached the town square, the only businesses that were open this early, as usual, were the bakery, the diner, and the gym. I went into Sugar to get a bottle of water since I hadn't planned this third-of-a-marathon trek this morning and didn't have my own bottle with me.

As soon as I stepped inside, the aroma of sugar and fresh-baked carbs enveloped me. I ordered an apple cinnamon muffin, congratulating myself on the choice that was healthier than a donut. At least this had fruit in it, right?

Olivia London was working the counter. She was a few years older than me, but we ran into each other often and were friendly. I kept our conversation focused on the array of goodies in the display, hoping she wouldn't notice or ask about my backpack, which screamed *walk of shame*. By the time I turned toward the door to leave, Chloe Henry was stepping up to the counter to order, so Olivia's attention was diverted.

As I walked back outside, I realized the rest of the town might already know Ian Finley had showed up, depending on whether he'd made any appearances before arriving at Naomi's last night. The best way to find out was to check the Tattler app.

On the sidewalk outside of Sugar, I went toward the right side of the square instead of left, even though the left route was more direct to Naomi's. The left route passed in front of the Dragonfly Diner, where I worked, and the gym, where there were sure to be people on the machines in front of the windows, watching passersby. The right path would have fewer people to run into.

I stuffed the water into my backpack, took a bite of the muffin, and opened the Tattler on my phone. As I walked along the sidewalk, I scanned the topics.

The Rusty Anchor had hosted a surprise appearance of Everly Ash last night, playing some of her new songs to a crowded beer patio.

Kizzy Estes, live-in mother-in-law of Emerson Estes, met up with an "old friend" in Vegas and ended up eloping and moving to Sin City permanently.

Patrick, one of my coworkers at the diner, had announced his engagement to Sebastian Dumas.

Dr. Holloway's llama had gotten loose again and made her way downtown.

Elsa Karasinski had moved to an assisted living facility in Memphis and was closing Grandma's Attic.

Poor Ms. Karasinski, but she'd turned eighty-one years old last spring. No one was sure how she'd been handling her store of knickknacks from the last century, either financially or physically.

There were no mentions of Naomi's brother. He wasn't known in town, as he wasn't from here, but if he'd stopped by any businesses and mentioned his name, word would've gotten around because of his connection to Naomi. Everyone, not just the artists who used the studio, was curious about what would happen with their property.

I turned left at the corner, and my gaze went to the Grandma's Attic storefront. The windows were already papered over with Store Closed scrawled in large letters on each side of the door. I frowned, thinking of the dear lady and wondering how she must be handling this giant change in her life.

When I was almost past the store, I spotted a much smaller For Rent sign with real estate agent Darius Weber's photo, posted in the lower corner of the window.

I glanced at it as I walked by, then halted abruptly when I noticed the second-story apartment above the store was also available. Of course it was. Ms. Karasinski had lived up there for years, and now she was moving to assisted living.

With my hands shaking, I entered Darius's number into my contact list and walked on, past city hall, past the rest of the businesses on this block, until I hit the paved path that led to the residential neighborhood northeast of downtown and eventually to the road to Naomi's.

I kept my phone unlocked, with Darius's info up on the screen, my thumb hovering over the call button as I walked. On the one hand, it was as if the universe had set up this opportunity for me, just when I needed it. On the other, I knew Ms. Karasinski's apartment would demand a commitment of a year.

What if my plans changed before that year was up? What if I couldn't handle the rent for a full year?

With a self-derisive laugh, I said, "You don't have plans, so they can't change. And you don't even know how much the rent is."

I pushed it out of my mind as best I could and dropped my phone into my bag. Savoring my muffin, I kept walking at a quick pace toward the edge of town.

Once I'd made it to the county road to Naomi's, I chugged some water to wash down my breakfast, the thoughts starting to crowd in.

Should I call the real estate agent? It wasn't even seven o'clock yet. That was too early, wasn't it? Maybe not if you were in real estate and always hungry for the next deal?

Should I talk to Dakota first? I knew it was too early to reach her, but I could leave a message for when she got up. She'd already given her blessing on searching for places, so until I knew more about Ms. Karasinski's apartment, I didn't need to talk to her. The rent might be too high for us anyway.

Instead of taking action on any of it, I dug my phone out and pushed play on my running playlist, regretting that I hadn't brought my earbuds. I started running again, along the left side of the county road, the tunes half-audible as my phone bounced around in my backpack. It was enough to keep my mind from wandering too much to looming decisions and scary thoughts.

A couple hours later, I reached Naomi's driveway. I had a side stitch from the muffin, and my legs were extra Jell-O-y thanks to a night of little sleep, but I'd made it. Unfortunately the same car as last night remained in the driveway.

I hadn't figured out what to do about Ian and how not to get shot or assaulted if he was the violent type, so I pulled out my phone, paused the music, and brought up Darius Weber's contact info again.

With another glance down the half-mile driveway toward that car, I hit Send to call the real estate agent, planning to leave a message since it was still early.

"Darius Weber. How can I help you?"

My brows shot up, and I stopped my pacing. "Um, hi, Darius. This is Harper Ellison. I was calling about Ms. Karasinski's apartment." I swallowed, my mouth sandpaper dry. "Is it still available?"

Five minutes later, I ended the call and bit my lip, wondering what the heck I'd just gotten myself into.

"Good stuff," I said out loud, trying to reassure myself. "You need a place to live. Here's a place to live...in the perfect location."

My heart thundered on as I walked slowly toward Naomi's house.

I was the first to call about the apartment. The rent, if I split it with Dakota or another roommate, would be more than I was paying now, but anyplace that wasn't condemned would be more than I was paying. If I kept working at the diner and watched my spending, I could handle it.

Darius had explained the apartment was still full of Ms. Karasinski's belongings, as she'd had to move suddenly after a fall last week. It was, in Darius's words, *a bit of a challenge.* He said if I could squint past all the stuff, I could see it later today.

Without giving myself time to think about it, I'd agreed to see it. Nothing else.

I needed to see if Dakota could join me, or someone, maybe Piper or Shawna or Maribella, who I worked with. But first... I was almost to the house that had been my home for three years.

I studied each window on this side, looking for movement inside or a sign of what was going on. Was Ian still passed out on the couch? Or dead?

That would solve some of my problems. I laughed at the awful thought, then sobered as I stared at the front door. What now? Walk in like I always did, because I lived here? Or knock like a stranger, which I was? Neither one felt right.

I settled for knocking because I wasn't in the mood to get shot. As I waited for him to answer, I tried to think back on whether Naomi had ever mentioned whether her brother had a gun or was a violent type, but the truth was, she hadn't told me much about him.

The door whipped open, and there stood the man in question. He narrowed his eyes at me, not speaking. I didn't know how he usually looked, but today he looked like hell, with bloodshot eyes, scruff on his jaw, and weariness in his expression. He'd changed out of the wrinkled suit from last night and was wearing athletic pants and a Henley.

"Hi," I said tentatively. "I'm Harper. Naomi's roommate."

His shoulders lowered slightly as he averted his gaze to the ground, seeming defeated or annoyed or...regretful?

"You came by last night?" he asked in a voice rough with fatigue and most likely a severe hangover.

"Yes. With my...date."

Ian walked away from the door, toward the kitchen, leaving it open for me to follow, so I did.

I stopped at the doorway to the kitchen, where he stood on the opposite side, his back to me as he filled a glass with water.

"I suspect I owe you an apology," he said, not turning around.

"You don't remember me coming home? Telling me to leave?"

He drank half the glass, then rubbed his temple. "I have some memory of it."

I stood there tensely, waiting to see what he'd do next, ready to bolt for the front door if he got nasty again.

"What did you say your name was?" he asked.

"Harper."

He slowly turned to face me, leaning his weight

on the cabinets. "I'm sorry for the way I acted. I... wasn't in my right mind."

"Scotch can have that effect," I said lightly. "Been there."

I didn't like this guy, didn't trust him for anything, but I needed to get along with him well enough to have a chance to move my stuff out. Even better would be to find out what he planned to do with the studio.

"You lived here with my sister?"

I nodded. "For three years. We were good friends." I willed my emotions to stay level. "We didn't have a formal lease, but I paid her rent every month. I could show you payment records on my phone—"

"That's not necessary."

I leaned on the doorframe, lowering my guard by a degree but not relaxing enough to enter the room. "Your aunt Sharon tried to contact you after Naomi... She said she left a dozen messages."

"Yeah," he said. "I was in Thailand, off-grid for two months." His lips slipped into a frown momentarily. "I didn't know until a week ago. This is the soonest I could get here." The quiver in that last word told me what his words didn't. Not getting the messages about his sister bothered him.

"You and Naomi weren't very close, right?"

"We were...different. Opposites, you could say. It's been a few years since I talked to her."

"I'm sorry to hear that."

He turned his gaze out the window that looked over the driveway. "We fought about this place when our grandfather left it to us. I wanted to sell it then."

"She didn't," I said with certainty. "She loved this place. The farmhouse. The land. The studio."

"That outbuilding out back?"

It was technically a farm outbuilding, I supposed, but Naomi had made it so much more. "Have you been inside?"

Ian let out a sardonic chuckle. "No. I didn't make it past the scotch."

There was enough self-derision in his tone that I kept quiet, wondering for the first time if there was more to this guy than I ever expected.

"I came back to take care of business," he said. "Drove straight here when my plane landed yesterday to take stock of what would be involved." He dropped his gaze to the floor and rubbed his temples. "When I walked in the door..." He shook his head, his eyes closed, then swallowed. "Everything about this place is so one hundred percent my sister... Damn." His voice cracked, and he took several seconds to speak again. "We hadn't talked for five years. I thought I was still mad at her. Then I walked in here, and it was as if she might glide into the room at any second. The colors are her. The decor is her. I could swear it even smells like her, light and airy and sweet."

I had the same thought every time I walked inside, even though it'd been weeks since Naomi had been here in the flesh. I could still smell her sweetness.

My caution toward this guy slipped several degrees and was replaced by sympathy. I could tell just from looking at him his sister's death had hit him harder than he'd anticipated.

"I'm not a big drinker," he continued. "I didn't expect to be blindsided by her loss..." He covered his eyes, then roved his hands down his face. "I saw the scotch and got a glass to dull things a bit."

"Did it work?"

"Not nearly enough."

I nodded. "I tried the same kind of thing a couple of times. Vodka instead of scotch. It doesn't matter how much you drink. When you sober up, she's still gone."

"Yeah," he said on a pained exhale. "I'm sorry you walked in on that. Sorry you had to go somewhere else last night. Please tell me you didn't sleep in your car."

"I didn't sleep in my car." That would've been smarter, I realized now.

He drank the rest of his water, set the glass on the counter resolutely, as if he was closing the topic of last night. I needed to do the same.

"Do you know what you're going to do with this property yet?" I asked. "A lot of people are wondering."

"I'm going to sell it."

Even though that wasn't surprising, it felt like a punch to the gut.

"I'll give you time to find a place to live," he said, as if my reaction showed on my face. "I'll move to a hotel."

"It's your house."

"I own it, but it's your home. Contrary to what you saw last night, I'm not a complete asshole."

I studied him and found I believed this was more Ian Finley than the guy from last night. There was no question he was grieving his sister in addition to being hungover. Something in my gut said I could trust him on some level. Maybe if I spent more time with him, I could convince him not to sell. To keep the studio open. So many people relied on that space to escape into their art.

"Do you own a gun?" I asked.

"Do I what?" He said it with a chuckle of disbelief. "No. I don't own a gun. Do you?"

"No. I have a lead on a place to live, but it

would take a bit for it to be ready. I don't exactly know how long yet."

"That's fine. I'm not unreasonable...unless I've had a bottle of scotch."

"Thank you," I said. I watched him for a few more seconds, finding nothing to dissuade me. "You're welcome to stay in one of the other bedrooms instead of a hotel." I had a lock on my door, but I didn't think I'd need it.

He studied me right back, his head tilted. "If you're sure you're comfortable with that, I'll take you up on it."

"I'm sure. I'll be out in less than a month." I couldn't let myself think too hard about what I'd just indirectly committed to. I obviously couldn't stay here. "If it goes into September, I'll pay a pro-rated rent."

"That's not necessary," Ian said. "Being able to stay here will help me a lot. I'll be taking stock of what needs to be done, seeing to any repairs or upgrades. I'll stay out of your way as much as possible and give you a heads-up on any projects that might be disruptive."

I nodded just as I caught sight of an SUV pulling up in the driveway. My heart lurched when I recognized it as Max's. "I have one more condition to add to our deal."

His brows went up in question.

"That guy from last night? He's going to show up at the front door in about thirty seconds. I'm going out the back, to the studio. If you can get rid of him, I'll buy you dinner sometime."

Ian followed my gaze out the window as Max got out of his vehicle. With a half grin, Ian said, "I can handle him."

"Thanks." I returned his smile. "We'll shake later. I gotta go."

Without waiting for Max to knock, I beelined right the hell out the back way to my refuge.

Chapter Twelve

Max

I pulled up in Harper's driveway and put the SUV in park, scanning the house for any sign of activity. The windows revealed nothing, but movement behind the house, nearly out of my line of sight, caught my eye.

I was ninety-eight percent sure that was Harper. She'd scurried into the studio like a frightened mouse. I clenched my jaw hard enough to break a tooth. She'd obviously gone into the house while Naomi's drunken, asshole brother was still there.

I was out of the vehicle in a heartbeat, torn between storming into the house to unleash on the brother and following her to the studio to make sure she was okay.

Concern for Harper won out.

I strode across the gravel, keeping an eye on the back door of the house, half expecting that crazy son of a bitch to burst out in a fit of anger and go after her.

I let myself into the studio and paused for my eyes to adjust to the dimness. I was in an entryway that opened onto an expansive, high-ceilinged room. At first glance, I didn't see Harper, but I heard someone to the side. When I took a step into the room, I spotted her bending down and taking out a storage bin from a locker.

Her dark hair was pulled up sloppily, several strands spilling down along the sides of her face. She wore short running shorts that showed off an expanse of feminine legs and a cropped top that revealed the skin at her waist.

I stood there staring for longer than necessary, knowing I needed to alert her to my presence. I got caught up in the way her running clothes revealed so much of her tempting flesh. Then my gaze caught on her face. Her lips. The lips I'd had mine all over last night. Unreasonably, irrationally, the urge to kiss her again pulsed through me and nearly had me stepping toward her.

Tamping down on that idea before I did anything stupid, I scanned her for any sign of distress or injury. She appeared to be in no immediate danger.

As she pivoted around and set the box on the closest worktable, I cleared my throat, causing her to jump out of her skin.

"Sorry," I said. "Are you okay?"

"What are you doing out here?" She glanced behind me at the door, as if expecting someone else.

"Checking on you. Did he threaten you?"

"Who? Ian?" She looked behind me again in the direction of the house, her irritation written all over her face. "I'm fine."

She wouldn't meet my gaze, so I wondered if she wasn't leveling with me about the guy in her house or if she just didn't want to see me. The thought that I might be less welcome than the volatile dude inside took the wind right out of my sails.

And yet, in the next breath, it hit me again how warranted her anger toward me was.

Now that I knew she was physically unharmed, I needed to apologize.

Harper's focus remained on the plastic bin filled with what looked from here like colorful polished stones. She rifled through the bin, pulling out a stone here and there, laying some of them on a tray, setting some back into the bin, as if she was looking for something specific. As if she didn't care I was in the same room.

The irony of that struck me. For most of my life, I'd been unable to walk into a room or a business unnoticed. Because I was an athlete, anonymity had been impossible from the time I was in high school. How many times had I wished to be unnoticed? Just a regular guy living a private life? And now that Harper was acting completely oblivious to my presence, I longed to be acknowledged by her.

This girl had the power to turn my life on its head.

I cautiously walked toward her table, my footsteps and her clinking of stones the only sounds in the cavernous room.

When I reached the opposite side of her worktable, I halted, waiting to see if she'd acknowledge me.

She did not.

She continued her search, setting out stones that were all a similar pinkish-purple color.

"Harper," I said into the gaping silence, "I'm sorry I was an asshole last night. You didn't deserve to be treated that way."

Her gaze lifted to mine at last, those milk-chocolate eyes penetrating mine as if she was weighing my words. "I didn't. I don't." She returned her attention to the stones, pulling out an oval-shaped one and setting it beside the others. "Thank you for apologizing." She fiddled with more stones before adding, "I'm sorry I kissed you."

Her words hit hard, causing a pang in my chest. Ego? Pride? "Ouch."

Harper glanced up at me and narrowed her eyes. "You obviously didn't want me to."

Therein lay my conundrum. "Let's get one thing straight," I said quickly, hating that look in her eyes that said she thought I wasn't attracted to her. "The first thought of kissing you came the instant you opened the door to me at your house, looking like a dream in that sexy-as-fuck dress."

Her gaze popped up to mine again, her eyes going dark with heat.

Maybe I shouldn't have been so honest.

There was something about her though.

I'd known her for two days, for all intents and purposes, and she already had a way of making me want to level with her like I'd leveled with no one else.

As the silence lengthened, her brows shot up. "So I didn't read you wrong all night?"

"You didn't read me wrong, but it's complicated." I cringed at the cliché.

Her chest rose with a deep inhalation as she went back to searching through the box of stones.

I could bow out right now, tell her I didn't want

to get into it, or even lay the blame on her dad for why we couldn't be together. But that was only the simple, surface, easy reason. I'd never told anyone my reasons for not dating now that I was a father, but something about Harper Ellison made me want to show my cards. I wanted her to know it was me, not her.

I leaned my elbows on the high-top table, giving myself one last chance to *not* go into this sacred topic.

Harper already knew more about me than any woman I'd dated, because she'd asked. She seemed to instinctively understand me better. I knew from the get-go she wasn't after my money, didn't care about my previous fame. Knowing she wasn't scoping me out as a potential husband made it easier to reveal the Max no one else ever saw.

"The reason I was such a jerk last night is because I was pissed at myself for getting distracted from Danny. I can't let that happen. Danny comes first," I said with all the conviction in my soul. "I intentionally haven't dated since...since he got here." I paused and urged the thickness in my throat to recede, wondering when the punch of Jamie's death would have less power over me.

"Danny turned out to be okay," she said. "You didn't get distracted. You took your monitor with you. You were listening for him. It's not your fault the batteries quit while we were out there."

I could argue with that, but I didn't bother. The monitor, Danny's dirty diaper, those weren't the issue. "It's a small example of the bigger picture. A relationship takes energy and time. I can't afford those. Danny deserves as much of my energy and time as I can give him. Jamie named me as his guardian because he trusted me to put his son first."

Harper set down the stones she was holding and turned her full attention to me. "You're a wonderful father to Danny, Max. I saw it last night, but even before that, I heard how good you were with him. People talk in this town." She let out a half laugh. "All the damn time. And what I've always heard is how dedicated to Danny you've been. Like it or not, this town judges everybody, and if you weren't measuring up, word would've gotten around."

"This town often judges based on a partial picture. Limited knowledge."

"That's true," she allowed. "I know I only saw you with him for a few minutes, but there's not a doubt in my mind you love him to pieces and would do anything for him." She walked around to my side of the table and sat on top of it, inches away from me. Touching my arm, she said, "Max."

I met her gaze.

"Hear me. You're a wonderful, dedicated father to Danny. He's a lucky little boy to have you."

That lump in my throat pulsed back even bigger than before. "There's nothing lucky about losing both your parents before you're a year old."

"No." She squeezed my arm. "No. Absolutely not. But aside from that, if that had to happen, he lucked out that your cousin made you Danny's guardian."

"It's such a coincidence," I said, my voice going hoarse with emotion. "Jamie and I were as close as brothers growing up. One reason we were so tight is that we bonded over our asshole fathers. Both of them deserted our families. Both of them pretty much forgot their kids existed."

"Wow. That sucks. How old were you when your dad left?"

"I was thirteen. Jamie's dad left a few years before that."

Frowning, she asked, "Where's your dad now? Is he still alive?"

I shrugged. "Last I knew he was living in Arizona, married to wife number four. I heard that from my mother. I don't keep in touch with him."

"And Jamie's dad?"

"He's in Memphis. He came to Jamie's funeral, but I didn't talk to him. Didn't have anything to say to him."

"That's rough," she said after a few quiet seconds.

"Jamie and I swore we'd be much better fathers. And he was." My voice cracked. I fought to get myself back under control. "He was so dedicated to Danny."

"And he knew you would be too."

I nodded, unable to get any words out.

"That's a lot of pressure," Harper said quietly. "You care so much. You're already leagues ahead of both your dad and Jamie's."

I grunted.

"You nearly lost your mind over Danny having a dirty diaper," she said pointedly.

"That wasn't the issue, and you know it. The issue was that I was out cavorting in the lake with you when Danny needed me."

She laughed. "*Cavorting?*"

I might have cracked a little smile at her tone of disbelief.

"We were sitting in shallow water talking for most of that time," she said. "I'm not sure I've ever *cavorted* in my life."

"You were definitely cavorting." My smile grew along with my relief at the lighter subject. Latching onto the break in seriousness, I turned my attention to the tray of magenta stones. "What are you doing here with these stones?"

"Looking for my next project." Harper hopped down off the table, walked around it, and opened the locker she'd taken the bin out of earlier. She drew out another box, set it on the table, and removed the lid. She lifted out a tray that contained several pieces of jewelry—a deep purple teardrop-shaped pendant, a pair of smaller round earrings with light-blue-and-white patterned stones, a necklace with three triangular black stones spaced out along a silver chain. More earrings—some with clusters of smaller stones, some with single larger stones, all the pieces artfully set in silver.

"Did you make these?" I asked in a little bit of awe.

She pulled another tray out with more than a dozen rings in it, in similar styles, with colored stones set in silver. "I did. I kind of have an addiction to gemstones."

I picked up a ring with five different-sized circular stones in deep blue, turquoise, and a translucent white.

"That's lapis, kyanite, turquoise, chrysocolla, and moonstone," she said.

"It's stunning. So this is what you use the studio for? You make jewelry?"

"I dabble in a lot of mediums." She laughed. "I've dabbled in nearly all the mediums."

"Is jewelry your favorite?" I asked as I picked

up a large, irregular-shaped pendant with a reddish-orange-and-white striated stone.

Harper bit her lip as she watched me run my finger over the smooth stone. "It is," she said hesitantly.

That she'd committed now as she hadn't been able to last night in the car didn't escape me.

"Harper, why don't you do *this*? Your creations are incredible. People would pay good money for these pieces."

"I've sold a few to friends."

"That's a start." I picked up an earring with a trio of dark-violet and smoke-gray stones. "You have a gift. You should do more with it."

"Maybe." She was back to being noncommittal.

"Wouldn't you rather spend your time doing this than waiting tables?"

"There's nothing wrong with waiting tables."

"No, there's not. It's one way to pay the bills. But this... A lot of people can wait tables at the Dragonfly Diner. Not very many people can create unique pieces like these."

"They're not really that unique. Lots of people make jewelry like this."

"This is a business in the making."

"And that's the catch," she said. "That B-word is a scary one."

"Business?"

"I know nothing about running a business. Just thinking about it gives me an anxiety attack."

"You could learn about it though. Take a class or hire a consultant."

"With what money?" she said, laughing. "I don't even know what a jewelry business would look like."

"Online would be a great way to start because there's no overhead. Fewer expenses."

"Right," she said. One by one, she put the pieces back into the trays. She held her hand out for the earring I'd picked up.

"You're just going to pack them back up? Put the box away?" I handed her the earring.

She put it with its mate, closed the box, then slid it into the locker.

"What would you suggest? Take them down to the square, put out a table, and get myself into *business*?" she asked lightly as she walked back around the table to my side.

"Well, no. But you should really think about the possibilities."

"I have a lot going on right now. I have to move—"

"Right. You're not staying here, right? With that psychopath?"

"He's not a psychopath. Ian and I talked. He apologized. I think last night we walked in on him when he was going through something similar to your bike destruction night, except the only thing he destroyed was his liver. He said walking into Naomi's house hit him hard."

If that was the truth, I could sympathize. I wasn't ready to trust the guy though. "And you believe him?"

"I do. He seems contrite. Embarrassed. We struck a deal that I could stay here until I'm able to find a place and move out."

"He'll be here too?"

"For a while."

I didn't like it. Not at all.

"It's fine, Max. There's a lock on my door, but I'm not going to need it."

"You don't know that."

"I trust my instincts. And I'll be cautious."

"I don't like it."

The way she raised her brows made me stop and realize I had no right to say whether I liked or disliked anything in her life. We'd barely known each other before last night, and we weren't embarking on any kind of a relationship.

"When are you hoping to move out?" I asked.

"I'm actually looking at an apartment later today. Mrs. Karasinski's, above her store. Any chance you could go with me as a second pair of eyes?"

"I need to pick up Danny."

"Where is Danny?"

"I left him with my brother. I wasn't sure what I'd find out here with Naomi's brother."

She nodded. "You could bring him along."

"I could," I allowed, fighting with myself. Because a part of me wanted to go with her. "But your dad would probably find out."

"My dad doesn't get a say in my life."

"But he has a say in mine if I want to keep my job."

"He wouldn't fire you for looking at an apartment with me." She rolled her eyes.

"Probably not, but he could make things uncomfortable."

Harper grabbed my T-shirt in a bunch near my navel and pulled me closer. "You know saying my dad would be bothered by us spending time together only makes me want to do that even more, right?"

Her face was inches from mine, her eyes peering straight into my eyes. I could smell her scent, not the same spice from her perfume but more purely Harper, with a hint of feminine sweat that I found disturbingly alluring. I realized I was leaning into her and tried to get control of myself.

"Do you and your dad not get along anymore? It always seemed like you did from afar."

"We get along. We love each other. But whenever he tries to control my life, I like to get under his skin. It's sort of a hobby." She shrugged unapologetically, grinning like the troublemaker she was.

Then her lips were on mine, and without thinking, I put my hand on her waist and pulled her closer. I reveled in the sweet-tinged taste of her, the softness of her curves against my hard angles, the feel of her delicate but talented fingers running through my hair.

When I could convince myself to pull away long enough to speak, I said, "I'd tell you you're trouble, but I think you know that. I think you thrive on it."

Her lids slowly opened halfway, and she peered up at me. "If trouble means I like kissing you, I can own it."

"I like kissing you too. But we can't keep doing this. I can't do a relationship, Harper."

"Same. I don't do relationships. But if you keep chasing after me, I'm probably going to kiss you," she said, her tone playful.

I growled. "Chasing after you?"

"First to the lake last night, then here." She shrugged. "It's like you have a hard time resisting me or something."

"I have a hell of a hard time resisting you." Which meant I needed to stay the fuck away from her after this. I couldn't resist going in for one last kiss though. "I have to leave now," I finally said, managing to end the kiss again, fighting to back away from her.

Harper seemed as reluctant to stop as I was, but she merely nodded, as if she knew we were about two heartbeats from taking things further.

"Bye, Harper," I said. I walked toward the exit, stopped when I was almost there. "Keep your guard up around Naomi's brother."

"Yes, sir." A smart-ass to the end.

I couldn't deny I liked that about her. I liked a lot about her.

That didn't mean I could have her in my life.

I walked out the door. Breathing in the steamy summer air, I felt as if I'd avoided a close call.

If I didn't want to get burned, I'd have to do better at staying away from the open flame named Harper.

It'd been a wild couple of days, but I had game film to review, algebra quizzes to grade, and most importantly, a little boy to raise.

Chapter Thirteen

Harper

I'd been using art as an escape since that first class I took from Naomi years ago.

Today I'd gone out to the studio to avoid Max. I'd pulled out my polished gemstone collection without a goal beyond busying myself, soothing myself by running my fingers over the smooth surfaces, until Ian got rid of him. Obviously nothing had gone to plan.

The rubies had caught my attention, and I'd mindlessly pulled out all the pieces I had with no project in mind. After Max's appearance—or I should say, after kissing the hell out of Max *again*—I'd decided to turn one of the polished pieces into a ring. Only once I was halfway through the first stage of the project did it hit me that ruby is known for strengthening courage and passion.

Maybe that's why I kissed him.

Ha. If only I could blame a little polished rock.

I'd kissed him because, well, he was intense and hot and not expecting it. And fun as hell to kiss.

A better question would be, why *wouldn't* a girl kiss him?

Because she liked it too much, maybe, a voice in my head whispered.

I knew he'd told me about his dedication to Danny specifically to remind me there was no chance for something serious between us. Hard truth: That only made it easier to kiss him. If I thought he wanted a relationship, I'd run and lock myself in my room. Max had made it clear there was no chance of a real thing.

Between that and his sexy face and his athletic body? He was tough to resist kissing. That it threw him off-kilter was a bonus.

As I walked down the sidewalk toward Grandma's Attic, though, the joke might've been on me. I couldn't get Max out of my mind. How his lips felt. The way he'd taken less than a second to return the kiss. Those big hands on my waist, at the small of my back, lightly clutching my ass. I could easily imagine what it'd be like with no clothing between us and a mattress beneath us.

A smarter girl would promise herself to avoid Max, to stay away from the temptation. I was more apt to get myself in trouble, because honestly? I would not mind getting naked with Max Dawson one bit.

Approaching Mrs. Karasinski's storefront, I scanned the area for Dakota, who'd easily agreed to meet me here after her shift at Henry's. I didn't see her yet.

Movement inside the store caught my eye, and I realized Darius Weber was waving at me. He'd told me he was showing the shop to a prospective business owner before my appointment.

I heard my name and spotted Dakota hurrying toward me from across the square.

"You made it," I said when she was a few feet away.

"Just got off work. Demand for cold adult beverages is high today, so I'm running late."

"All good. Darius is still in the shop with someone."

The door opened then, and Darius greeted us. "Hello, ladies. Why don't you come in out of the heat."

"Thanks," I said as we followed him in.

Grandma's Attic was an appropriate name and

more acceptable in polite circles than, say, Grandma's Crap Collection. The store looked the same way it had for years. It was overflowing with knick-knacks and figurines, tchotchkes and trinkets, some of them probably still here from decades ago. It was like a garage sale with one-of-a-kind items, brand-name collectibles that targeted people Mrs. Karasinski's age, and a fine and casual dinnerware section that had probably kept Mrs. K in business over the years.

The store as a whole was chaos to the eyes. I was sure some people might see a treasure trove, but I just saw a mess. Always had. Bless that dear woman's heart.

"We're running a little behind, so I'm going to leave Cambria down here while I take you two upstairs," the real estate agent said.

My eyes went to the side of the store he gestured to.

"Cambria Clarke! What are you doing here?" I rushed over to the girl I'd gone to school with. We'd been in the same grade and the same friend group. At least half that group had scattered after high school, most of us growing apart. I knew Cambria lived outside of town.

"Harper! It's been ages. Hi, Dakota. It's good to see you both."

"Hey, Cambria. Are you opening a business?"

Dakota asked. Dakota had been a year ahead of us in school, but everyone knew just about everyone in this town.

"I'm...thinking about it." Cambria glanced at Darius and smiled. "Thinking pretty hard. I want to open a store to sell my candles. This"—she swept her arm out—"is a little more than I'd planned on though."

I wondered if she meant just square footage, as it was a generous-sized storefront, or if she was also referring to the, uh, shit show of old merchandise.

"It's a lot for candles," Dakota said.

"I've played with the idea of adding some gift items, home decor, that kind of thing, but I'm not sure. It's a lot more than I planned to take on."

My conversation with Max about selling my jewelry popped into my mind, but I kept quiet. That was a crazy thought. As crazy as it'd been when Max had suggested opening my own business.

"You can't beat the location," Darius told her. "You'd get the traffic here to sell whatever you decide to sell."

"That's true. I wouldn't have to market as aggressively to get people in during tourist season." Cambria glanced around thoughtfully again. "Do you mind if I stay a little longer to think about the possibilities?" she asked Darius.

"Not at all," he answered. "Let me take Harper and Dakota upstairs and get them started. Then I'll be back down to check on you."

"Thank you. Good luck, you two." Cambria waved distractedly and seemed to turn her attention to her thoughts again.

We followed Darius out the back way into a vestibule with an exterior door and a stairway going up.

"Your stairs are inside, which is hard to find in these downtown buildings," Darius said. "No shoveling or salting in the winter."

"No shoveling's a plus considering I don't own a shovel," Dakota said.

"Same." I went up after Darius.

At the top landing, Darius stopped and faced us. "Okay, I need you to go in with an open mind."

"Oh, hell," Dakota said. "Is that code for *It's a disaster?*"

Darius chuckled, which I didn't take as a good sign. "Mrs. Karasinski's apartment is as...*full* as her store. She's a sweet lady, but she's definitely a *collector.*"

"What you're saying is it's a shit show too," I said, already wondering what other rentals might be available.

I hadn't started my search in earnest yet, but I was pretty sure there was nothing else downtown.

Places on the square were rare. When someone moved in, they generally stayed for a good long time. I'd heard when Cash Henry moved in with his then-fiancée, Ava, his apartment above Bergman Hardware had been rented out within six hours.

After living in the country for three years, I wouldn't mind being within walking distance of everything. We'd have to act fast if we wanted this place.

Darius unlocked the door, then paused before twisting the knob. "You'll need to squint past the belongings. Look at the structure, the room sizes, the features like the skylight and rooftop patio out back. Focus on the potential."

"You're scaring the crap out of me," Dakota said.

Darius pushed the door open and let us enter first.

"Oh. My. God," I said.

"You did not exaggerate," Dakota added.

I blinked and tried to breathe. "I'd say you understated."

"Is she a hoarder?" Dakota stepped past me, her head going back and forth as she took in all the clutter.

"All of this will be removed within the next week," Darius assured us. "The owner said she'd replace the floors and paint all the walls. It's gonna look fantastic once we take out Mrs. K's belongings."

"Poor woman," I said, because she was sweet as pie, but how did someone live like this?

"I know this isn't ideal," Darius said with a smile, "but I've had three other calls on it today. I've got two showings so far tomorrow. I'm not trying to pressure you, because it will be rented fast regardless. I just want you to know that, if you like it, you'll need to act quickly."

Dakota and I exchanged a look that spoke of nervousness, maybe a little excitement, and a good dose of what the fuck.

"The kitchen appliances were replaced three years ago. There's a stackable washer-dryer in the bathroom, which is large especially considering when this was built. The bedrooms have windows looking out on the square."

"Too bad there's no balcony," Dakota said.

"The patio out back looks over the woods. Mrs. K has it crowded with old furniture but that will be removed. Try to—"

"Squint?" I asked.

"You're catching on," he said. "I'll be back to check on you in a few minutes. Take your time."

He pulled the door closed after him. Dakota and I looked at each other with our eyes wide, then burst out laughing.

"This is awful," she said. "It's no wonder Mrs. Karasinski fell. How could she not trip over all the crap?"

"I'm trying hard to see past it, but I'm struggling."

Dakota gazed around at the living room. "Okay. It's not huge, but we could fit a couch and a chair or two. A coffee table."

"Maybe some shelves over on that wall," I suggested.

"Let's look at the bedrooms."

They were on the front of the apartment, and each one had a window seat, currently piled high with clutter, but I was starting to imagine the potential.

"Oh," Dakota breathed out when she went into the bathroom. "Look at this."

I poked my head in the door and saw an old-fashioned claw-foot tub. There were towels and blankets filling it, but I could imagine bubbles and a glass of wine. "Nice."

The kitchen was small but functional with a large window to the back.

"Let's go to the deck," I said. "It feels like there's not enough oxygen in here."

Dakota laughed. "You're not one of those tidy freaks, are you?"

"I never thought so, but compared to this?"

"Everyone is," she said before I could.

We stepped out to the deck, built on the roof of the lower level. It wasn't large, and it too was full of crap, but with a cute bistro table and chairs, it could be the perfect spot for morning coffee.

"Sit," Dakota said, planting herself on an old wicker love seat. "I am dying to know how last night went. I saw the pics. You were a knockout. That dress was killer. I saw you and Max dancing. It looked like you were getting along well?"

I lowered myself to the worn cushion next to her, letting my mind catch up to her change in subject. "The gala was good. He was fun."

"Max? Was fun? Did you get him drunk?"

"Stop," I said. "He didn't drink, but we danced. And he was exactly what I needed to get through the award acceptance."

"Borrrring. Tell me you spent the night with him."

Laughing, I said, "I did."

Her eyes went big, and she grabbed my arm. "What? My brother got lucky? I mean, don't tell me details, but I hope it was good."

"I'm sorry to bust your bubble, but your brother did not get lucky." I explained to her about finding a drunk, mourning Ian and that I'd slept in Max's guest room.

"That sounds more like Max. Always so careful these days."

"I did kiss him," I said, grinning.

Her head whipped toward me. "*You* had to put the moves on *him*? You know what? I take it all back. You deserve so much better than him," she said lightly.

I laughed again. "I did what you wanted. I got him out of the house."

"Plus kissed him. His head probably spun around at that."

"You said you didn't want details," I said.

"I don't. But if you've got some psycho living at Naomi's, we need to get you out of there, like, yesterday. Unless you'd rather shack up at my brother's."

"No." It was only a half lie. I didn't want to shack up, only sex him up till his head exploded...or other body parts. Keeping a grin to myself, I said, "I think we should jump on this place. They're taking all the crap out, redoing the floors..."

Nodding, Dakota said, "It could be a kick-ass place to live." She frowned. "Tell me the rent again?"

I told her what we'd each owe and what Darius had estimated the utilities at.

"I was thinking about increasing my hours at Henry's," she said.

"You could cover it even now, right?"

"I could. It'd be pretty awesome to not live at home anymore."

I shuddered. "I don't know how you do that."

"My mom is not your dad."

"Fact. So? What do you think? Are you in?"

As she studied me, a grin made its way across her face. "Let's do it."

"Yes!" I hugged her, and we swayed back and forth with excitement. "Here's to new adventures, roomie."

"Let's go tell Darius."

We didn't bother going through the rooms again. I was ready to get out of that cluttered space. We thundered down the stairs, laughing, exhilaration and excitement bubbling up inside of me.

Signing a lease was a big deal for us, but living with Dakota would be good. It was past time for me to get out of Naomi's overly quiet farmhouse that echoed with memories. I could take the memories with me and leave behind some of the loneliness.

"We'll have to be quieter when there's a business open," Dakota said. "I hope it's Cambria's."

We entered the store and found Cambria by herself behind the checkout counter, which appeared to have been partially cleared off.

"Hey, ladies. How'd it go?" she asked.

"Have you been up there to see it?" Dakota asked.

Cambria shook her head.

"It looks like down here," I told her. "We're doing it anyway."

"Congratulations," Cambria said.

"They're shoveling out all the shit," Dakota added. "Where's Darius?"

"He went outside to take a phone call. It sounded like someone asking about the apartment."

"It's ours, bitches," Dakota said. "What about you? Did you decide to go for it?"

"I'm still thinking," Cambria said. "I had in mind something about a third of the size of this, but that back room would make an ideal space for candle making. I use an old barn now, but it's close to falling down, and it won't work once the weather turns cold."

"What kind of candles do you make?" Dakota asked.

"I do special shaped ones, like animals, pine trees, canoes, sandcastles. Lake themed stuff. Plus scented tapers and columns and votives, all handmade."

"You sell them at the farmers market, right?" I remembered seeing her at a booth a time or two.

"Every week. I've been selling online and at craft shows and art fairs, but I'd like something a little more settled and stable. It takes a lot to travel around the state and set up and take down every weekend. Sometimes those are a bust, and I've wasted a lot of time."

"You'd keep busy all summer here," I said. "Plus holidays."

"Weekends," Dakota said. "Could you make enough candles to keep the place full though?"

Cambria shook her head. "Not with this much square footage. I was planning to carry candleholders, incense, things like that, but here I'd need more."

"How do you feel about jewelry?" I asked before I could think it through.

Cambria tilted her head.

"Oh, my God, you should see Harper's designs," Dakota said. "Do you have pictures?" she asked me.

Swallowing hard, wondering what I'd started, I pulled out my phone and swiped until I found some of my more recent creations. I let Cambria peruse them.

"These are gorgeous. I love your style, Harper." When she got to the end of them, she asked, "Where do you sell them currently?"

"Um, I mostly don't. I have a couple boxes full."

"Just sitting there going to waste," Dakota said oh-so helpfully.

"You should see Dakota's ceramics. Her mugs are big and beautiful. Show her," I prompted.

By the time Darius came back inside, Cambria had raved about Dakota's creations, and we'd helped her brainstorm other possibilities for merchandise if she decided to rent this spot. It was fun to think about. She was cautious about taking it on, though, understandably.

"What'd you two think of the apartment?" Darius asked when he reached the counter.

I looked at Dakota to make sure she didn't have cold feet. She nodded subtly.

"We'll take it," I said.

"Excellent. A lot of people are going to be sad to miss out," Darius said. "We'll just run a background check and a credit check tomorrow. Then we can fill out paperwork and get the lease signed. Mrs. K's son has a company coming to move his mom's belongings out next weekend. The property owner can get the flooring replaced, and then it'll be yours."

He shook my hand and then Dakota's.

"And what about you, Cambria? You ready to take the leap?" Darius asked.

"Not quite yet," she said. "Can I sleep on it?"

"Of course."

"Do you have anyone else looking at it yet?"

Her blue eyes looked contemplative and a little cautious.

"I had a call, but they didn't seem serious," Darius said. "I can let you know if any other inquiries come in."

"Please. It's a great space. I just need to pivot my business idea a bit."

"That's fair." Darius led us all to the front door, let us out, locked up, and told us he'd be in touch tomorrow. After shaking our hands, he said, "You ladies have a good evening."

"You too, Darius," I said.

We watched him walk off. Then Cambria said, "I don't suppose you two have thought about going into business, have you?"

"Not too much," Dakota said, laughing.

I shook my head and thought again about my discussion with Max this morning, but there was a big difference between selling my jewelry online and opening a full store in downtown Dragonfly Lake.

"I might be willing to consign my pieces to you, but I'll be honest. Opening a store scares the crap out of me," I said.

"Me too," Cambria said with a laugh. "I might take you up on the consignments. I have a lot of thinking to do tonight."

"You do. Good luck with it," Dakota said.

Once Cambria headed off, Dakota and I decided to go to Humble's Pizza for a slice and a celebratory toast.

Arm in arm, we walked down the sidewalk toward the restaurant. My stomach was jittery, but I wasn't sure if it was from excitement about the apartment or something else. Something like a gut feeling I should think more about Cambria's offer.

One major life step was enough for today, I decided, and did the best to put the rest out of my mind so I could enjoy the evening.

Chapter Fourteen

Max

I awoke sitting up on the sectional in my living room, my feet on the coffee table, my body sweating, and my dick hard.

As I blinked awake, I took a few seconds to get my bearings. The sun had set. It was still Sunday evening, just after nine according to my phone. I'd been grading quizzes after putting Danny to bed. I'd dozed off and had one hell of a hot dream featuring the sexy troublemaker who'd kissed me this morning. In my dream, she'd done a lot more than kiss me.

"Fuck," I said out loud as my blood pumped south.

I refused to give in to the urge to finish myself off to thoughts of my boss's daughter. I wasn't some eighteen-year-old who needed to rub one out just because of a forbidden dream. Instead I got up and headed toward Danny's room to check on him, a surefire way to cool my jets.

On the way through the kitchen, I started counting backward from one hundred by threes to get my mind off the discomfort in my sweatpants.

I opened Danny's door enough to see inside. He was asleep, so I snuck to the side of his crib to watch him for a few deep, peaceful breaths. As I'd hoped, my love for my son took over, and my body chilled the hell out. I reached out, wanting to run my fingers over this amazing little guy's cheek but stopping myself so I wouldn't disturb him.

I watched his chest rise and fall a few more times the way I'd obsessively done when he'd first come into my care. The never-ending anxiety that something bad could happen to him was like an old bathrobe by now. Familiar but ugly.

Content that he was sleeping soundly, I crept back out of his room, relieved my erection was gone. I returned to the pile of math quizzes on the coffee table and dug into the last two of the night, hoping equations would keep my mind off Harper.

When I finished, I put the graded quizzes in my work bag, and thoughts of the brunette with the brown eyes returned in full force. I wondered what she was doing. Back in the studio creating jewelry? Or was she in the house with Naomi's unpredictable brother?

I didn't like the second possibility. She might trust him, but what if her instincts were wrong? I didn't know her well enough to have a gauge of that yet.

I picked up my phone to check on her. That was all.

> Is your housemate leaving you alone?

I typed in the words but didn't press Send. We weren't this familiar, were we? I didn't want to be a text buddy. Couldn't really afford to open that door.

I couldn't handle not reassuring myself she was okay with her unstable roommate though.

I pushed Send.

After thirty seconds, bubbles showed she was typing. I didn't allow myself to think how relieved I was.

An eternity passed before a message appeared, making me wonder if she'd rethought replying.

He's beat on my door three times. Don't worry, it's locked, plus I moved my dresser against it.

I straightened and was on the verge of calling her when the next message came through: a winking emoji and a laughing emoji.

I should've guessed. Sagging into the cushion, I shook my head, eventually getting to the point where I could smile. As always, Harper was trouble walking.

Why couldn't I seem to leave trouble alone?

I was still trying to come up with a reply when she sent another message.

Max? I was teasing. I'm fine.

Before I could answer that, she sent a photo of herself, which revved my pulse right back up.

She was waving and smiling, an open-mouthed, smart-aleck grin. Her dark hair was down except for a braid on each side of her part that went from her forehead to the back. Her eyes shone with mischief and a sparkly shade of lavender shadow. Her lips were glossed in a muted tone, her cheeks pink with a natural flush, and she wore a necklace with a light-purple, oval stone and earrings that coordinated, all of them set in silver. I was sure she'd made the pieces herself.

I couldn't see more, couldn't tell where she was beyond outside. I tried to tell myself I didn't care, but I couldn't pull it off.

No doubt she was trying to throw me off, as she liked to do.

I sat there shaking my head, grinning like that eighteen-year-old boy I wasn't, weighing my options, halfheartedly attempting to talk myself out of giving it right back to her.

I lost the battle and typed in one word.

Hot.

She didn't immediately reply, so I hoped I'd thrown her off.

When a full minute or two passed and she still hadn't said anything, my confidence slipped. Had I misread her?

Maybe she was driving and couldn't answer.

Or maybe my text flirting game was outdated and lame.

I stopped waiting for a reply, busying myself by prepping my bag for work tomorrow. I went to the kitchen to make my lunch as I always did before bed, but before I could pull out ingredients for a chicken wrap, there was a quiet knock at the front door.

My adrenaline started pumping at the thought it might be Harper. It was after nine p.m. on a Sunday. Who else would be at my door, particularly after our back-and-forth? Still, when I looked out the peephole and saw her standing on my doorstep, there was a punch to my chest that took the wind out of me and made my mouth go dry.

I opened the door and tried to look puzzled instead of really fucking happy to see her.

"Hi," she said a little shyly. "Is Danny asleep?"

"He is."

She relaxed a degree. "Do you mind if I come in?"

In response, I opened the door wider and stepped back. I was running possible comments through my mind, smart-ass ones, flirtatious ones, but I held them in, because suddenly the stakes were a lot higher with her staring up at me in the flesh.

"Am I interrupting anything?" she asked as she glanced around.

"Just an ill-advised flirtation via text messages with this hot girl I know."

Her shoulders relaxed even more, and her smile widened, became more natural.

"What brings you by?" I asked. We weren't on

booty call level, though if she kissed me right now, I didn't think I could resist the temptation.

"I just wanted to talk," she said quickly, shutting down my line of thinking in a heartbeat.

Well, mostly. Because the parts of her that hadn't shown in the photo were just as alluring as that pic she'd sent over.

Her legs were showcased by a short lavender skirt with silver buttons down the front. On the top, she wore a white, thin-strapped tank that contoured to her curves and bared a two-inch strip of skin at her waist. On her feet were minimalist sandals with wedge heels, making her legs about two miles longer.

"Talk," I parroted as I reined in my thoughts. "We can talk. Inside? Or we could sit on the deck."

"The deck's good. It's cooled down a lot."

I flipped the living room and kitchen lights off except for one under-cabinet one to avoid attracting bugs and went to the thermostat and flipped the AC off. Then we went out the back. I left the slider open, closing only the screen, so if Danny needed me, I could hear.

"Have a seat," I said, gesturing to the outdoor sectional that faced a fireplace. It was cooler than the daytime but not nearly enough for a fire.

Harper leaned down and removed her shoes, then sat in the corner of the sectional and pulled her legs up under her, her knees to the side. "This is amazing," she said, sinking into the lush cushions. "It's more comfortable than any furniture I own. Which isn't a lot actually. That'll have to change soon. Dakota and I are signing a lease."

"Mrs. Karasinski's place?" I asked as I sat at a right angle to her, keeping a few inches between us despite my desire to slide up against her.

"Yes. In spite of it looking just like the inside of her shop." Her eyes widened meaningfully.

"There's a lot of stuff in her shop if I remember right."

"You do. I can't wait to see the apartment once the crap is all gone. The bedrooms each have a window seat looking out on the square. There's a deep, claw-foot tub that looks unused, and the back deck has a view of the woods." Her eyes sparkled with excitement.

"Congratulations. You can't beat the location. How soon can you move in?"

"A couple of weeks. They have to empty it, and then we're getting new floors and paint."

"The sooner you're out of Naomi's—"

"Ian's fine. Stop worrying. So when we were looking at the apartment, the agent was also showing the shop downstairs to a potential business owner."

"Anything good going in?"

"Well, maybe. Do you know Cambria Clarke?"

"I had her in an advanced class years ago."

"She graduated the same year as me," Harper said. "She's thinking of opening a shop to sell her candles."

My brows shot up. "I haven't been inside that store for a long time, but that'd be a lot of candles, wouldn't it?"

She laughed and nodded. "A shit ton of candles. So she's rethinking her business plan, possibly broadening her focus." Harper paused and inhaled deeply. "I said I might be open to her selling my jewelry."

"Hell yes. That's great, Harper. I think it'll sell easily."

She had a pensive expression, as if she was going to say more. She bit her lip, then said, "She asked us whether we'd ever thought about going into business."

"Like owning the shop with her?"

"I guess so. A partnership. I said signing a lease was a big enough commitment for one day. But I can't get the idea out of my mind. I was sitting at Humble's, celebrating with Dakota, and I kept thinking about what a shop like that might look like. After Humble's, we went to the Fly. There were lots of people out tonight, and I still kept thinking about Cambria's question."

"Do you think she meant it?"

"I have no idea how serious she was, but maybe?"

"So candles and jewelry?"

"And Dakota's ceramics. Cambria mentioned gift items and home decor. We could have hand-made soaps and body care, picture frames, stickers... Lots of possibilities."

She was animated, noticeably excited. "It sounds like you're legitimately considering going into business with her," I said.

"I don't know. It's...scary."

"It's outside your comfort zone. That's often a good thing. It means you're stretching. Growing."

"It's *so far* outside of my comfort zone."

"Why is it?"

"Business owner? Me?" she said, her voice pitching high. "I told you I don't know a thing about running a business."

"You have a unique product line in your jewelry. Plus ideas for other lines. Business is something you can learn. I'm betting Cambria has some business acumen, or she wouldn't be looking to open a store."

"I don't really know. We've sort of fallen out of touch as adults." She went thoughtful and quiet again, then asked, "It would be crazy to pursue this, right?"

"Maybe it'd be crazy not to."

She laughed as if she thought I wasn't serious.

"Harper, you told me barely twenty-four hours ago you needed to find purpose. Something that excites you."

She sighed. "You're going to use my words against me, aren't you?" she said.

I laughed quietly. "You're going to fight what's right in front of you, aren't you?"

She leaned her head back into the cushion, peering at the ceiling fan on the overhang that sheltered this part of the deck.

"Tell me what scares you about it," I said.

"Everything," she said without thought.

"Let's break that down."

She lifted her head to frown at me. "You're going into teacher mode now."

"It's what I do. It seems like you showed up tonight to talk through this, right?"

"Maybe I came over because you called me hot."

"If that were the case, you wouldn't have told me about this business opportunity. You would've avoided it by kissing me. Again."

With an adorable pouty look, she said, "You don't have to call me out."

"Just calling 'em like I see 'em."

"It's not too late for me to go the kissing route." She said it like a threat.

The way my body reacted, it was anything but a threat.

"We had our one date last night," I said as if I wasn't tempted to lean over and kiss *her* this time. "Besides, you'd still have the same problem weighing you down afterward."

"Logical people are annoying," she said, but the fact that she didn't kiss me told me she really did want to talk out her decision, regardless of acting grumpy.

I held myself back from touching her in support. "If you went into business with Cambria, what's the worst thing that could happen?"

"I could fail," she said with zero hesitation.

That quick response took me aback. "People fail all the time."

"I don't."

"You've never failed?"

Harper bit her lip, thinking. She scrunched her nose up and said, "Not really. No."

I tilted my head and gave her a skeptical look.

She shrugged. "You can't fail if you don't really try."

"You haven't tried at anything? Ever?"

That was so opposite of my life in sports that I couldn't fathom it. And school... I'd always strived for good grades and graduated with a four-point-oh average.

"Just ask my dad. It frustrates the hell out of him." A ghost of a grin tugged at her lips for a second then disappeared.

"Wouldn't he be happy to see you take a chance on this?"

She covered her face with both hands, then slid them down to her mouth.

"Speaking as a parent," I continued, ignoring the inner voice that said I had no idea what I was doing as a parent, "I'd think he wants you to find success and happiness, whatever that might look like."

With her hands still in front of her mouth, she tapped her index fingers together repeatedly, agitated, not meeting my gaze. Then with a gusty exhalation, she spit out, "It's not about my dad. It's a me thing."

She was obviously struggling, and I could no longer resist touching her. I spread my palm over her lower thigh, above her knee.

"I'm scared of failing," she said in a quiet voice. "Of embarrassing myself. Always have been. I know my dad just wants me to be happy. I've tried to make myself believe I've been happy all these years drifting along, but deep down, I hate that I'm a scaredy cat. I hate that I can't seem to put myself out there and do anything meaningful." She squeezed her eyes shut tight. "Hate it."

"You do meaningful things. Look at the gala last night. You had everyone tearing up."

"That was for Naomi."

"That was meaningful."

Her hand landed on mine, but it almost seemed incidental. She was clearly lost in her thoughts, and I'd bet they weren't kind toward her.

"Harper. Give yourself some credit."

She pressed her lips together and shook her head. "You don't understand."

"Why don't you explain?"

Though she hadn't shed any tears, her breath in was shaky.

"Come here." I lifted my arm and made a place for her to sit in the crook of it.

Her short skirt made shifting awkward, but she settled in next to me, her legs stretched out on the perpendicular side of the sectional, and rested her hand on my thigh.

"Tell me what I don't understand," I said.

She trailed her finger back and forth on my leg, over the fabric of my sweats. Her eyes tracked her movement as her strokes went from short ones to longer ones. I'd already been struggling to ignore the effects her nearness had on me. But with her finger inching farther up my thigh...

I caught her hand in mine and wove our fingers together. Her gaze shot up to my face.

"Getting a little too close," I told her.

Her brows shot up, as if she was considering a full-on diversion tactic.

"We're talking about important stuff. You're not going to distract me," I said, meaning it.

She slumped back against my side, not talking but not trying to pull her hand out of mine either.

After several minutes ticked by, I felt her take in a deep breath. Then she said, "My family is a bunch of high achievers."

"Yeah?"

"Every single one of them. My sister is a junior partner at a big law firm in Boston. My brother makes a boat load of money as a stock analyst in New York and is happily married to Brian. Both my siblings were straight-A students. Ashley played volleyball and basketball. Jon played varsity soccer and went to State on the swim team. My dad, well, you know him. Everybody respects him. He's all about achievement, grades, activities, volunteering. My mom lives in San Francisco, and she's an interior decorator who caters to high-profile clients. Apparently small-town ranch homes and lake houses weren't enough for her."

"That's a lot to live up to, huh?"

She scoffed. "You think? I grew up hearing all

about how Ashley aced her government test and got voted class president. Jon was the valedictorian. My dad earned his doctorate when I was in grade school. I remember in first grade, Ms. Tanney raved about both my siblings. In front of the entire class, she said she expected great things from me."

I grimaced, guessing Ms. Tanney must've meant it in a positive, encouraging way, but obviously that wasn't how Harper had taken it.

You never knew, as a teacher or a coach, how things might land with any particular student. Every kid was different. Every kid was motivated by different things. There was no one-size-fits-all in teaching.

"I figured out early on it was easier to not try," she continued. "I already knew I couldn't do better than my older siblings on grades, so why try? I guess it stuck."

I pulled her to my side a little tighter. The teacher in me hated to hear that, but I'd had students over the years in a similar position. Add Harper's overzealous, well-meaning dad to the mix, and I could begin to understand how she'd taken the road that had worked for her. It was a shame she'd felt like less before she'd even gotten started.

"So yeah," she said. "I don't have a lot of experience going after things I want."

"But you might want this."

"I don't even know. Maybe? I don't know the first thing to do." She hesitated, then asked, "What would you do?"

"I'd get more information," I said easily. "Talk to Cambria. Find out what she's thinking. Discuss possibilities with her. Did she ask my sister too?"

"Yes, she was talking to both Dakota and me."

"The three of you should meet then. You can't decide on anything until you understand more of the variables."

"You're using math words," she said, acting disgusted.

I laughed. "Math people do that sometimes. It fits though. You need more information."

"Yeah." She was still for a few seconds. Then she stood abruptly, walked to the railing, and looked out toward the lake.

I missed having her against me the second she stood. Leaning forward, elbows on my knees, I watched her in the darkness, her back to me. A few strands of her hair rustled in the breeze. My eyes were drawn to the silhouette of her body, the womanly curves of her hips, the inward dip of her waist, the sexiness of her long legs and bare feet. I knew her toes were painted in a magenta polish even though I couldn't see it from here.

Now that she was at a safer distance, I couldn't

deny how much I wanted her. I wanted to know more of her secrets.

What kind of panties was she wearing under that short skirt?

How sweet would her nipples taste?

What kind of sounds did she make when she came?

My blood pounded through me as my dick grew hard. I stood, acknowledged I was making a poor decision, and went to join her at the railing anyway.

Chapter Fifteen

Max

I settled in next to Harper at the railing, our sides touching, both of us looking at the dark lake and the lights on the distant, opposite shore. With my blood thrumming through me, I fought to get my mind on her dilemma, where it should be.

"Getting more information from Cambria does not mean committing," I told her. "One baby step at a time."

Harper turned to face me, resting an elbow on the railing. Peering up at me with those gorgeous but unsure brown eyes that made me want to pull her into me to reassure her. "What if she wasn't serious?" she asked in a quiet voice.

I gripped the railing with both hands, battling the urge to turn toward her. Being face-to-face would make it too easy to touch her. "Then you know. But what if she was?"

Her chest rose with an inhalation. "That might be even worse. Max?"

I met her imploring gaze. A sly smile slowly spread over her lips. "It seems like you're afraid to face me."

I chuckled because she'd read me so easily. "It seems like you're about to pull your kiss-and-divert move."

"If you don't want me to kiss you, all you have to do is say it."

Gazing down at her, I took in the playful sparkle in her eyes, my attention getting caught up on her lips as she moistened them.

My blood pounded harder, straight to my dick. I clenched my hands on the railing, trying to curtail the urge to run them all over her body, pull her into me, feel every inch of her.

With our gazes locked, the air between us charged, time seemed to stand still.

"I want to kiss you," I ground out quietly, intently. "I want to touch you all over. Taste every bit of you. Push my cock inside you until you feel it in your chest."

With her eyes blazing into mine, she said, "Then do it."

I swallowed, still managing to hold on to the control that was unraveling like a very thin thread. Debating with myself.

"Your dad..."

"Has no place in this conversation," she whispered. "He'll never know."

I glanced toward the house, in the direction of Danny's room.

Harper laughed quietly. "He'll never know either."

For three heartbeats that nearly pounded right out of my chest, I watched her as I tried to convince myself she was wrong.

I couldn't do it.

And I could no longer resist her.

Turning toward her, I palmed her cheek, my hand shaking with need. With my other hand, I pulled her flush against me, then trailed my fingers down her back to her ass, my erection pressing against her.

The next heartbeat, my lips were on hers, devouring her, tasting her, breathing her in as if my life depended on it.

I turned our bodies so mine pressed her into the

railing as her arms went around my neck and her knee rose, her foot trailing up my leg, bringing her core into direct contact with my dick when her skirt crawled upward. A guttural groan rumbled from my throat as I felt her heat and softness through my sweats.

"Max," she whispered, "we should go inside."

"Right," I said on a shuddering exhale. I was half out of my mind, on the verge of drilling into her right here, where anyone could see us. I needed to rein myself in and quit acting like an animal. I nibbled on her lips, then wove our fingers together. "Come on."

Coaching myself to get my head on straight as we went inside, I locked the slider behind us and pulled the drapes, then glanced toward Danny's side of the house.

"Go check on him," she said.

Knowing that would ease my worries, I nodded and went toward his room. I paused outside his door, listened for any stirring before opening it. Prayed like hell he wasn't awake, didn't need me.

His room was silent, so I pushed the door open enough to lay eyes on Danny. With a baby sigh, he stirred, turning his head from one side to the other, but he slept on.

I watched him for another few seconds to assure myself he was out.

Without a sound, I pulled the door shut, then hurried back to the living room to find it empty. What the—

I realized a low light came from my bedroom. I went toward it, shaking my head, relieved as hell she was still here. When I came around the corner to where I could see inside my room, I stubbed my toe on the doorway as I took in the sight before me.

Harper was stretched out on my bed, naked from head to toe, her head propped on her elbow, hips curving up like an hourglass, breasts spilling onto the mattress. She'd turned on the string of blue LEDs around the tray ceiling, casting the room in just enough light for me to feast my eyes on her.

"You're fucking gorgeous," I managed. I closed the bedroom door and whipped my shirt over my head.

"Danny's okay?" she asked.

"Sleeping soundly."

"Monitor's on?"

I forced my gaze away from the vision she was, to the dresser, where the red power light shone back at me. As I nodded, I slid my sweats and boxer briefs down my legs, my cock jutting upward as soon as it was free. Harper's gaze centered on it, and her top leg rose, opening her to me. I knew this image of her, spread out on my bed like an offering of heaven, would be with me till the day I died.

She held up a condom packet she must've brought with her, because mine were in the master bath in a drawer somewhere, not having been accessed for more than a year.

"I love the way you think," I said as I lowered myself to the mattress next to her.

"I love the way you look," she countered.

With a growl of a laugh, I touched her at last, spreading my hand over the soft skin at her waist, running my fingers down to her ass, up her curves, to the side of her breast. With my thumb, I found the tip of her nipple and rubbed it, eliciting a gasp from her.

As if in retaliation, she grasped my shaft and stroked it. I caught my breath as my eyes rolled back into my head. As soon as I was able, I reached down, entwined our fingers, and dragged her hand upward. "Not yet." I kissed her lips, teased her lightly with my tongue and teeth. "First I want to taste every square inch of your body."

I kissed along her jawline, to the spot beneath her ear, then nibbled at her lobe as I closed my palm around her soft, ample breast.

"Not sure I can hold up to that without coming apart," she said after a gasp.

"Ohh, you're going to come apart." I kissed her lips, our needy breaths mingling. "Over...and over... and over."

In the sexiest feminine growl I'd ever heard, Harper said, "Love me an ambitious man."

I proceeded to show her how ambitious, laving my tongue over her, roving my hands across every bit of her soft, irresistible skin, learning her body and what drove her the most wild.

Her first orgasm came with my tongue between her folds. Her second exploded from her as I suckled her nipple and fingered her clit. I was lowering my mouth between her legs again, loving the way my name sounded from her lips as she climaxed, when she tugged at me, pulling me up to her mouth as she panted.

"Max, please."

"Please what?" I asked, then kissed her fully, our tongues tangling and twisting as we ate at each other's mouth.

She kneaded my ass with one hand, cradling my body between her legs. "I want the next one to be with you inside."

I nearly lost my load as she dipped her fingers between my legs. When I could speak again, I said, "What the lady wants..."

The sweetness of her giggle as she did wicked things with her fingers turned me inside out. I fumbled around the bed with one hand, trying to find the condom, not sure I could get myself sheathed fast enough.

Harper held up the packet, and I swiped it out of her hands, ripped it open, and slid it on. Bracing myself between her legs, I lifted one of her knees, opening her fully to me. I settled my cock at her entrance, squeezing my eyes shut with the effort it took to not rut into her like a wild animal, in case she wasn't ready.

"Max, you're killing me." She arched her body upward as she grasped my ass in both hands and pulled me into her, impaling herself with a slow, needful moan.

The sensation of being inside her, of her slick heat closing around me, clenching me with toe-curling friction, was nearly enough to make me come instantly. Fully seated, I paused to catch my breath and pull my shit together. "Give me a second," I said tensely, willing my body to hold out against the ecstasy that was Harper Ellison.

She gave me a few seconds, maybe ten. Then she contracted her inner muscles around me. I gritted my teeth.

When I could breathe again without coming, I pulled most of the way out and slammed back home. "Trouble," I said, unsure whether I meant it as a complaint or the highest praise.

"You seem...to like trouble," she said between my thrusts.

I didn't even try to deny that. I wasn't sure I could still speak.

With our bodies covered in sweat, moving as one, I drove into her, fighting a fine line between giving in to my own orgasm and holding on to make sure she came first. I was starting to learn the noises she made as her climax neared, loved how she communicated her pleasure so clearly with *oh, yes* and *oh, God*, and finally, as I was starting to see a kaleidoscope of colors and stars, my name fell off her lips, and her orgasm gripped her.

I tumbled over the next second, clasping on to her for dear life as sparks of fiery pleasure shot through me. I buried my nose in her long, silky hair and knew I'd associate her exotic scent with the most exquisite of pleasures until my dying day.

We lay there breathing hard, not talking. I had to let my body come down before my brain would start working. I'd come so hard I wasn't sure if I'd ever be the same again.

As soon as I realized I was lying on top of her and she was bearing most of my weight, I managed to roll off-center, so I was only half on her, not willing to give up all the skin-to-skin contact yet. I'd be content to lie here like this for a few days. Who needed food?

My son would need food.

The thought of him brought me back to reality faster than I wanted.

I fought off coherent thoughts and let myself just be with Harper for a while longer. I became aware of the way her breasts rose and fell as her breathing evened and slowed. Her skin, like mine, was covered by a sheen of sweat. I found the strength to lift my head and prop my chin on one arm as I gazed down at her. Her hair was strewn in every direction across my pillow. Her nipples were still erect, tempting me. I trailed a finger over one, causing her to shiver. A sexy, vixenish smile stretched over her swollen lips.

She had the look of a woman who'd been thoroughly sated. That had me feeling pretty damn good until she said, "You're not too bad, Max Dawson."

My brows shot up as I tried to discern if she meant that or if this was post-sex smart-ass Harper. "Not too bad?"

She let out a light, feminine laugh. "Yeah. That was pretty okay."

Her smugness registered, and I relaxed. "You weren't half bad yourself."

Harper laughed and leaned up to kiss me, pulling my head to her. Her kiss was fervent, her tongue plundering my mouth as if to put an exclamation point on the reaction she wasn't able to admit to.

I'd take it.

"Be right back," she said. She slid gracefully off the bed and went into the bathroom. I watched her walk confidently away, her hips with a slight sway to them. Every last ounce of that confidence was justified and then some.

I took care of the condom, then pulled the blankets back as I finally registered a chill in the air. Waiting for her, I lay on my back, legs under the covers, my hands behind my head, staring up at the dim blue lights. Endorphins still raced through me, leaving me in a contented, blissful state.

I liked sex as much as the next guy, but over the years, there'd been a lot of women who tried too hard, as if they thought they could land the former-NFL guy if they just wowed me in the sack. They were the types who tried to take the lead or wanted to get extra kinky. Sex could be calculating, I'd learned, but with Harper, it was different.

Harper had more of a you-get-what-you-see aura about her, as if she wasn't up for putting on airs for anyone and especially not this has-been athlete. She just...was.

It was refreshing as fuck.

The bathroom door opened, and my eyes locked onto her naked body and her pretty face again as she walked toward me. Instead of lying next to me, though, she sat on the edge of the mattress and picked up her underwear.

I frowned. I hadn't committed to being done with her yet, was pondering how long until I'd be ready for round two.

"What are you doing?" I asked, rolling to my side and propping up on my elbow.

"I need to go," she said matter-of-factly. Almost cheerfully.

I frowned, thinking of what another hour could bring us.

She must have read my thoughts, because she leaned over, kissed me briefly, and said, "My car's out front. The longer I'm here, the more likely someone will recognize it."

That brought reality home abruptly.

I sat up and did my best to look indifferent. To appear unworried that someone might've already seen her car. To seem not disappointed as fuck that there'd be no round two.

Harper was playing it smart. I was grateful one of us had our wits about us.

As she dressed, I pulled my sweats on commando, went out the bedroom door to the deck, grabbed her shoes, and carried them back to her.

"Thank you," she said, taking them from me but not putting them on.

I followed her out of my bedroom. At the front door, she stood on her tiptoes and pressed a quick kiss to my lips, said, "Night, Max," and walked out.

After I closed the door, I stood there letting it sink in that, for once, someone was in more of a hurry to end our night together than I was.

Chapter Sixteen

Harper

My seven a.m. shift at the Dragonfly Diner came way too early the next morning, even for an early riser like me.

I hadn't gotten much sleep at all. I'd like to say it was strictly from thinking about Cambria's proposition, but there was a lot of mooning over Max in there too.

No, not mooning. Just remembering.

Last night with Max... It was *hot*. Like, best-sex-of-my-life hot, and I'd had my share of good sex.

I hadn't been able to get him out of my mind even once I got home. After three orgasms, I should've been able to move on, but instead I'd lain there and relived our sexy times. That wasn't my usual MO. Usually it was nice while it lasted, and then I carried on with the rest of my life.

Max had spiced up my dreams for the short hours I'd slept. Then I'd woken for the day with my mind on him, my body jonesing for another go-round.

That was probably a red flag, but honestly, for sex that good, who cared? We'd said it was one and done, but if I had my way, Max and I would have a repeat...or a dozen.

"Your best customer's here," Monty, the owner and morning cook, said as I stopped for Rosy Mc-Namara's and Nancy Solon's breakfast orders at the window.

I picked up the plates—a scramble and a Dragonfly Dust Waffle—and turned toward the front of the restaurant to see my dad ambling to the counter. He greeted nearly everyone on his way.

"Hey, Dad," I called as I passed nearby.

"Good morning, Harper."

Rosy and Nancy's table was in the front corner by the window. "Here you go, ladies," I said as I set their plates in front of them. "Looks like Monty put an extra dose of sprinkles in your waffles, Nancy."

"Ooh," Rosy said, checking out her friend's

plate, which was, in fact, about twice as colorful as usual. "He knows they're your favorite."

"He ought to. How long have we been coming here?" Nancy asked.

"Can I get you two anything else right away?" I asked, doing a quick check that there were enough creamers on the table for Rosy. She used three per mug of coffee and normally had at least one refill.

"We're good, darling girl," Rosy said.

"Tell Monty these waffles are even better than usual." Nancy had drowned her plate in syrup the second I laid it down and already had a bite in her mouth.

"You got it."

I checked in with Chloe and Ava Henry, who were deep in conversation, then headed toward my dad.

"How's my favorite server this morning?" he asked as I stopped on the opposite side of the counter from him.

"I'm good. How's it going?"

"Couldn't ask for a better day. I saw the pictures from the gala. You looked mighty pretty."

"Thanks, Dad. You want the usual?" I picked up the coffeepot, flipped over his mug, and filled it.

"Sure do. How'd it go with Coach Dawson?"

My body went hot just from the mention of his name. I turned away to put the coffeepot back on the warmer, summoning an expression of nonchalance before I faced my dad again. "Great. He ended up knowing several people there and introduced me around."

"That worked out well then," he said.

Maybe it was my imagination, but I could swear, as he raised his mug for a sip of coffee, he perused my face like only an over-concerned father could.

I worked to keep my face blank as I wrote his order down and sent it back to Monty, though my boss probably already had the corned beef hash cooking and the egg ready to go.

"Max was a gentleman," I assured him, which was the truth. *If* we were only talking about Saturday night at the gala. Which we were.

"Order up, Harper," Monty called through the window.

Grateful for the save, I picked up meals for Hank and Shirley Moody. "Nancy sends her compliments to the cook," I said, grinning at my boss.

He grunted, but I thought I saw a shy smile as he averted his face, putting all his attention on the food sizzling on the grill as I hurried off.

When I came back to deliver my dad's breakfast, he watched me instead of digging into his food.

"You look tired today, honey."

With a lighthearted laugh, I said, "I'm tired every day. I must need new makeup."

"Were you out late last night? On a Sunday?"

Fighting to blank my expression, I wiped at a coffee stain on the counter. "With a seven o'clock shift this morning?" I flashed him a look like he should know better, and I didn't feel bad at all for the misdirection.

While I didn't care for my sake if my dad knew I'd been at Max's, I'd protect that information fiercely for Max's sake because it mattered to him. I didn't think my dad would fire him, but I also didn't want him to warn Max away from me again, and I absolutely didn't want Max to regret being with me.

My dad eyed me as if trying to discern whether my implication was the truth. Time to deflect.

"I have exciting news. Dakota and I are going to be roommates. We're signing a lease on Mrs. Karasinski's apartment."

"Above her shop?"

"That's the place. We can move in as soon as they clean it out."

He nodded thoughtfully. "Will you be able to handle the rent?"

I bit down on my irritation that he thought he had to ask that question. I might not be a lawyer or a stock analyst, but I knew better than to commit to a lease if I didn't make enough money to cover rent.

"As long as my wonderful customers keep tipping generously."

That was one thing I had to give my dad full credit for. He tipped me well but not ridiculously over-the-top, this-is-my-daughter well. That would feel like charity.

"We'll see how the service is today," he teased.

"That's fair." I went to the kitchen window where food was up for a table of early-bird tourists.

After making a round of all my tables, I refilled my dad's coffee.

"Thank you, honey. Monty's lucky to have you for all these years."

That seemed like a dig at me for staying at what I knew he considered a dead-end job for so long. But Dakota had told me many times that I was over-sensitive about this issue where he was concerned, so I let it roll off.

As I cleared Chet Hogan's place three stools down, I wondered what my dad would think if I told him I was considering opening a business with Dakota and Cambria. Probably that we were reckless.

Frankly I wasn't sure he'd be wrong.

That balled up nervousness lodged in my gut again. It was anxiety, but there was also a kernel of excitement when I imagined being a store owner with my friends and not pouring another cup of coffee.

Though I'd shut down the topic last night with Max, I'd been mulling over his words ever since. He had a valid point—I didn't have enough info to decide about opening a business. There'd be no risk in meeting with Cambria and Dakota to learn more. *If* Dakota was even contemplating the possibility.

I made a point of not mentioning any of it to my dad. He'd never let it go if he knew I was remotely considering such an endeavor. And if it didn't go anywhere, he'd be even more disappointed that his daughter was "stuck" being a server due to lack of ambition.

I carried the water pitcher around to my tables and refilled Nancy's glass without interrupting their conversation. Something stirred in me, something like hunger. Not for food but for having a direction in my life, an endeavor that made my blood buzz.

The seed had been planted at Max's two nights ago when I'd seen my life for what it was—empty and without deep meaning. Running into Cambria yesterday, mentioning my jewelry to her, and having her jump on it so easily... That seed had been nourished, encouraged, as if someone had sprinkled fertilizer on it and watered it.

This wasn't a position I'd found myself in before, and it wasn't comfortable. But there was just enough jittery excitement bubbling around in me that I couldn't ignore it.

I decided to contact both Dakota and Cambria after my shift.

Chapter Seventeen

Max

Monday morning was a Monday in every sense of the word.

Last night, reality had gradually seeped in, crowding out the incredible high from getting naked with Harper and keeping me awake for hours.

I'd crossed multiple lines that went against my personal code *and* my professional code. I'd made a liar out of myself where my boss was concerned, allowed my dick to make a decision instead of my brain, and exposed myself to a mind-blowing bliss I didn't currently have room for in my life.

It'd be too easy to become addicted to Harper Ellison.

I'd finally managed to drift to sleep about an hour before my alarm went off. Then I'd apparently turned off that alarm instead of snoozing it. I'd woken to Danny's cries nearly an hour later and bolted out of bed with my adrenals pumping.

I'd had to skip my morning run with Danny in the jogging stroller, our weekday father-son ritual that served as a peaceful, meditative time for both of us, with me pounding the pavement in an even rhythm and Danny taking in the sights as the town came alive for the day.

When I'd dropped him off at my mom's house, I'd barely had time to tell him goodbye. As irony would have it, Danny was fussy to begin with, so I'd left my mom with a cranky, unsettled toddler.

On the short drive to the high school, I'd realized I'd forgotten my coffee. I hadn't merely walked off and left a mug of it on the counter. No, I'd not even remembered to brew a cup.

Now I had about two minutes to get my ass into my classroom and get organized for the day.

Instead of entering through the front door and walking by the main office like I usually did, I used the side entrance by the gym. Both were about the same distance from my classroom in the math wing, but this way I had less chance of running into Bob Ellison.

I was a guilty son of a bitch, and I knew it.

There were clusters of students who'd arrived early: outside the band room, at lockers, roaming the halls. My colleagues were here and there, some on morning supervision duty and others discussing their weekend. I made eye contact with no one, busying myself with my phone as if checking my calendar for the day.

When I rounded the corner into the math hallway, Lisa Brimm and Dean "Mills" Miller were outside their rooms, chatting across the hall.

"Morning, Coach," Lisa said, her voice chipper with an edge of *knowing* to it. "Good weekend?"

"Sure. You?" I kept going toward my room, and they closed ranks and walked with me.

"Not as good as yours, judging by the photos," she said.

As I'd anticipated, there'd been no shortage of them on the Tattler.

"The boss's daughter," Mills drew out. He did have the courtesy to say it quietly, so only the three of us could hear. "I'm shocked Bob okayed that."

"Old news," I told him, not surprised he'd been out of the loop. Mills was a good work friend, a few years younger than me, and what I'd affectionately call a math nerd. He was an intellectual guy who didn't keep up on the social scene. Normally I liked that about him.

"Are you and the principal's daughter a thing now?" he asked as he pushed his glasses higher on his nose.

"We're not a thing, Mills. Why are you so obsessed with this?"

I saw him shrug out of the corner of my eye. "You could have any woman you want in this town. I find it interesting you singled out the one who could get you in the most trouble."

"I didn't single her out."

"*She* bid on Max in the auction," Lisa said.

"How do you manage to miss *everything*?" I asked Mills, ready for the topic to switch from me to him.

He laughed. "Years of practice, my friend. Level with me. How are you handling Bob with this?"

We'd reached my classroom, and I faced my coworkers. "There's nothing to handle," I lied. "Harper needed a date for an event in Nashville. She bid on me to take her. I took her. End of story."

I was still waiting for my dick to get that message.

Mills lifted his palms in surrender. "Okay. Got it." He exchanged a look with Lisa that I could easily read. It said, *Oversensitive, much?*

Hundred percent accurate, and I needed to

tone it down and get my head in a space to interact with dozens of moody, hormonal teenagers for the next ten hours, God love 'em. Without coffee. Because venturing to the teachers' lounge for a cup of marginal brew would risk running into Harper's father.

The hall was filling up. One of Mills's students called out a question from his classroom doorway, so he headed that way.

"I better do the same," Lisa said. "Have a good day, Coach. Hope the kids don't latch on to the gossip and give you too hard a time."

"Thanks a lot," I said.

The kids I could handle. Probably.

I darted into my classroom, thankful to have first period as my planning time. I needed to do last-minute prep for my second-period Algebra II class. Prep I'd planned on doing last night.

That thought naturally led to the steamy memory of what I'd ended up doing instead. As I unpacked my bag and put it in my coat closet, I couldn't get the image out of my head of a naked Harper, lying in wait, stretched out on my comforter.

This wasn't the place for those kinds of thoughts even if she weren't my boss's daughter. There was no room for weakness in a roomful of teens. I prided myself on keeping my private life out of the classroom, but this morning I was struggling to get any of it out of my head.

Once I sat at my desk, missing my caffeine, overheating from my thoughts, I ran my hands over my face. "Let it go," I muttered.

"You okay, Coach?"

I jumped out of my skin at the sound of Bob Ellison's voice nearby. Like, two feet away, I realized when I opened my eyes.

"Morning, Bob," I said, forcing my usual cheery professionalism into my voice.

"You don't look like it's a good one."

I scrambled mentally like a quarterback facing down aggressive linebackers. "Forgot my coffee. Nothing worse than facing a bunch of rowdy teenagers without caffeine."

Unless it was facing your boss after sleeping with his daughter.

"There's some in the lounge."

"Yeah. I'll have to grab a cup." It would be better than nothing now that avoiding my boss was a moot point. "What can I do for you?" I asked, knowing he had to have a reason for appearing in my room at this hour.

"Your team played quite a game Friday night. Congrats on win number one for the season."

"Thanks." I relaxed a little. "If Brant keeps it up, he'll get some attention from colleges in the next year." Our starting running back was only a sophomore and had come close to setting a single-game record for yards rushed. In the first game of the season.

"He's something else. Fun kid to watch," Bob said as he took up a casual stance against the wall. "Tanager had a decent game too."

"He's fighting to keep his starting job," I said of the first-string defensive end. I was warming up to the topic like I always did. Our kids were coming along well for it being so early in the season. I couldn't wait to see what they could accomplish.

"I saw the photos of you and my daughter," Ellison said abruptly, just as I'd started to relax. I should've seen that coming.

I pulled out a reply that put his focus on how amazing his daughter was. "I wish you could've heard Harper's award acceptance for her friend. It was a tearjerker. Poignant, to the point, and profound. And one hundred percent off the cuff." I shook my head. "I don't think I could do half as well with a prewritten, well-rehearsed speech."

Pride flashed in his eyes as he shook his head. "She's something else. Don't think I'll ever understand her. She doesn't do anything the tried-and-true way, but she somehow seems to do okay."

"She did more than okay. I wish I'd thought to

record the crowd's reaction. They gave her a standing ovation as they dabbed at their eyes."

I bit down on my tongue before I could praise her more. There was a fine line between sounding like a teacher who recognized a job well done and a guy who'd fallen under Harper's spell in a non-teacher way.

"I warned you away from my daughter at the auction—"

"Yes, sir," I interrupted, hoping like hell my facial expression didn't reveal that I couldn't get her out of my mind. My heart raced, and I stopped breathing.

I tried to think of something else to say that would reassure him but wouldn't be a lie. Nothing came to me, because facts were facts. I'd had sex with Harper last night. If he knew, he'd shit-can my ass on the spot.

He straightened from the wall, advanced to the side of my desk, put his hands on it, and leaned forward. I braced myself.

"The more I looked at those photos of you two..." He paused.

I waited.

I got up the nerve to meet his gaze, and he shook his head, exhaled, as if he was trying to figure out how to say something.

"The more I think about it, Max, the more I think you could be the best thing for my daughter."

My brows shot up. I studied his face, looking for an explanation. There was a spark of challenge in his eyes.

"I'm not sure I heard you right," I said.

"You did." He stood tall, folded his hands behind his back, principal style, and paced. "You're a few years older than her. A heck of a lot more settled. You've got a stable career, two of 'em, actually. You've lived in the same place for years. What I'm trying to say is that maybe what my daughter needs is a strong, stable influence in her life instead of these young punks who hook up and won't commit to more."

I knew fifty percent of that equation was that Harper didn't want more, but it wasn't my place to tell him that.

Still reeling from his one-eighty, I sat there dumbfounded. "I'm flattered you feel that way, Bob," I finally said.

I couldn't deny there was a part of me that was tempted by the idea of pursuing Harper. But it was a small part. Not a logical one.

"It's hard for a father to let go of his daughters, in particular. Tough to think any man could be good enough for them. Scaring every male off is a knee-jerk reaction no matter how old she is."

"I can imagine that now that I have a child."

"Harper needs some stability in her life, whether it's from a career path or a relationship. Hell, I don't know. Between you and me, she could stand to grow up a little."

I didn't respond, knowing Harper herself was having similar realizations. I believed she'd get there. On her own.

"I appreciate what you're saying, but I have to respectfully disagree that I'm the guy. Danny's my focus. Now and in the future. My cousin trusted me to take care of his son." I shook my head, those familiar heavy emotions rolling over me again. "I can't put into words how that's affected me, but it's life changing."

"Parenthood is like that no matter how you arrive at it," my boss said.

"I'm sure it is," I said, knowing no one would understand where I was coming from, and that was okay. "Bottom line, your daughter is an amazing woman who deserves a man who can give her the world."

"Yes, she does."

"That man's not me."

"I respect that, Max. I do." He stopped his pacing, faced me, and slid his hands into his front pants pockets. Nodding once, he said, "That's fair. I just wanted you to know I changed my mind. If you were to get involved with my daughter, you have my blessing."

"That's good to know, sir. I'll take it as a compliment."

Bob nodded, pivoted, and walked to the door. There he paused, looked at me, and asked, "You're sure you're not the guy?"

With a chuckle, I said, "I'm sure."

He walked out, and I expelled a breath.

Holy hell.

My mind was thoroughly fucked with.

But I'd meant what I told him.

I had to be sure. I had to be resolute.

Harper was a temptation. A fucking wet dream. But I couldn't be the man she deserved.

Being a single parent was hard as hell. Danny already lost out more than he should to my two jobs. Adding the distraction of a relationship would eat even more into time with my boy.

As much as I wanted to get to know Harper better, I couldn't let myself go there.

Chapter Eighteen

Max

Every year, Principal Ellison hosted a back-to-school barbecue on the beach for the staff and their families.

He and the office staff had the food catered by a local restaurant and supplied coolers full of nonalcoholic drinks. We could bring our own adult beverages as long as we made it to work tomorrow, as it was a Wednesday evening. I was down for water tonight since I'd just finished football practice on a hot field. We hounded the players to drink plenty, but sometimes the coaching staff had a hard time following our own rules.

I'd been to the barbecue every year since I was

hired except for last year. Last year, my cousin's death was recent, and Danny had only been in my care for a few weeks. Truth be told, on top of grieving, I'd been too nervous to take him to the beach, so he and I had skipped it.

We were in a different place this year, I realized as I carried him along the side of the road toward the beach. Though I still often felt like an imposter, all too aware of how many ways I could screw up this little human, I guessed we were making progress.

"Look at us, little man," I said to him. "Guys' night at the beach. We'll eat some dinner and play in the sand with your trucks." I had an overstuffed diaper bag over my shoulder, complete with trucks and a sand bucket, beach towels around my neck, and his booster seat in my other hand.

There was no such thing as traveling light with a toddler.

"Tuck," he said joyfully.

"We brought your dump truck and your bulldozer. How's that sound?"

Danny didn't answer, his eyes glued to the gathering that came into view with my every step.

There were clusters of people standing and talking, most of them in swimsuits, coverups, wide-brimmed hats, ball caps. Though it was after five, the late-August sun still beat down hot. Danny and I would be taking a dip to cool down at some point.

Several grade-school-age kids splashed and chased each other in the shallow water. A trio of middle-school girls stood in bikinis, trying to look grown-up, their incessant giggles proving otherwise.

I spotted Mills talking to Lisa and her wife, Beth Ann, along with Michael Clausen, the biology teacher, and his wife, Kristina. Ty Bishop, who taught econ and coached the varsity basketball team, was playing two-on-two volleyball with Jasmine Hughes, Amber Ullman, and Amber's boyfriend. I laughed as Jasmine spiked one emphatically on six-foot-four Ty and scored.

"Bah," Danny said, pointing at the volleyball in the sand.

"That's a volleyball," I told him, loving his inherent interest in all things sports related.

Some baby babble came out of his mouth that I thought meant *volleyball*. I smiled and kissed his forehead.

"Hey, Coach." Several people greeted me as we arrived.

"Hi, guys," I said. "Can you say hi, Danny?"

My son burrowed his head into my chest, which elicited several *awws* from nearby women.

"Such a doll," Jody Rivas said.

"Need some help, Max?" Rissa Raymond was

suddenly in our space, reaching for the diaper bag. She was single, transparent, and persistent in her quest to worm her way into my life. I'd never given her any reason to believe I was interested.

"I've got it. Thanks," I told her in a friendly but noncommittal tone. Without making eye contact with her, I continued toward Mills, Lisa, and Beth Ann, greeting everyone as I passed, leaving Rissa behind.

"Ooh, here comes that handsome little boy," Beth Ann cooed as I approached. She waved at Danny. "Hello, Daniel. Remember me?"

Instead of hiding, Danny nodded shyly. He'd met her a few times, and she always fussed over him enough to make an impression.

"Want to set up by us?" Lisa asked, gesturing toward an umbrella, a large blanket spread over the sand, and a single beach chair next to it.

"I forgot to pack a blanket," I muttered.

"You can share ours," Beth Ann said. She took the booster chair from me. "We'll set this up on the blanket, and your daddy can sit right next to you," she told Danny.

I gladly let her take the chair and followed her. Lisa moved their bag so there was more space.

"That's Mills's chair," Lisa said. "Food just started arriving so we should be able to eat soon."

"Are you hungry, Danny?" Beth Ann asked as I lowered him to the ground.

Standing next to me, Danny held on to the bottom of my swim trunks and nodded.

"I heard there's chicken nuggets," Beth Ann continued, bending down to Danny's level.

"She's good with kids," I said to Lisa as I dug out Danny's bib and sippy cup.

"She's ready for us to have one," Lisa confided.

"Yeah?" My brows went up as this was the first I'd heard of it. "Are *you*?"

Lisa's smile as she watched her wife was softer than the ones she used at work. "We've started the process."

"Congrats," I said, handing Danny his water.

"A little early for that, but thanks."

"Water for you?" Mills joined us, holding out an ice-cold bottle to me.

"Thanks, man." I took it, opened it, and downed half of it.

As I screwed the lid back on, my hunger hit. I scanned the food-serving area, set up under a large white awning closer to the road than the lake.

Joanna, one of the office staff who always oversaw the food at these events, was unloading food onto the long folding tables. I glanced to the other end of the tent, expecting to see Bronwyn, the school secretary.

Instead of Bronwyn's bottle-blond head, I saw dark, glossy hair in a messy pile on someone who bent over a rolling food carrier. There was something intensely familiar about that color, that shininess...

At that instant, Harper stood, sliding a covered tray from the carrier onto the table. As hungry as I was, I ignored the food, my gaze locked on my boss's breathtaking daughter.

She wore a slate-blue bikini top, a long, flowered skirt with a slit up to her hip, multiple necklaces that, even from this distance, I'd bet were her creations, and large hoop earrings.

My stare got hung up on her, and my dick stirred in my swim trunks.

Fuck.

What was she doing here?

"Good thing you two aren't a thing," Mills quipped.

I glared at him. His grin said he'd witnessed every second of me watching Harper.

Luckily Lisa and Beth Ann were focused on my son, with him demonstrating the bulldozer at work.

Mills leaned closer, his smug smile disappearing. "I'm just a bystander, but she's pretty tough to ignore, huh?" Instead of smart-assery, his tone was empathetic. I let my defensiveness come down a notch and nodded.

"That's one way to put it. I'll just keep my distance."

"Looks like if you want food, you'll have to interact."

"It's not a problem."

I was glad I'd spotted her ahead of time, because when I went through the food line, I'd have to manage a balance between politeness and warmth that would fluctuate depending on who was around us and how close they were.

Not a fucking problem at all.

I kept a close eye on the serving status as Mills and I talked about upcoming statewide test dates. As soon as the call went out for us to fill our plates, I scooped up Danny and headed that way. If there was a long line behind me, I couldn't be expected to do more than say hello, please, and thank you.

As Danny and I approached the long tables of barbecue pork, homemade buns, cold fried chicken, and more from Henry's Restaurant, I set him beside me and took his hand. I stacked two plates, then piled food for both of us on the top one.

There were a few people in front of us, and the line moved slowly. I tried my best not to gape at the vision that was Harper Ellison. She looked like a goddess in that bikini top, with her flat, bronzed abdomen exposed and her skirt hanging low on her hips.

"Hi, Max," she said before I was directly in front of her. Before I was ready.

"Harper." I smiled, reining it in enough so it hopefully didn't radiate the lust that pumped through me. "I didn't expect to see you here."

She brushed a lock of hair out of her face. "My dad begged me. Bronwyn had an emergency root canal this afternoon and wasn't up to the task."

"Understandable. Well, we're glad you're helping out." I cringed inwardly at my lameness. Extra points for sounding like a stuffy teacher with no connection to her.

"Who is this handsome boy?" she said, her eyes on Danny.

I took two full seconds to understand she was a step ahead of me in pretending she'd never met my son. Considering it'd been the middle of the night when she had, I appreciated the act.

"Can you say hi to Harper, Danny?" I said.

When I thought he would duck into my thigh, he surprised me by peering up at Harper with a shy smile. He didn't say anything, but the eye contact alone was notable.

"You enjoy your nuggets, cutie-pie," Harper said to him. Her gaze drifted over me for an extra second as if acknowledging our secret that she'd previously met Danny.

With a half smile and a nod, I moved forward in

line. I forced my thoughts to the fruit selection in an effort to keep from reacting to that look from Harper.

Ty Bishop was in line behind me. He was an inch or two taller than me and twice as loud as he kept an ongoing dialogue with anyone and everyone around him, most of whom were female. He was a few years younger, good-looking, athletic, and unlike me, he loved attention from women. He could have it.

"Hey, pretty lady," he said to Harper as he came up even with her.

I clenched my molars together as I leaned over to ask Danny if he wanted watermelon or apple slices.

My son pointed at the apples.

"Hi, Ty." Harper's smile at the basketball oaf was audible.

Her use of his name, as if she knew him well, grated on my nerves. I reminded myself he was closer to her age than I was and possibly ran in the same social circle as her, unlike me.

"Guess we got an upgrade to the food servers this year," Ty said.

I rolled my eyes, then scolded myself for showing any reaction.

Harper laughed, and I hated that the musical

sound that turned me inside out was directed at him.

My son tugged at my hand, diverting my attention from Harper, who was offering Ty an extra-large serving of potato salad.

"Dat," Danny said, pointing at the watermelon slices, so I piled some of those next to the apples, then moved us along, farther from Harper and her suitor.

Back at our places, I settled Danny into his booster, added food to his plate, and dug into my own dinner.

I'd made it through the necessary interaction with Harper without apparently drawing undue attention. Now I just needed to avoid looking at her for the rest of the evening.

Chapter Nineteen

Harper

Most people would probably help their dad with a picnic jam out of the goodness of their heart.

My heart must be a little less full of goodness, because my main motivation for saying yes when my dad had asked me to fill in for poor Bronwyn was the chance to spend the evening with Max.

Or, I should say, to spend the evening in the same place as Max.

I didn't expect him to go out of his way to interact with me. I knew we couldn't let on that there'd been anything between us beyond one date. But when he'd strode onto the beach with his little boy in his arms, the view had improved tenfold. Considering the scenery at the lake was normally beautiful in and of itself, that was saying a lot.

I'd done my best to act nonchalant when he'd brought Danny through the food line. Then I'd made a point of taking my own full plate to the opposite side of the party and sitting with Dorie Ludwig, who I'd graduated with, and her mom, Corinne. Both of them were natural redheads, bookish and super smart, and English teachers at the high school.

Dorie and I had never been particularly close, but she and her mom were easy to talk to and welcoming.

After eating, the three of us went over to the dessert table and grabbed mini slices of Cash Henry's famous hummingbird cake. I couldn't seem to help myself—as we stood in a trio and oohed and aahed over our glorious desserts, I allowed my eyes to skim in Max's direction for the hundredth time. He was sitting next to Danny, bending over him as if his son had said something, and laughing. As he straightened, his hand on his little boy's back, Max's eyes met mine for an instant. It wasn't the first time tonight, and I couldn't help wondering if he was having the same problem I was of keeping my gaze to myself.

"You ladies look like you could use an adult

beverage." Ty, who was an incurable flirt, butted into our circle of three, rolling a cooler behind him. "Can I interest you in a bottle of hometown-proud Rusty Anchor beer?"

Dorie declined, but her mother chose a Beach Babe Pale Ale from his not-small selection. It was a classic Ty Bishop move that served as a way to flirt and interact with more people. That was just who he was.

"Harper," he said, putting his arm around me, "it's come to my attention that you're in desperate need of a brewed beverage this evening. What can I get you?"

Laughing, I said, "Do I look that bad?"

"*Au contraire*, pretty lady. You look particularly stunning."

I rolled my eyes and laughed. "Thank you, kind sir," I said, playing along.

"You're too much, Ty," Corinne said.

She wasn't wrong, but I took a Sandbar Wheat, let him open it, then thanked him.

"Anytime, darlin'." He gave me a side hug, leaning close to my ear and saying so no one else could hear, "You're the hottest girl here, for real."

With a smile, because Ty really was harmless, I said, "You're the flirtiest." I raised my brows to convey that wasn't necessarily a desirable claim to fame. Dorie and Corinne had welcomed Francesca

Gibbons, another English teacher, into the group and listened raptly as she explained why she was so late.

"That's what you do to me, Harper," Ty said in a low, more serious voice. The others paid no attention to us.

It was all an act, I knew. Ty could throw out meaningless lines faster than a professional fisherman. He'd hit on me plenty in the past, but he knew not to cross a line, with me or anyone else. That was just Ty.

"You know you'd have better luck with girls if you didn't try so hard, right?" I teased.

"That's a myth," he said emphatically. "Ladies love me."

"Of course they do." I shook my head, laughing. He had a good heart, and I knew someday he'd find the right woman for him. Probably someone who loved his lines and his try-hardness. That woman wasn't me, and we both knew it.

"If you're not going to marry me, I better move on to find someone who will," he said with a wink.

"Thanks for the beer, Ty."

Before he walked off, he grabbed my hand, lifted it to his lips, and kissed it.

I shook my head and grinned.

As he rolled his beer cooler away, my eyes were

drawn across the crowd to find Max watching me. He wasn't smiling.

As if he realized he was staring, he turned his attention to the group of math teachers he was with. I tuned into Francesca's tale of helping Dr. Holloway, the town vet, catch his pet llama who'd gone on the lam yet again.

Not two minutes later, my phone buzzed in the pocket of my skirt. I pulled it out and saw Max's name, which threw my heart rate into overdrive. I angled my screen to be sure no one could see it, unlocked it, and read Max's message.

> Something going on between you and Bishop?

I pursed my lips to hide the satisfaction that brought. I weighed how to handle the question as I pretended to be engrossed in Francesca's story.

I could mess with Max and tell him yes, but I didn't want to play games.

I texted my answer.

> No.

> He's hanging all over you like a monkey on a banana tree.

I hid my laugh and again tried to act as if I wasn't one hundred percent into my phone.

I quickly typed in a single word.

Jealous?

I'd seen him stiffen and frown in the food line when Ty had called me pretty lady the first time. I could tell he'd tried to stifle any reaction, but I'd been watching for one, hoping. And I'd seen it clear as day.

Max took a couple of minutes to respond. I could see he, too, was trying to engage with the people around him. But finally, my phone vibrated. I discreetly took a peek.

Yes.

I felt lighter than air, as if someone had pumped helium into my chest. I bit my lip and fought the urge to glance his way. I lasted a few seconds. When I looked toward where Max had been standing, he was gone.

For a heartbeat, I panicked that he'd left, but then logic caught up, and I realized there was no way he could pack up his son and all the kid equipment that fast. Sure enough, I found the two of them a few feet from their original spot, digging through their diaper bag. I sighed, happy they were still here, then rededicated myself to participating in the conversation around me.

Later, when Joanna and I were finishing packing up what little food was left, I heard talk of a high-stakes volleyball match. Normally I'd be game to join them, but I wasn't dressed for it in this long, flowy skirt, so I ignored the loud recruitment going on around me.

I tuned back in when I heard my dad, who'd apparently decided to play, say, "Come on, Coach. We need your height against Ty."

Behind me, Max's low-pitched laugh sounded, awakening something deep inside me and making me *want*. "I promised Danny we'd get in the water," he said.

"You want to go swimming, Danny?" my dad said.

It was all I could do not to turn around and see if Danny responded. Turned out I didn't need to, because my dad laughed and said, "You do. What if we asked Harper over there to take you so your daddy could be on my volleyball team? Would you like to go swimming with Harper?"

I turned around, unable to ignore them.

Danny was peering at me with his sweet blue eyes and the beginnings of a grin. He wore shark-print swim trunks and a life vest with mini floaties on his arms. The cutie was impossible to resist.

When I glanced up at Max, though, I felt like a bucket full of cold reality was poured over me. He was frowning.

"He doesn't go to other people easily," Max explained.

Except Danny had taken my dad's hand and was willingly coming toward me, his eyes big.

I met Max's gaze again, expecting him to be smiling as I was, but instead he scowled.

"He'll be just fine with Harper," my dad assured him. "We don't have a hope of winning without you on our side of the net."

I could tell Max didn't like it, but he finally relented, just as Danny reached me.

"Do you mind, Harper?" my dad asked.

Any other time, I'd resent my dad forcing me into something. "How could I resist such a handsome little guy?" I asked, meaning it. I picked up Danny.

Again, I looked at Max now that he was so close, but he avoided eye contact, instead sizing up his son to make sure he was okay with this change in plans, then turning to my dad and saying, "Let's go kick their butts. Quickly."

When he followed my dad past me after kissing his son, he finally acknowledged me—with a frown.

For an instant, I was stunned at his open rudeness. When I noticed Danny staring at me unabashedly, his blue eyes ever curious and long lashes angelic, I commanded myself to shake it off and snapped on a facade of indifference.

"Are you ready to get in the water, big guy?"

Danny whipped his head around to point at the lake.

"I'll take that as a yes. We have to make a quick stop first, okay?"

I carried him over to my bag under the food awning and dropped my phone inside of it. I lowered Danny next to me and said, "I can't swim in this silly skirt, can I?" I slid it down my legs and stuffed it into my bag, then slipped my flip-flops off. "I'm ready if you are, Danny boy."

I picked him up again, a smile stretching across his face as he studied me. Impulsively, I kissed his forehead because he was so damn cute, and then immediately realized what I'd done.

I'd kissed Max Dawson's kid with a level of familiarity that might lead people to think Max and I were closer than we were. As if I were angling to be Danny's new mommy. My mouth went dry at the thought of the M-word. That was not my jam and wouldn't be any time soon, no matter how lovable this little boy was.

No one appeared to have seen my slip-up.

There was no taking it back anyway. With a shrug and a little more caution, I carried Danny to the waterline and set him on his feet.

We waded, his hand in mine, stopping frequently for him to bend down, splash, and giggle. That giggle was everything. How anyone could be around it and not feel better about the world was beyond me.

When we neared the volleyball court, where the game was in progress, Danny pointed and said, "Boy bah."

"That's right. Volleyball. Aren't you the smartest boy ever?"

He'd stopped, entranced by the game. When Max's team scored a point and cheered, Danny pulled his hand away from mine and clapped awkwardly, beaming. "Dada!"

"You want to watch Daddy?" I asked. Looking at Danny's face, I didn't need a verbal answer. He was animated and engaged, joy emanating from him.

This was the excuse I needed to watch Max in action. *Thank you, Dad.*

We ended up sitting in shallow water, at Danny's insistence. I sat crisscross applesauce, and Danny plopped on my lap, kicking his feet from time to time.

Max on a volleyball court was a thing of beauty.

And then he took his shirt off. Yes, I'd seen his stellar chest and abs before, but I'd never get sick of that view.

The sun sank in the sky enough that Danny seemed to get a little cool before the game was over. I pulled him out of the water, got towels for both of us, and dried him as his lips chattered. A search through his bag produced a set of dry pajamas, so I changed his diaper and put on the cat pj's.

By the time the game ended and Max extracted himself from his team's victory celebration, Danny was dry, warm, and mellow, content to sit on my lap and watch the action from a distance.

"Good game," I said to Max as he packed up the rest of their belongings and prepared to leave.

"Thanks." He didn't even look at me.

I stood, holding Danny. Once Max had his bag over his shoulder, he took his son from me, seemingly extra careful not to touch me. Smart, but it made me want to touch him even more.

"Come here, Danny boy. Looks like you're ready for bed."

"Dada."

Max's math teacher friends had gathered around us and were packing up as well.

"I'll see you all tomorrow," Max said to them, his normal Mr. Social tone in place. Before he walked off, he looked right at me, then said with less warmth, "Thanks for watching Danny, Harper."

"Good night."

When he didn't reply, I did my best to keep a blank expression on my face, but inside, I was screaming *WTF?*

As I went to find my dad and make sure he didn't need anything else, I couldn't get two things out of my mind. One, Max hadn't had the courtesy to say goodbye to me. Two, I was pretty sure he didn't trust me with his son.

Neither one sat right with me.

Chapter Twenty

Max

Once I got Danny to bed, I had nothing to keep me from going over the barbecue in my head. More specifically, the end of the barbecue.

I knew damn well I hadn't handled anything right with Harper, but if I'd had a conversation with her or looked her in the eye—or allowed myself another eyeful of her in that bikini—it would've been all I could do *not* to kiss her.

The party had tuckered Danny right out. He fell asleep practically the second I put him in his crib.

Since I'd sweated like a pig during the volleyball game, I grabbed the monitor and headed for the shower. With my mind still on Harper, I turned the water to cold and stood under the spray long enough to shampoo and soap up.

As I was drying off, my phone dinged with a message. I walked to the counter where it was sitting and saw Harper's name. The benefits of the cold shower wore off in a millisecond.

Is Danny in bed yet?

He is. He was nearly asleep on
the short ride home.

Almost a minute passed before the three bubbles appeared. Like a dumb ass, I stood there and watched the screen instead of pulling on sweats. My blood was pounding through me by the time her next message came through.

Can I stop by? I have some
questions.

My radar went off. *Questions* was damn close to *We need to talk.*

And yet my dick went hard anyway.

That's fine.

With my heart rate elevated, I wrapped a towel around my waist and hurried to the other side of the house to make sure Danny was still asleep. He hadn't moved. I watched out of habit to make sure his chest went up and down, then ducked out.

The next second, there was a light knock at the front door.

I checked out the peephole to make sure it was Harper. My dick went even harder at the sight of her. She was still in her bikini, with the skirt back on. Even now, I could see her perfectly in my mind's eye in that two-piece swimsuit. It wasn't particularly skimpy, was appropriate for an office beach party, but she was perfection in it.

For a moment, I considered pulling on pants.

Against my better judgment, I opened the door and let her in as I was.

"Hi," she said, her gaze going to the tented towel, her brows going up. When she made eye contact, her pupils were enlarged.

"I just got out of the shower."

Harper pressed her lips together and nodded, seeming to withdraw. She breezed past me and went toward the living room. By the time I locked the door and followed, she'd sat on the chair. Not the sectional.

I lowered myself to the edge of the middle cushion of the sectional, my jets good and cooled from her standoffishness. I kept my eyes locked on hers, doing my damnedest to ignore the rest of her body.

"What's going on?" I asked, leaning forward, elbows on my knees.

"Why don't you trust me with Danny?" she blurted.

I opened my mouth to answer, but no words came to me at first. I tilted my head, puzzling over the question. "I trust you. I wouldn't have left him in your care during the game if I didn't."

"That's not the impression you gave off."

"What impression did I give off?"

"It was clear you didn't want me to watch him. Your hesitation was embarrassing. I might not have a lot of practice with kids, but I'd never let anything hurt Danny."

I stared at her, stunned. "I..." I closed my mouth, ran my hands over my face, realized I needed to level with her. "First, let's get something straight. I trust you with my son."

She narrowed her eyes like she didn't believe me.

"I've left him with you twice now. If I didn't trust you, that never would've happened."

"Then why did you act like that?"

I glanced out the window at the black night, my eyes drawn to her reflection. "I don't want Danny to get attached to you, Harper," I finally said on an exhalation. "He likes you. He seems to like you more than he likes most people. The fact that he went with you willingly tonight?" I shook my head. "He's never done that with anyone outside my immediate family."

"Never?"

"Not with anyone. I've probably been overprotective." I knew damn well I'd been overprotective. "I don't want anything to hurt him. Ever. And I know there's gonna be shit in life that tears him up. Look what already happened to his parents. But if I can prevent him from getting hurt, you better believe I'm going to protect him with everything I have."

"You think I'd hurt him?" Her tone was incredulous.

"I think if he grew attached to you and then you stopped coming around, he'd get hurt."

Understanding sparked in her eyes. "I see."

"Do you?"

"If you date someone, you don't want Danny to get to know them in case it doesn't work out." She still looked skeptical.

"Precisely."

"Except we're not dating."

"No."

"So it doesn't quite hold up."

"Same concept. Danny could get hurt, and I won't risk that."

"Danny would only get hurt if I spent time with him. Right now, he might like me, but if he never saw me again, he wouldn't miss me."

"Maybe," I acknowledged. I hoped she was right. It was damn hard to know what went through an eighteen-month-old's head. "I'm sorry you felt embarrassed tonight. That wasn't my intention. There was a lot running through my mind as to how to act around you. Everyone knows we went to the gala."

"I know."

"That was supposed to be all it was."

"Yep." Harper stood. "Except it isn't."

Before I could stop myself, my gaze dropped to her generous breasts in the bikini top, the expanse of her bare abdomen, her sexy belly button, the hint of her hip bones, and the skirt that left one long leg exposed.

I went hard instantly.

"No." My voice came out rough and husky. I sat back against the cushion, revealing the effect she had on me. "It isn't."

I stopped breathing as she stepped toward me, closing the space between us, one foot at a time. When she reached me, she went down to her knees. With her hands on my thighs, she leaned closer.

Her gaze darted to my lips, then back into my eyes. Then her lips fluttered over mine, just a tease of a touch. Her breath stuttered out, and I felt it whisper over my skin.

I was dying to grasp her gorgeous ass and pull her into me, but I held back, waited, my heart hammering. I was curious to see what she would do.

"Our night together was a secret," she said just above a whisper.

"Yes."

"Nobody knows I'm here now."

"Where's your car?" I asked. I'd been too wrapped up in the sight of her at my door to check for her vehicle.

"It's parked downtown, near the Fly."

"You walked here?"

She nodded. "Because I can keep a secret." She smiled meaningfully. The gleam in her eyes was alluring as fuck. I clenched both my fists to keep from reaching for her. "I'm thinking…"

She leaned forward and kissed me full on the lips, none of that fluttering, flirting crap. Her hand trailed up my jaw, to the back of my head, as her tongue plunged inside my mouth.

I couldn't hold back any longer. I filled my hand with one of her luscious ass cheeks, molding it, drawing her closer. Before I could really get started,

Harper broke off the kiss. I was gratified to see she was breathing as hard as I was.

"I'm thinking we have some serious chemistry."

I let out a gravelly laugh. "We do."

She ran both her hands up my thighs again, closer to my dick but not nearly close enough. "We already agreed my dad can't know about us."

I swallowed and nodded because what she said was true. I could tell her he was okay with us, but something kept me quiet.

"And no one else can know about us."

"Right," I said.

She flicked a glance toward Danny's room. "If we're not an official couple, Danny will be fine. He won't get attached to me because he won't know I'm here."

Every drop of blood in my body pulsed to my dick. "I see where you're going."

Her lips curved into a sexy, vixenish smile. "It'd be a shame to let this chemistry go to waste." Her mouth was a breath from mine again.

"Crying shame," I said.

"It's your call. Fling? Or I can leave."

"No fucking question," I managed, about to climb out of my skin if I didn't get inside her in the next three seconds. "Stay."

She peered into my eyes, her lids heavy with need. Just when I thought she'd lean forward and seal our lips together again, she reached for my towel and whipped it open. Her hand closed around my shaft, and I groaned. It felt like heaven and left me aching for more at the same time.

The next second, she gave more when her mouth closed around me and her tongue swirled around my tip. My eyes rolled back in my head. I ran both my hands through her hair, fumbling around until I found the hair band holding it up. I struggled with it, trying not to yank her hair out, but I wanted it down, flowing over her shoulders, tickling my thighs, free for my fingers to burrow through.

Without lifting her mouth from my cock, she reached up with one hand and freed her hair. I opened my eyes to see it cascade down like a dark waterfall. Her eyes met mine as she took me farther in, until I hit the back of her throat and moaned in ecstasy.

For the next few minutes, she owned me, working some kind of witchcraft with her tongue and her hands. I felt like I'd been transported to some other plane where time and space didn't exist, only sensation.

When I was on the brink of exploding, I bit my lip and managed to pull her up, her mouth coming off me with a pop. Her lust-filled eyes questioned me as I guided her closer to my mouth.

"Was that not working?" she asked.

I let out a rough chuckle. "Incredible. But I want you to ride me."

"Yeah?"

"Fuck yeah."

She stood, still fully dressed. I expected her to rectify that, but she went to the chair where she'd first sat and picked up a bag I hadn't previously noticed. She dumped out the contents and rustled through it until she held up a condom packet.

With a glance toward the large windows facing the lake, she eyed the sole lamp that was on, walked over to it, and clicked it off, leaving only a dim light from the kitchen. It was just enough to see as she slid her skirt down her thighs and kicked it to the side. With her swimsuit still on, she straddled me, her core hovering inches from my needy cock.

I reached behind her and unfastened her top. Before she could slide it down her arms, I palmed her sumptuous breasts like the treasures they were, bringing them to my mouth, hungrily tasting one, then the other. Her necklaces jingled together as she arched into me, holding her breast to my mouth as if she couldn't get close enough.

I feasted on her, suckling her nipple, teasing my tongue over her pebbled flesh, savoring the taste of her. With my free hand, I kneaded her ass again, losing myself in the sensual indulgence that was her body.

I heard the condom being ripped open. Then her fingers were on my dick as she positioned it on the tip and slid it down to the root, squeezing me in the process, drawing a gasp of pleasure from me.

With a needy sigh, Harper lowered herself to my lap. I opened my eyes to see her holding her bikini bottoms to the side. She slid down me with a moan, turning me inside out.

I worked my hands under the thin material over her ass, massaging her cheeks as if they were bare. She paused when I was all the way seated in her, a look of ecstasy on her face. Then she ground her body against mine, circling, deepening our connection.

She seemed to be fighting herself, trying to stay in control, moving in a slow circle then stopping, biting her lip. I let her take charge even as I was dying to thrust into her.

Finally she slid partway off me in a slow, torturous motion. Her bliss-filled groan nearly shot me to the stars. Then she slammed home again. All I could do was hold on as she did exactly what I'd asked her to and rode me like a fucking goddess.

Her hair was everywhere, her breasts bouncing, our bodies moving as one until she cried out and contracted around me. That was all it took for me to come so hard I couldn't breathe, could only hold on to her for dear life and ride out my shattering orgasm.

I eventually became aware that Harper's gorgeous body had gone limp as she breathed hard near my ear. I wrapped my arms around her tightly, catching my breath too. I'd be content to stay like this for hours. Maybe weeks.

"That," Harper said eventually. She had a lethargic, satisfied smile on her face. "That's the chemistry I was talking about."

My agreement rumbled out of my chest. "Mm-hmm."

She lazily lifted her head and kissed me.

I brushed her hair behind her ear and cradled her cheek. "Stupendous chemistry."

"Please tell me we can keep doing that in secret."

There wasn't a man on this planet strong enough to say no to what she was offering, our bodies still intimately connected, her irresistible breasts pressed into my chest. I still needed to make sure we were on the same page though.

"As long as there's no strings and no feelings. No one gets hurt. Not Danny, not you, not me."

"I'm good," she purred. "Single and free with some mind-bending sex on the side is my jam."

I chuckled and wondered how I'd gotten so

fucking lucky. "Sounds perfect. I need to take care of the condom."

She pulled away from me and shifted to the side. I took a minute to summon the strength to get up and walk away.

When I came back from the bathroom, Harper was stretched out on the sectional, still in the bottom half of her bikini, though it was askew. I leaned over the back cushions from behind the sectional and scooped her up into my arms cradle style, eliciting a quiet squeal of surprise.

"What are you doing?" she whispered.

"Taking you to my bed for round two. We messed up the first time."

"What?"

I dipped my fingers into her bikini bottoms. "We forgot to get these out of the way. We'll need a replay."

With a sexy laugh, she said, "I like it when you talk all footballish, Coach. Let's see if you can get a touchdown."

"Trust me. I know how to score."

As I carried her to my room, there was a quiet but pesky voice in my head warning me that getting involved further, making this a recurring thing, wasn't wise. I ignored that voice, set her on my bed, and peeled her swimsuit down her legs.

Chapter Twenty-One

Harper

Serving eggs and burgers on almost no sleep wasn't my favorite thing to do. Today I'd made it through my eight-hour shift thanks to the power of endorphins and erotic memories of my night with Max.

He was incredible, and I was in lust. The man was the best lover I'd ever had, with that fit, athletic body, impressive stamina, and an insistence on pleasing his partner early and often. I'd lost track of the number of orgasms he'd given me. Literally lost track. I'd had two- and three-O nights before, but last night's count would require two hands.

I was a little in awe that I could still walk.

I grinned as I drove from Naomi's house, through town, and headed out the other side of Dragonfly Lake toward Cambria's place in the country.

I'd wondered how Max was faring throughout the day. We probably hadn't slept for more than an hour when I'd walked back to get my car just before five, before anyone was out and about. He'd hated that he couldn't drive me, but Danny was sound asleep, and I'd reminded him this was a small town with zero serial killers.

As far as we know, he'd said seriously. The concern in his eyes had warmed me to my toes all over again. Then I'd brushed it off, distracted him with a slow, deep kiss, and waved goodbye as I left. He'd let me borrow a T-shirt to put over my swimsuit so I'd be a little less conspicuous if anyone saw me. It was huge on me, so I'd tied it at the waist and rolled up the sleeves for my walk of shame.

It was one thing to refill coffee mugs and write down orders on no sleep, but quite another to teach teenagers algebraic equations. I wanted to check in with him later this evening, after football practice, but I'd be smart to rein myself in and wait a few days before contacting him. This wasn't supposed to be an every-night kind of fling. Which I was starting to think might be an absolute shame.

As I drove along the road out of town, following

the directions from my phone, I turned my thoughts to my meeting with Cambria. Dakota would join us as soon as she got off work. I'd brought a bottle of wine to soothe my nerves as much as anything.

Business meeting? Me?

The situation seemed kind of crazy, but the more I imagined working with these two women to build something unique and hopefully lucrative, the more I warmed up to the idea.

My map app directed me to a gravel driveway surrounded by tall trees. I drove past the remains of a building that looked to have burned down long ago and pulled up to an adorable cabin that appeared either newish or extensively refurbished. There was an old barn a few hundred feet away that looked like one strong wind would destroy it. That must be where Cambria made her candles; there was no way she could find space for that in her tiny home.

I got out and headed to the front door. There were two steps up to a cute porch with a high-top table and four chairs on one side and two rocking chairs on the other. Before I could knock, the door opened, and Cambria came out with a welcoming smile, a brown-and-black dog darting out ahead of her and a smaller white-and-brown one sauntering after.

"Hey, Harper. It's good to see you."

We hugged. "Thanks for having me, Cambria. Who are these guys?"

"That's Roscoe," she said, pointing at the bigger one. "Slowpoke here is Jethro."

I let Jethro sniff my hand, then scratched his ears. "Such a handsome boy." I stood up. "Your house looks incredible."

Her smile told me she loved it. "It was a long road to get it looking like this. Do you want a tour? It's only six hundred square feet, so it's more like a minitour."

"I'd love to see it."

As she showed off her place, she told me how it'd come to be hers. "This land was part of a farm years ago, but most of it was sold off, and the farmer died, leaving it abandoned. There used to be an old farmhouse, but it burned to the ground after a lightning strike."

"I saw the remains of it," I said.

"It happened years ago. The grandson of the farmer inherited the property and finally decided to unload it as is, with the building remains, the ancient barn, and this, which, at the time, was a hundred-year-old, no-frills but solid bunkhouse. I'd been saving for a house, but I didn't want to be right in town, and I wanted something, well, kind of funky."

"This is funky in a very good way."

The main floor consisted of a living room with a fireplace, a kitchen with an island and two stools, a small bedroom she used as her office, a bathroom, and a laundry closet. A wooden ladder went up to the loft, which was a gorgeous bedroom with large windows, rustic ceiling beams, and a sitting area opposite her bed.

"I got the property dirt cheap, so I was able to use my savings toward a complete refurbishment. They gutted it and started from scratch. I'll be paying it off for a while."

"Worth it. But I can't imagine going through that process," I said.

She'd obviously taken a big risk, and it appeared to have paid off.

"It was stressful to have construction going on for so long," Cambria admitted. "We came up against so many challenges due to it being a rustic, century-old building."

"You can't tell it now. This is amazing." I laughed. "To think I was nervous to sign a one-year lease on Mrs. Karasinski's apartment a few days ago..."

"Talk about location though. Do they have her belongings out yet?"

"This weekend." I remembered the bottle of wine and held it up. "Do you like moscato?"

"I do. Let me get glasses. We can take them to

the barn, and I'll show you where I work. You'll see why I need a better space."

With our glasses full, Cambria and I walked to the barn, the dogs accompanying us.

"When my house was finished three years ago, this place was in a little better shape. It's taken a beating from the weather and needs a new roof. It's the one thing I miscalculated in moving here."

She showed me her supplies, all in waterproof containers because the roof leaked.

"What are you working on?" I asked. A few dozen identical cylinders I suspected were silicone molds sat on the worktable.

Cambria stepped up to the table. "I got a huge order last week at a craft fair. They've been setting overnight, and I need to take them out, do a quality check, wrap each one in cellophane, and get them ready to ship. I promised they'd go out by tomorrow."

"That's a tall order. Need some help? If you show me what to do, we can work on them while we wait for Dakota."

"It's okay. I can do it later tonight."

"Unless we pour too much wine down your throat. Then you won't want to do it later. I don't mind helping."

"Seriously?"

"Show me these candles, please." I took a sip of

my wine and set the glass on a shelf so I wouldn't spill on her work. The smaller dog was curled up in a doggy bed in the corner. Roscoe sat on semi-alert outside the open door.

Cambria picked up one of the molds and popped out a dark green pine-tree-shaped candle with a wick sticking out the top. She trimmed the wick and showed me what she looked for as far as flaws. This one passed the quality check, so she added a sticker to the bottom and demonstrated how to wrap it and tie a ribbon and tag around the cellophane. Next, she unveiled a squirrel-shaped candle and repeated the process.

We had twenty candles done, nearly half the order, when Roscoe barked as Dakota drove by. I texted her to come to the barn.

"Hey, girlfriends," Dakota said a couple of minutes later when she appeared in the open doorway, Roscoe at her side, apparently having decided she was friend instead of foe.

"Hey, you," I said. "You're early."

"Seth let me go because we were slow this afternoon. Tourist season is winding down."

"Harper brought wine," Cambria said. "We were prepping an order I need to ship out, but we can stop and get down to business."

"Ooh, these trees are super cute," Dakota said. "What are we doing? I can help."

"Thirty to go," I told her. I was starting to get the hang of tying the ribbon just right.

Cambria poured wine for Dakota, and I explained the steps I'd learned earlier. We worked for another hour or so, chatting as we did.

"Guess who sat at the bar during my shift today," Dakota said as she unveiled another tree.

"The pope?" I said, focused on getting the ribbon just right.

"Naomi's brother."

"Ian?" My roommate had been in and out, but we hadn't talked much. He kept to himself and spent a lot of time outside, taking inventory of the property, I guessed.

"The one and only," Dakota replied. "You made him sound like an ogre that first night he showed up. You failed to mention he looked like *that*."

"He seemed like an ogre when he was drunk," I said. "So you talked to him?"

"I did. I tried to convince him not to sell."

I'd told everyone who'd shown up at the studio Tuesday about Ian and his plans. Though not a surprise, the news didn't go over well.

"A lot of people depend on the studio," I explained to Cambria. "Dakota more than most."

"Naomi's kilns are good ones. I can't exactly put one in an apartment," Dakota said, "even if I could afford one."

"You know, you could probably make your candles there too," I said. "Have you been there before?"

Cambria shook her head. "I've always meant to check it out, but I never needed it until now. I've been spoiled having a workspace in my backyard."

"What did Ian say?" I asked Dakota. "Did you convince him?"

She shrugged with a little laugh. "I got him thinking about it."

My brows shot up. "How'd you manage that? The one time I brought it up, he didn't really listen, just insisted he wasn't sticking around."

"I've got some feminine wiles." Dakota's smile went smug, but she kept her eyes on her task.

"So you flirted, and grumpy Ian is moving to Dragonfly Lake now?" I teased.

"Ha. I suggested some possibilities. Businessy ones, like find a manager for the studio. Turn the farmhouse into a bed-and-breakfast. He actually seemed to listen."

"Interesting," I said slowly, eyeing my future roommate. "It'd make an awesome B and B." Ian just didn't seem like the type to run one. But really, I didn't know him at all. "You should come over before I move out and work on him some more. It sounds like you have influence."

Dakota laughed. "I don't know about influence, but I can bother him some more."

"Sounds like you better bring those feminine wiles," Cambria said as she finished tying one more ribbon. "You guys are the best. It would've taken me till midnight by myself. Now all I have to do is box them up and put the mailing label on."

"We make a good team," Dakota said. "And speaking of, we should probably talk about this business thing."

Cambria eyed the ceiling before leaving her work on the table for a few hours. "Why don't we sit on the porch. I've got snacks we can munch on while we talk. And more wine if we need it."

"More wine is always a good option," I said. That bubbling feeling was back in my gut, the mix of excitement and nerves.

"Come on, Jethro," she said to the snoozing dog.

The three of us walked to the house. Cambria insisted we sit at the high-top table and let her bring the food out, so Dakota and I did exactly that with both dogs settling nearby.

"How was the picnic last night?" Dakota asked me once we were alone.

I'd forgotten I even mentioned I was going since it'd been last-minute.

"Typical teacher get-together," I said noncha-lantly. "Food from Henry's, BYOB, a cutthroat volleyball game. No one got stupid drunk. No one did anything scandalous. It was over by eight."

"Did you see Max?"

"Yep." I took a drink of wine. I hated keeping a secret from her, but Max was her brother. She might've been the one who dared me to bid on him, but I wasn't sure how she'd feel about us sleeping together—more than once. I wasn't going to find out either, because Max and I agreed to tell no one.

Which was killing me more than a little.

"That's all?" she asked. "Just yep?"

"Yep," I repeated. "He was there with Danny. He hung out with the math teachers."

"What about you?"

"I sat with Dorie Ludwig and her mom."

The door opened, and Cambria carried a tray out with a cheese ball and crackers, summer sausage, and chocolate-covered nuts. Plus a bottle of chardonnay.

"You're my kind of human," I said as she slid the tray to the center of the table.

Not only did she have excellent taste in snacks, but she'd saved me from more questions about Max.

We emptied the moscato into our glasses as we filled our plates with food.

"So," Cambria said as she slid onto her chair. "My mind has been going nonstop since Sunday. I feel like it wasn't a coincidence that you two came along when I was mulling over how to pivot."

"Maybe it was fate." Dakota popped a chocolate almond in her mouth.

"I almost didn't even look at the shop when I saw the square footage," Cambria continued, "but being on the square..."

"You can't beat that location," I said.

"Exactly. So my mind was spinning the minute I saw it, coming up with possibilities. Then you two mentioned your jewelry and your ceramics."

"We'd just been talking about how some of us regulars at the studio have quite a stash of our work because we don't have a good way to sell it," Dakota said.

"Let me tell you some of my ideas and see what you think." Cambria had opened the chardonnay inside and poured some in our now-empty glasses. "Sorry for not washing those out first. Party foul."

"I'm not a purist," I assured her.

"Same." Dakota held her glass up. "To laid-back bitches."

We clinked, laughing.

"Tell us what you're cooking up," I said after taking a sip.

"My candles; your jewelry, Harper; your ceramics, Dakota; and I know a girl who makes soaps, lotions, that kind of thing. I think she'd jump at the chance to sell through a retail store. I've researched some other product lines that would fit what I have in mind—candle holders, crystals, geodes, stickers, incense, some other decor, and gift items. Basically an eclectic mix of handmade merch and unique items we can order from smaller suppliers."

"I love it," Dakota said easily. She said it so fast that my head whipped in her direction. "What?" she asked me. "You don't?"

"No, I do," I said. "I'm intrigued. I can picture it. Sort of an earthy, artistic vibe?"

"Yes!" Cambria said. "I had an idea for a name." She made a face as if hesitant to tell us. "What do you think of Earthly Charm?"

I let it roll through my head for a second. "I like it."

"It's perfect," Dakota said. "You're good at this."

Cambria laughed. "Trust me when I say I've been obsessing." Her eyes were wide with enthusiasm that was contagious. "So there's a couple of different directions we could go."

She paused to take a bite of sausage, and I didn't miss her use of the word *we*.

I gulped some wine and waited.

"I'd love to have partners. You two if you're interested. We could open this business together as co-owners, either apply for a small business loan or find investors, and develop it together, equal shares.

Or if that's more than you're wanting to bite off, I can be the sole owner, and I'd love to have you as my first two employees."

I blew out a breath with an overwhelmed *wooo* sound. "That's...big. Both options are a huge deal."

"Huge deal," Dakota said. "Thank you for including me."

"If you hate it, no hard feelings," Cambria said in a rush.

"I don't hate it," I said. "I'm a little freaked out about the partnership. Are you sure about that?"

Cambria picked up an almond but didn't put it in her mouth. "I'll be honest. I'm freaked out too because it's a big endeavor to open a store on the square. I was originally thinking a tiny storefront with a large enough back room to do my work in, but then this opportunity came out of nowhere. I'm a risk taker, so I want to do it either way, as long as I can get financing. But I'd love it more if you two were in it with me. If it was *our* business."

"You know I'm a bartender, right?" Dakota said. "I can make a mean mimosa and a killer martini, and I can make change when I have to, but I've never owned a business."

"If you've sold your mugs, you technically have," I pointed out, surprising myself because, by those standards, I was in business too.

"This is such a bigger scale," Dakota said. "How long do we have to think about it?"

"However long you need, as long as nobody else gets serious about that storefront. Darius said he'd give me first dibs." Cambria looked to me. "What are you thinking, Harper?"

"I'm thinking I need more wine."

We all laughed, and I held my glass up for her to refill.

I nodded. "I need to make enough money to pay the rent and live on."

"I plan to include payroll in the financing," Cambria said.

"This girl is smart," Dakota said.

"We can totally do this," Cambria said, her eyes lit with excitement and determination. "Going into business together would be an adventure."

I laughed giddily and wondered if the wine was hitting me. Because I liked adventures and was really considering this. "I need to make sure you understand that, like Dakota, I'm great at customer service but inexperienced with business stuff."

"You're both creative and smart and have good taste," Cambria said. "I like business. I've watched a ton of videos about it and learned a lot. That said, I'm green too. We'll figure it out together."

I met Dakota's gaze and lifted my brows. "Thoughts?" I asked her.

With her grin widening, she shrugged. "Where's the downside? I love the Henrys, but I could use a change. It's outside my comfort zone, and they say that's supposed to be a good thing."

"Yeah." I'd lived most of my life deeply ensconced in my comfort zone. If I wanted to be more like Naomi—and I did—I needed to seriously up my game.

"Worst-case scenario," Dakota continued, "the store doesn't make it, and we have to find new jobs." She shrugged again. "But with the collective creativity and girl power at this table? I don't see how Earthly Charm doesn't rock this town."

I swirled my wine in my glass, watching the pale-yellow liquid swish around, my heart hammering. I'd never been an over-thinker. I went by my gut. Right now my gut was screaming to take the chance.

"I think we should go for it," I said. "I'm in."

Chapter Twenty-Two

Max

Today I was leaping over the line from unwise and careless to downright stupid and reckless. It couldn't be helped though.

Moving day had arrived for my sister and her new roommate, none other than the woman I'd slept with every single night for the past week and a half. And by sleeping, I meant minimally sleeping and mostly fucking every which way, including loose.

I kept thinking the spectacularness of sex with Harper would fizzle out, but our nights together were so incredible that the sleep deprivation didn't bother me.

The night after we'd agreed to our no-strings fling, she'd come over again after Danny was asleep, bursting with the news that she'd committed to the business venture with Cambria and my sister. I knew what a big step it was for her, and the teacher in me was so damn proud of her for taking the leap.

Who the hell was I kidding? That wasn't the teacher in me; it was the man who was getting to know Harper with all her strengths and quirks.

Even if we hadn't been sleeping together, I would've felt the same. Harper was easy to like. She was funny, creative, and carefree in a way I'd never be, not to mention sexy as sin with an insatiable drive that kept up with mine.

Surprisingly, we found we could talk for hours, which didn't help with the sleep deprivation. We'd delved into long, middle-of-the-night conversations on everything from the creative process to the psychology of teenagers, from the best spots on the lake for stand-up paddleboarding to our respective first dates.

As for her lack of interest in a commitment?

I was one lucky sucker.

Was it a good idea to spend every single night together? Unequivocal no. But I hadn't found it in me to suggest a night off.

It was nearing ten a.m. on the second Sunday of September. Harper had snuck out of my place a mere five hours ago to her car, parked in a random spot downtown, and driven herself back to Naomi's one last time.

Dakota had asked me to help her move. After all the times she'd watched Danny, I couldn't say no, so today I'd spend hours with Harper, her dad, my sister, and our brother, Levi. My mom was helping by watching Danny at her house. Acting as if Harper didn't affect me would require an award-winning performance and a megadose of restraint. For hours.

My siblings and I arrived with Dakota's first two loads before Harper and her dad got to the apartment. All that was left for our next trip was living room furniture from my mom's basement that she was donating to the cause.

We were down to the last few boxes when I walked out of Dakota's bedroom and straight into a view of Harper in the living room, bending over to prop open the main door, her perfect ass pointing right at me from under a pair of pink running shorts.

I stopped dead in my tracks because I hadn't heard them arrive and had not been fucking prepared for that view.

"Good morning, Max." Her dad's jolly voice pulled me out of my stupor as he entered the apartment. His gaze lingered on me a second too long, as if he knew damn well what I'd been staring at.

"Hi, Max," Harper said, cheery and nonchalant as could be, but I was sure she knew what kind of view she'd given me. With her, there was a good chance she'd done it intentionally.

"Morning," I said, my voice rough. "We were starting to wonder about you."

"Thought maybe you came to your senses and changed your mind," Levi said as he came out of Dakota's room.

Dakota followed with an exaggerated sigh. "Hey, roomie, need a brother? I'm selling mine."

For half a second, Harper's gaze met mine and flared with meaning. "No, thanks. One is more than enough." She laughed as I checked whether her dad had witnessed our silent exchange.

My boss was too busy examining the apartment like only a father could. He inspected the locks on the windows, then eyed the kitchen appliances. I tried to act as if I wasn't battling a hard-on in my jeans and went down the stairs for more of my sister's boxes.

While I finished emptying my SUV and Dakota unpacked boxes in her room, Levi helped Harper and her dad unload Bob's truck. As much as I wanted to be the one to assist, it was better this way. I was having a hard time acting unbothered.

The truth was, I was bothered as fuck just by being in the same apartment as Harper.

By the time we had all three vehicles empty, it was after noon.

"That's all of Harper's stuff," Bob said as my sister, brother, and I congregated in the as-yet-unfurnished living room. Harper was in her room, assembling a bookshelf. "Did I hear you had a couch somewhere?" he asked.

"I've got the living room pieces at my mom's," Dakota said. "We'll need Levi's truck."

"Is that a two-person job or three?" Bob asked.

"Levi and I can get it, can't we?" Dakota asked our brother.

"Piece of cake," Levi replied.

"Tell you what," Bob said. "You two go get that last load. Max, you can help Harper assemble those shelves. I'll order pizzas from Humble's and bring them back for all of us."

I eyed him to gauge whether this plan was another veiled attempt to leave me alone with his daughter, but he avoided looking at me as my siblings voiced hearty approval of his offer.

Within three minutes, the others left Harper and me alone in her apartment.

I knew my boss was matchmaking, and that was fine. I could be alone with his daughter and not act like a sex-starved animal in mating season, no problem.

To prove it, I went into her bedroom to see if I could help with the shelves.

Harper stood, eyeing the living room. "Did everyone leave?"

"They're all gone." I kept it to myself that her dad had done that on purpose.

She closed her bedroom door, and before I could blink, she threw her arms around me, pressed her body into me, wrapped a leg around mine, and kissed me hard.

I filled my palms with her ass, drawing her closer as I turned and pressed her into the closed door.

With a gasp, she broke off the kiss. "How fast do you think you can make me come?"

That was all it took for all my blood to pound to my dick. "How fast can you get your panties off?"

She shoved her shorts and underwear to her ankles and stepped free in less than two seconds. Next thing I knew, she had my fly unzipped and was reaching into my boxer briefs, freeing my steel-hard cock.

"Fuck, Harper."

"That's the plan," she purred.

With a hungry growl, I lifted her up, pinning her bare lower half between me and the door. Her legs circled me, centering her core right where I needed it. I pressed my dick into her even though my jeans still constricted me. The little bit of skin-to-skin contact above my boxer briefs was a taste of hot, damp heaven, but I needed more.

Spreading one of my hands across her gorgeous ass to support her, I shoved my other hand down my side to get rid of my pants.

"Fuck," I gritted out again, stopping before I freed myself. "I don't have a condom."

Harper let out a shaky, needful breath. "I'm on birth control," she said in a rush. "And clean. I've always used a condom."

"I'm clean too," I said.

She slid her fingers into my pants, dragging them down to my thighs. I didn't even bother to take them off farther, because before I could make sure she was okay with this, she raised herself enough to slide down on my dick.

"Not gonna last long," I managed through a clenched jaw.

"Kind of the point of a quickie." Her breath came out in a gratifying gasp as I thrust into her—hard.

Then I rutted into her exactly like a sex-starved animal in mating season. She didn't appear to mind as she clung to me with both arms and locked her legs behind me as if holding on for dear life.

I knew I was.

I closed my eyes and nearly bit through my lip in an effort to make sure she came before me. At the first contraction of her muscles around me, I lost it and plunged over at the same time as her, grunting as I emptied myself into her.

"It's not official because I didn't check the clock," Harper eventually said, still catching her breath, "but I'm pretty sure that was under five minutes. A good first effort."

I laughed, my body jerking and causing Harper to contract around me again, which felt incredible even now. "You're gonna be the death of me," I managed. "And no, I'm not complaining."

As my blood gradually trickled into my brain once again, I wondered how long it'd been since everyone had left and, more importantly, how long till they returned.

I kissed her, then slid her down my body, severing our connection. "You need to put yourself back together before they return."

Her dad might be playing matchmaker, but I was sure he hadn't had a quickie against her bedroom door in mind.

Harper bent down and pressed a kiss to my spent cock. "Might want to put that thing away," she said, looking pleased with herself.

Jesus. What this woman did to me...

As she picked up her shorts and underwear and hurried off to the bathroom, I pulled my pants up and tucked myself in, in need of a shower. I could smell sex in the air. What had I been thinking, for fuck's sake?

If I'd been thinking, none of that would've happened.

I couldn't get myself to regret it though.

———

Harper

By the time my dad returned with pizza, we had the sofa, chair, and coffee table in place, and the apartment was starting to feel like a home.

Max's mom, Brenna, had followed Levi and Dakota over, bringing Danny for lunch with the family. She sat on the sofa with Danny on her lap, my dad next to her, and Levi on the opposite end. Max was in the easy chair. Dakota had brought out a kitchen chair, and I sat on the floor, my back against the wall opposite Max.

We were all worn out and hungry from hauling everything up the stairs—and some of us from a life-altering quickie in the bedroom—so the pizza hit the spot. The mood was light, with Dakota and her brothers giving each other a hard time and my dad talking to Brenna and Danny. From time to time, Dakota and I discussed ideas for how to decorate. At Dakota's request, Max started a list on his phone of items we needed to buy.

"We could put a Christmas tree in that corner," Dakota said, pointing.

"It's not even Halloween yet," Levi said, shaking his head.

Dakota eyed me. "How do you feel about a life-sized skeleton for Halloween?"

"As long as we can dress him, I'm all for it."

"We can name him after one of our exes," Dakota said enthusiastically, making everyone laugh.

I caught Max glancing at me and met his gaze, just for a second. I'd never longed to be able to do something as much as I wanted to go over and climb into his lap in that oversized chair and just...*be* with him. Be touching him. Not even sexually, although I was always up for that.

I could easily imagine this gathering in a different context—two families brought together by a couple, by Max and me, maybe for holidays, maybe for a casual dinner. Maybe I was overtired, because I was getting downright sappy and wistful for something that would never be.

"Ooh," Brenna said as she set her empty plate on the coffee table. "It's time for a diaper change, isn't it, Danny boy?" She kissed his temple and scooted to the edge of the cushion, preparing to stand with him.

"I've got it, Mom," Max said. He scooped up Danny. "Let's go, stinky boy. You could use a refresh." He held his son out in front of him, parallel to the floor like a plane, and made airplane noises, grabbing the diaper bag on the way to the bathroom.

Max closed the door, but I could hear his running conversation with his son as he changed him. Something about that made my insides warm and mushy. I couldn't help but wonder what had gotten into me. Was it sentimentality over finally, officially having my own place with one of my best friends?

"Your son is a good father," my dad said to Brenna.

"Yes, he is," she agreed. "He sure didn't have a role model for it, but somehow he picked up how to be a caring man."

"Max is a nurturer," Dakota said matter-of-factly. "He loves to help people, encourage them, teach them."

What she said was true. I'd never considered that to be on my list of desirable traits in a man, but...God, it was hot. I loved all of that about Max. I didn't get to see him with Danny very often, which was probably a good thing, because it turned me inside out and made me want to...

I caught my breath, then glanced around to see if anyone had noticed. No one paid attention to me, thank goodness, because I had, in that moment, realized a very bad thing.

I wanted more from Max. I wanted a real relationship. A long-term one, where we lived together, loved when we wanted to, and took care of Danny as a team.

God help me, I was pretty sure I'd fallen for Max.

Maybe it was just lust on steroids? It was so fast. It'd only been a few weeks since our date at the gala. But no. This wasn't just wanting his body. It was more.

He came out of the bathroom at that moment, Danny walking at his side, his little hand in Max's, and swear to God, that image did nothing to make me feel *less*.

My mouth went dry, and I was suddenly shaky inside. I turned my attention to picking up plates and tidying the living room. Anything to ignore the man who'd ravaged the hell out of me in the bedroom less than an hour ago.

In the kitchen by myself, I threw away the paper plates, my heart pounding.

I'd screwed up, and I couldn't let Max know.

Because real feelings were never supposed to be part of our deal.

Chapter Twenty-Three

Max

I was dozing when I heard my bedroom door to the deck ease open. Rolling to my back, I watched Harper's silhouette as she closed it behind her and locked it, then tucked the key I'd given her into her shoe when she took it off.

With a sleepy smile, I let out a contented growl and pulled my blankets back for her.

For the two weeks since she'd moved, Harper had continued to come over most nights once she closed the studio for the evening. With my sister as her roommate, it'd become twice as complicated. Sometimes she waited until Dakota went to bed. Sometimes Harper turned in early, then snuck out once Dakota was in her own room. And there were a few times when the two of them went out together or stayed up late talking, and we had to skip a night.

I kept my mind occupied with a movie or an audiobook on those nights, trying not to admit to myself how much I missed her. I knew we'd gotten reckless by spending so much time together, but then I rationalized that we both had needs, we liked meeting each other's needs, and this arrangement would end soon enough, so why not enjoy the hell out of it for now?

I was bothered that she had to deceive my sister, so a few nights ago, we'd talked about coming clean to her. In the end, we'd agreed that would put too much pressure on what we had, so we were keeping the secret. I wasn't proud to admit how relieved I was.

Harper wore running clothes when she visited me in case someone saw her en route. Normally she shed them first thing, then joined me. Tonight I couldn't help but notice she crawled in fully clothed. I pulled her against me anyway and kissed her hello.

"Everything okay?" I asked, getting the distinct impression something was off.

She sighed as she snuggled into me. "Cambria heard back from two different banks today about a small business loan. Both of them said no."

"Damn. I'm sorry to hear that." I kissed her forehead.

"She has a big loan on her property, I have almost no credit history, and Dakota's is limited and not stellar. On paper, we look like a bad risk. They apparently don't care that the business plan Cambria created—with Seth Henry's help, I might add—is incredible or that our products are locally made and have the potential to sell like crazy or that the three of us are determined as hell to make this work."

I closed my eyes, genuinely upset for her. "Have you had time to come up with a plan B?"

"That's why I'm so late getting here. The three of us went out for drinks to discuss it and ended up closing down Henry's, then continuing at our apartment. We're going to keep trying until we find a way to make it work. There're a million banks out there, credit unions, and we found some small business grants we could apply for. We talked to Holden Henry about finding investors, and he gave us a few tips from when they were searching for the brewery."

"Those are good ideas," I said, caressing her cheek with one finger, wishing I could do more to soothe her.

In a different situation, I would seriously consider investing. I'd heard some of their plans and wanted to see both Harper and my sister succeed. I couldn't exactly offer up seed money to my secret fling. Maybe I'd get Dakota talking about it and see if she brought up the idea. There was a fine line between being supportive of my baby sister and being domineering. She'd accused me of the latter many times.

"Worst-case scenario, we could ask for a much smaller loan, and Dakota and I could continue our current jobs and help Cambria when we can."

"That wouldn't be ideal. It's not easy to split your time or your brain between two different jobs."

"I bet you know something about that," she said. "It's our last choice, but we want this. I want this to work out so much, Max. I was scared to death to say yes, but ever since then, I'm in it one thousand percent. I can't imagine *not* opening Earthly Charm."

"I know. I can see it in your eyes every time you talk about it, at least when the lights are on." I smiled, because we did spend the majority of our time in the dark. "That's the element these bankers don't consider."

"Exactly."

"I believe in you, Harper. If you need help with something, let me know. I could hook you up with my financial guy and see if he has any advice."

She kissed me lightly, distractedly. "Thank you.

I appreciate that." She let out a big, tired sigh and cuddled in closer to my chest.

A few minutes later, her breathing evened out. She was obviously worn out and worried and in need of a good night's sleep. I kissed her forehead lightly again, wanting her to have everything she wanted—the good night's sleep and the financing for the store.

Her even breathing didn't take long to relax me, and I fell asleep with her in my arms.

———

Harper's alarm went off at four thirty a.m. like it did every night she stayed with me. She'd figured out if she left by five, she'd get home before the town came awake, as nothing opened until six or seven. Most mornings we woke and indulged in an extra orgasm or two.

Today she snoozed her alarm, then curled back into me. After a few rounds of snoozing, she bolted upright and rolled out of bed.

"I didn't mean to snooze it so many times," she said.

"You needed the sleep. I guess I did too." Still dazed, I rolled over and hugged her pillow, watching as she pulled her hair on top of her head, preparing to leave. Before she headed to the deck door to sneak out, she came over to me, planted a thorough kiss on my lips, and said goodbye.

I inhaled her scent on my pillow after she left and let myself be lazy, knowing I had another half hour before my alarm would go off.

Just as I was about to doze off, a thought occurred to me and woke me right the hell up.

Harper and I were supposed to be fuck buddies, in this whole thing for the incredible sex, but last night we'd merely *slept*. No middle-of-the-night half-awake sexcapades. No morning oral. She'd never even undressed.

I hadn't realized it until now. In fact, I'd been all on board. It'd felt natural to hold her when she was upset, to be there for her in a way that wasn't physical.

That was a problem.

Wide awake, anxiety pumping through me, I sat up on the side of my bed, about to head for the shower when my phone buzzed.

I picked it up and read the message from Harper.

> I just saw that llama between backyards near Fifth and Acorn. Aren't you friends with Dr. Holloway?

———

"Ben Holloway." My friend's voice was groggy with sleep when he answered his phone.

"Ben, it's Max. Your llama's on the lam again."

There was a pause, then, "Fucking llama. I checked on her at midnight, and she was fine. Where is she?"

"Last I knew she was near Fifth and Acorn in someone's backyard."

"What do you mean last you knew? Where are you?"

"At home."

"How do you know she's at Fifth and Acorn?"

Here's where it got tricky. "A friend told me."

"A friend." He said it as if he knew damn well it was a woman who'd spent the night. "Anyone I know?"

"Don't you have a llama to go catch?"

"Fuck. I've got a fever and so does Ruby. She's in my bed and we're both burning up and aching." He coughed, and it didn't sound like he had any business going out.

"You need to stay put. I can catch Esmerelda." I'd helped Ben before.

"You'll need the van."

"I'll come get it. I'll have to take Danny with me."

"I'd offer to keep him here, but you don't want him anywhere near this crud."

"No, I don't. Toss the keys by the back door, and I'll take it from there."

He sighed and swore again. "Thanks, Max. I owe you one."

"Just keep your phone on you in case I need llama-catching tips."

"You got it."

————

Harper

I'd seen Dr. Holloway's llama from a distance before, but I'd never expected to be the one responsible for deterring her from downtown.

Max had called on his way to get the llamamobile from Dr. Holloway's and told me our plan. Esmerelda was undoubtedly heading toward Sugar, the bakery on Main Street, for one of her favorite cookies, but the goal was to not let her get that far. If she got to the square, she'd draw attention, which made it harder to capture her. Not to mention, Max and I didn't want attention. The llama's safety and return to her pen took priority, of course, but it would suck to get outed by a llama on the loose.

I didn't know much about llamas, but this one was no dummy.

The sky was starting to lighten in the east. We were about three blocks west of downtown, and I was between Esmerelda and the bakery, trying to get her to turn back. When I approached her from the east, holding my arms out like Max told me to, she indeed stopped her forward progression. Instead of doing a U-turn and heading home, however, she meandered to the north a yard or two and aimed for the bakery again.

There were enough trees and sheds and fences and garages that I couldn't tell where she'd pop up next. I was fully entrenched in a game of hide and seek with a llama.

Even though it was serious business, I couldn't help but laugh every time I found her. She eyed me with that expressive, judgmental gaze as if to say, *Get out of my way, damn hussy!*

We were a few blocks from where I'd originally spotted her, so I hurriedly texted Max an update, keeping an eye out for the white-furred fugitive. I was trespassing like a criminal to cut her off at the pass, dodging fences, setting off security lights, and arousing a dog or two.

As I made my way around some overgrown bushes in a blessedly unfenced yard, I looked up to find the llama mere feet away. I let out a short yelp of surprise, then slapped my hand over my mouth. Maybe I startled Esmerelda too, because she hoofed it away from me, then cut into another yard. I was blocked by a tall privacy fence, so with tears of mostly suppressed laughter half blinding me, I went in the opposite direction, looking for the next unfenced yard so I could cut her off yet again.

When I found a path through, I ran, thankful I was a runner, because this hairy beast was pushing me. I got to the front of this particular house in time to see a white blur across the street, ducking into yet another backyard.

I texted Max that we were crossing Walnut Street and wondered how long it could possibly take to load up Danny, drive a few miles to the vet's house, transfer Danny to the van, and get his ass back here to help me. It was a small miracle I hadn't been spotted by anyone yet.

On the other side of Walnut, I found an unfenced yard and ran through it, my eyes peeled for white. A dog started barking, but it was far enough away I wasn't worried about immediate discovery. Esmerelda, however, was more concerned, as I found her about twenty feet from me, in a narrow alley, her head craned toward the dog. This might be the break I was looking for. Were llamas afraid of dogs? I could only hope.

Max had told me not to rush up to her no

matter what because she'd take off, so I froze and tried to figure out what to do. Just then, my phone vibrated with a message.

It was Max, asking for my location. I replied, explaining about the alley and the barking dog, who still hadn't shut up. Hopefully his people would assume there was a squirrel or a bunny.

When Max jogged up behind me, I was so relieved I wanted to tackle hug him, but I merely pointed at Esmerelda, who hadn't moved.

"You stay here and extend both your arms so she won't try to dart past. I'm going to approach her from the side, slowly. This could take a while, but slow is key."

I nodded, still catching my breath. "Where's Danny?"

"The van's parked right over there." He pointed at the street perpendicular to the alley. "I locked it, but we need to hurry. He's engrossed in a video on my iPad for now." Max handed me the keys for when he got the harness on Esmerelda.

I stood with my arms out as instructed, watching Max, keeping an eye on the llama, silently pleading with the animal not to take off again. Nearly ten minutes later, Max, the llama whisperer, had reached her side and was talking in a low, soothing voice.

Apparently she was as spellbound by Max

Dawson as I was, because she merely stared at him, letting him touch her side. Eventually he was able to get her harness on, and from that point, he basically had control. He slipped a lead through the harness and told me to unlock the back of the van.

By the time he hit the street with Esmerelda, I had the back doors wide open, llama ready. I'd opened the driver's door so I could keep Danny company. He was strapped in his car seat on the passenger side, still in his pj's, engrossed in a kids' show with talking animals.

Everything went smoothly until Max and his llama friend reached the back of the van. The animal refused to step inside.

"Come on, Esmerelda," Max said patiently. "Ben's been training you for this. You like the van."

"She didn't get a cookie," I said from a distance, grinning.

"Hell, I forgot. There's a Sugar bag between the front seats."

"You stopped and got her a cookie?" I asked as I ducked across the driver's seat.

"Ben stocks up for exactly this reason. I need you to open the side door, hold the cookie up so she sees it, then put it in that tray."

I did as he said, and before I could get to the tray behind the passenger seat, the llama hopped inside and came after me, or maybe the cookie. For a second, I thought I was a goner, but she only wanted the rainbow-sprinkled sugar cookie, not my fingers. With a squeal, I dropped the cookie on the tray and ducked out of the way, my heart hammering, exhilarated laughter pouring from me, my shoulders shaking with it.

Once I was safely on the pavement, I remembered to close the door at the same time Max shut the back one, and we had ourselves one captured llama.

Max came around the van, a handsome smile on his face as he shook his head. "That wasn't how I saw my Monday starting, but thank you."

With a quiet laugh, I said, "Thank *you* for showing up when you did."

He glanced in at Danny, who was oblivious to the llama just inches behind him, a mesh metal divider ensuring he was perfectly safe.

After a head shake of disbelief at his son, Max turned his attention back to me. "Mission accomplished. We make a good team."

"We do," I said. "A super-secret superhero llama-catching team."

"I'd offer you a ride home but..."

"Your van is full, plus the *secret* part." I smiled to show him I'd be fine.

After saying goodbye though, as I walked away

from the van and made my way toward the square, his words replayed in my head.

We make a good team.

I wanted to be a team with Max. I'd tried to shove that desire aside ever since moving day when I'd first had the thought. But the more we were together, the more I couldn't deny it.

I swallowed hard.

I was either going to have to work up the courage to tell him I wanted more or I was going to have to stop seeing him altogether.

Chapter Twenty-Four

Max

Being in sports for my whole life, I'd never had a shortage of guy friends, at least on the surface. But nothing had the power to forge deep ties the way single fatherhood did.

Our group of single dads met nearly every Saturday. We made a collective effort to ensure we all had childcare for those few hours each week, the others often sharing a sitter. My family made themselves available to watch Danny.

Some nights we played cards or darts. Sometimes we took my boat out. Every once in a while, we hit a bar, usually for a birthday or another occasion. We frequently had sports on the TV wherever we were.

Tonight I was hosting at my house for the first time. We'd be breaking in the lakeside terrace and taking my new grill, which was admittedly big enough for a guy my size to sleep on, for a test run. If the air temperature cooled enough after sunset, we might try out the fire pit as well. I'd had the terrace built in early summer but had been waiting on the back-ordered grill before having the dads over.

Danny was staying overnight at Levi's. My brother had picked him up midafternoon so I could get ready. I was serving ribeye steaks, grilled potatoes, and corn on the cob.

I'd told everyone to come to the backyard when they arrived. The grill was heating, and the drink cooler was full of Rusty Anchor when Chance Cordova and Luke Durham appeared at the side of the house.

"Welcome," I called as they came down the incline toward the terrace.

"We finally get an invite to the coach's fancy house, and we're relegated to the backyard. Feels like my childhood," Chance said with a big grin. He was a pretty boy who generated female attention wherever he went.

"You can go inside to use the restroom, but only

if you take your shoes off first," I joked. "Hey, Luke. What's up?"

"How's it going?" Luke owned a farm outside of town where he worked his ass off growing strawberries, apples, and Christmas trees.

"Good to see you," I said. "Is your dad with Addie tonight?" His daughter was four years old and full of energy.

"As usual," Luke said. "He might not be able to help around the farm much anymore, but he's the best grandpa known to man."

"Family's everything," I said, meaning it. "Help yourself to a beer. What's Samantha up to tonight?" I directed the question to Chance.

"She's grounded. I'll be checking her location to make sure she stays home. I wouldn't put it past her to cause trouble expressly to ruin guys' night."

At fourteen, Samantha Cordova was living up to the stereotype of a difficult teenager and making the rest of us appreciate the tame-in-comparison challenges of younger kids.

Ben arrived next, carrying a large thermal travel cup I'd bet was full of some kind of health elixir. Without a word, he set a bottle of top-shelf whiskey on a side table, then sat down.

"Thanks," I said, a little puzzled. "We'll have a glass after we eat." He gave a two-finger salute.

I'd put chips, guacamole, and salsa on the outdoor table, along with cut veggies and dip, mostly for our resident health-nut veterinarian. We four sat around the appetizers, digging in and listening to Luke's dad's latest medical challenges and Chance's experience being summoned to the middle school principal's office on behalf of his daughter.

"Compared to her, I was a model student," Chance said, shaking his head.

Chance and I were about the same age, but he'd moved to Dragonfly Lake as an adult, so I couldn't attest to what kind of kid he'd been.

"Being a teenager is hard," Luke said. "We can try all we want to be everything our kids need, but I imagine being a girl without a mother figure makes it even harder."

"I wonder if I could hire one," Chance joked. "Wanted: mother figure for fourteen-year-old hellion. Pay sucks. Father not interested in relationship beyond sex."

We laughed and drank to that just as West Aldridge rounded the house and headed toward us.

"There he is," Chance bellowed.

"Welcome to the party terrace," I said as he approached.

"Glad you made it," Luke said.

West didn't look particularly happy.

"Need a beer?" I asked.

"Got anything harder?" West didn't smile, nor did he help himself to the drink cooler.

"You okay?" Ben asked him.

"Just about didn't make it tonight," West said.

I was due to put the steaks on the grill now that everyone who was expected had arrived, but I stayed put, curious.

"What's going on?" Luke asked him.

West leaned forward, elbows on knees, and blew out a heavy breath. "April moved out two nights ago."

"Oh, shit," Chance said.

"What happened?" Luke asked.

I stood and dug a Lunker Stout out of the cooler, knowing it was West's preferred beer, opened it, and handed it to him.

He took it without a word and downed a third of it while we all waited to hear more. He'd met April close to a year ago. She'd moved in with West and his three little girls not long after.

"We haven't been getting along lately," West said. "Arguing a lot. About stupid things, big things, you name it. She got sick of it. Said we were toxic, and our relationship was doing more harm than good."

"I'm sorry, dude," Chance said. "That sucks."

West shrugged. "She's probably right. It was overdue. But my girls..."

He had six-year-old twins and a three-year-old.

Anxiety tightened in my chest before he could say more, because I knew where he was going.

"They're heartbroken," West said.

At their ages, those girls would bond readily with any woman West moved in, at least the first time. They'd just had a dose of the same lesson I'd learned as a kid. Same lesson my cousin Jamie had learned. Sometimes people you loved left for good. April might've only been there for eight or nine months, but for those little girls, that was an eternity.

"Damn," Ben said. "That's rough."

West crossed his hands in front of his mouth, and his eyes watered as he tried to regain his composure.

"I'm sorry, man," Luke said. "That's gotta make it hurt double."

"Quadruple," West said. "Once for each of us. I might be more upset on my girls' behalf than my own. Which says a lot about where our relationship was."

"In all the years since Erin died, I've never introduced a woman to Sam," Chance said. "I never want her to hurt like that again. There were times when I didn't think we'd get through her mom's death."

"Yeah." Ben nodded. His wife had also died too young.

"April loved those girls from the first time she met them," West said. "I didn't think it'd end up like this."

"Maybe she'll still want to see the girls?" Luke asked. He was coming from a unique spot among us. He and Addie's mom were on good terms. Not romantic and never married, but cooperating when it came to parenting. Jessie was full-time military, so Luke having custody worked for both of them. But he didn't have experience with losing a parent or a spouse.

"I don't know if I want her seeing the girls," West said. He sat up straighter. "Hell, I don't know much of anything other than I hate that my daughters' hearts hurt because I made a mistake and trusted the wrong person."

My mouth had gone dry, and my throat was clogged with emotion. Because that was exactly one of my biggest fears with Danny. He'd already lost his biological parents. I never wanted him to experience a loss like that again.

"You didn't know she was the wrong person," Ben said. "You need to cut yourself some slack."

"You'd never do anything to hurt your girls on purpose," Luke said.

"And yet they got their hearts crushed anyway."

West shook his head. "Fuck, guys. I'm sorry to bring the party down."

"No need to apologize," Chance said. "We get it like no one else gets it."

I got it so fucking much I hadn't been able to say anything at all. I tipped my beer back and poured some of the cold liquid down my throat, barely tasting it but appreciating the coolness.

"The biggest bitch of it all?" West said. "We hadn't even had sex for weeks."

"Ouch," Chance said.

"I miss sex," Luke said.

"Who doesn't?" Chance said with a laugh.

I felt Ben's weighted stare on me and tried to ignore it.

"I suspect Max might not," he said, grinning.

Everyone's attention turned to me, and I flipped Ben the bird.

"You got a girlfriend you forgot to tell us about?" Chance asked.

"I don't have a girlfriend," I said. "You asshole. I caught your fucking llama for you."

"That's what the whiskey's for," Ben said.

"I'm missing something," West said, eyeing the two of us.

"Max has a secret friend," Ben said.

"You don't know that," I said, not hiding my irritation.

"I do now." He laughed. "I've suspected you had something going on for a couple of weeks. You just confirmed it with your reaction."

"Asshole," I repeated, not putting much heat behind it. He didn't know enough to out Harper, so I'd take a little shit from these guys, and then it would pass.

"You gonna tell us about your lady friend, Dawson?" Chance asked.

"Maybe it's not a lady," West cracked.

"It's a female," I growled.

My confirmation elicited howls and hoots.

"Are we back in middle school or what?" I asked.

"Must be a reason you're keeping things secret," Chance said as he reached for more chips.

"It's a fling," I said. "Nothing serious. Just fun." Saying that made me feel itchy. I took another swig of beer.

Everyone's eyes remained on me, as if I was going to tell them more.

"It's not worth talking about," I continued. "I need to put an end to it soon."

"So she's just a fuck buddy?" West asked.

My gut churned as I nodded. "That's what it's supposed to be. I'm afraid if I let it go on much longer, one or both of us will get attached."

"Would that really be so bad?" Luke asked.

"Did you hear West's story?" I shot back rhetorically. "I've been that kid. My dad left when I was thirteen. Having a parent take off isn't something you completely recover from."

"What if you found the right person though?" Luke persisted. "What if you found a woman who'd stay? Be a mom to your boy?"

"How the hell do you figure out the difference?" West asked.

"Good damn question," Chance said.

"I can't risk it." I shook my head, resolute.

"So you're fine with being alone for the rest of your life?" Ben asked.

I pegged him with a half grin. "There's a happy middle ground."

"Sneaking around?" Luke frowned. "I'm all for a fling here and there, but I wouldn't mind finding a wife."

I shook my head. "We're all here because of a loss. Loss of a spouse, loss of a relationship. Loss of Danny's biological parents in my case. All of us. For every single one of us, shit went sideways and already affected our kids. I don't like those odds."

"You lost your cousin, which sucks, but Danny's not going to remember it," Luke pointed out.

"And Knox's Juniper," Chance said, referring to Knox Breckenridge, who was no longer single but often still joined us, just not tonight. "She was young enough when her mom deserted her that she probably won't have emotional scars."

"Danny's old enough now he'd get hurt just like West's girls," I said.

"It's a risk," Chance said. "We all gotta decide, if we're lucky enough to find someone we click with, whether it's worth that risk."

That much was true. I wouldn't fault anyone who wanted to take the chance, but I knew when the odds weren't in my favor.

Harper, by her own admission, wasn't the staying type. That very fact was why we'd gotten together in the first place. She didn't want anything serious. I didn't want anything serious. We'd had our fun and then some. I'd be stupid to hold on much longer.

"Screw waiting till after dinner," I said. "I'm breaking open that whiskey right now."

Chapter Twenty-Five

Max

Our dads' night ended earlier than usual—a lot earlier.

After we ate, Chance had checked his daughter's location on his phone, found her not at home, and left to spoil her fun.

Not thirty minutes later, West's babysitter had texted that Scarlett, one of his twins, was inconsolable and scared her daddy had left too, so West had taken off, putting a damper on our moods, because damn if we didn't feel for him and for his little girl.

The remaining three of us had shot the shit for a few more minutes. Then Ben and Luke had left by nine. I'd had the terrace cleaned up by ten after and had been sitting on the end of my dock ever since.

The temperature was cool enough to light a fire, but I was more content to sit in the dark, nearly surrounded by the water. Alone.

I didn't know how much time had passed, probably at least an hour, when I noticed the distant echoes of laughter from a party across the lake had died down. The insects were chirping at full volume when my phone vibrated with a message.

I knew before looking it was Harper. She usually messaged when all was clear on her end. I waited several heartbeats before pulling out my phone, a knot forming in my gut.

Beautiful, sexy Harper. She deserved so much better than what I could offer.

How's the dad party?

All done.

You guys quit early. Danny's at Levi's all night?

Yes.

I'll be over in a few.

When we first started this...*fling*...she'd always been careful to ask if it was okay, but somewhere along the way, our nights together had become a given. If we were both available, she spent most of the night in my bed.

We'd drifted over a line at some point.

Tonight, when I should've felt freer than usual with Danny out of the house, I was unsettled instead. It didn't feel right for my son to be gone, and it didn't feel okay to carry on with Harper.

I texted her one more time:

I'm on the dock.

Twenty minutes later, I heard her rustling through the grass, but I didn't turn around. She reached the dock, stepped onto the surface, and made her way to me with quick, light steps.

"Hi," she said as she sat down next to me.

"Hi." I looked over at her in the darkness. It killed me how pretty and young and happy and... expectant she was.

"What are you doing out here?" She glanced around as if making sure we were alone.

"Just...thinking."

"Anything good?" Her tone had dimmed, gone a little serious, as if she sensed my state of mind.

Instead of answering directly, I closed my eyes, wondering if I was really going to do this.

I needed to.

I knew I needed to, but fuck.

"This thing between us," I began, then swallowed, gave myself one last chance to reconsider. "It's run its course, Harper."

She was quiet for so long I turned to look at her again. She tilted her head and said, "Funny, I thought it was just getting good."

Ah, hell. There was a part of me that'd been hoping she'd agree right away. That would've made this suck-ass conversation a little less suck ass.

"You're incredible, Harper—"

"Oh, my God, stop," she said. "Max, stop. Can we talk about this?"

"Of course." I didn't like that idea, didn't think it would do any good, but I owed her a conversation if she wanted it.

"I..." She shook her head and hugged her knees to her chest. "I know we never set out to grow closer, but we have. I said I wasn't looking for anything long-term, but...we're good together."

Shit. This was not what I'd expected at all.

"What changed, Harper?"

She didn't answer right away, looking out over the water, lost in thought. "I guess I did," she said quietly. "Naomi's death affected me. Made me realize how lacking my life was. I've consciously started taking more chances. I have a great apartment on the square, and Cambria, Dakota, and I are on the verge of owning our own business, if we can just find an investor. It feels weird to say, but I'm loving it. The more chances I take, the more I want to keep taking chances because they're making me happy."

"I'm glad you're happy," I said lamely.

She lowered her knees and swung around to face me. "I've been wanting to talk about us for a while. Even though it isn't the deal we started out with, I want a chance with you, Max. Look at me."

I did as she requested, meeting her gaze that was filled with so much sparkle and honesty it hurt.

"I'm in love with you, Max, and I could swear you care about me too."

Her declaration knocked the breath right out of me. A dozen emotions swirled through me so intensely I couldn't begin to pick them apart or name them.

"I want more than your secret nighttime hours," she continued, gathering steam. "I want to spend time with both you and Danny, get to know your son better, be a couple out in public. I know you're worried what my dad will say, but all he wants is for me to be happy. If I tell him *you* make me happy, he'll be all for us being together."

Fuck.

I never should've kept what Bob Ellison had said to myself, but the only thing to do now was come clean. I rubbed a hand over my face, hating past Max, the one who hadn't leveled with her. "Your dad already gave me his blessing."

I was again met with several tense seconds of silence.

"What?" Her confusion was clear.

"I'm sorry I didn't tell you."

"What do you mean? When did he give you his blessing?"

"After the gala, he came to my classroom first thing that Monday morning. Scared the hell out of me because we'd been together the night before. I thought for sure he was there to bust my balls. He shocked me by saying he'd reconsidered. He thought I'd be good for you. If I wanted to pursue you, I had his blessing."

"Good for me? Why didn't you tell me this?"

"I should have," I said. I knew damn well I should have. "I guess maybe I was clinging to it as an excuse for why we can't be together."

She fumed quietly. I couldn't blame her.

"What's the real reason, Max? How about you be honest with me since I just bared my heart to you."

I considered diving into the lake, swimming for

as long as I could hold my breath, as a distraction, an escape. But I owed her the truth.

I sat there for ages, considering where to start, how to convey what was in my head. Maybe I was half hoping she'd get sick of waiting, give up on me, and leave. It would've been easier.

"I think I told you my dad left my mom for another woman when I was a kid," I began. "I came home from school one day, and all his stuff was gone. My mom's eyes were red as she explained he'd moved to Nashville. That messed me up good. I went through years of counseling to work through it. Thank God my mom got me counseling. Maybe you went through the same sort of thing when your parents split."

"My mom didn't desert me. I mean, she ended up across the country, but she visits. We talk often enough. And I was a senior in high school at the time, so I was older and focused on getting out of school, becoming an adult. Not trying to get through middle school or puberty."

I nodded. If my dad had wanted to stay in my life, maybe it would've been less traumatic. "He tried to take my brother and sister and me out for dinner a couple of times not long after he left. Levi was pissed at him. Dakota was too young to understand what was going on. I couldn't act like everything was fine. Each time, dinner was awkward and awful. The longest hour and a half of my life. He stopped trying after that. He called us on our birthdays. Couldn't be bothered with Christmas because he and his new wife liked to travel for the holidays." I shrugged. "It became easier to give up on him than to hope things would get better."

Harper's brow furrowed as she listened.

"I thought I was over it, but now I have Danny to protect, and that's brought a lot of the old stuff to the surface," I said. "Jamie named me guardian because he went through the same thing—his dad took off—and he trusted me to put Danny's needs first."

"So you're going to stay single for your whole life?" she asked, disbelieving.

"Until he's grown. I never intended to get married anyway. My parents soured me on the idea. I like my life the way it is."

"Lately you've been having your cake and eating it too." There was more than a little resentment in her tone.

"That was our agreement," I reminded her. "Casual, fun, short-term. No strings."

"Yeah, that's my bad. I'm the idiot who let myself feel things." There was heat in her words, and I suspected it was directed toward her instead of me. I didn't want her down on herself. I was the one with the deep-seated problems here.

She stood abruptly. "I'm sorry your dad hurt

you so bad, Max. I'm sorry I caught feelings for you. That was never my plan." She kicked the dock with her toe repeatedly. "I've told you before I would never intentionally hurt Danny."

I stood too. "Key word being *intentionally*. There's no way to know how long we would last, Harper. I can't put Danny in the position to lose again. He's already lost too much."

As much as I hated the idea of not spending nights with Harper anymore, Danny's needs had to come first.

"I feel sorry for you," she said quietly. "You could be loved. Both you and Danny could be loved if you'd just let yourself. By trying so hard to protect him, you're depriving him of more people to love him."

Her words rattled me a little, rousing my never-ending doubts regarding fatherhood. Maybe her point was valid, but Danny had *my* love, my family's love. There was no question he was well loved, adored, cherished.

She closed her eyes for a moment, a flash of pain crossing her face.

That single moment gutted me. Because I did care about her, more than I'd ever intended to. "I'm sorry, Harper."

It hurt like hell to end it, but it'd be so much worse the longer we were together.

I was doing the right thing.

"Yeah," she said in a scoff. "Guess that'll teach me to let my heart get involved. Thanks for the lesson."

I started to reach for her, to offer comfort, but I stopped myself. She didn't want comfort from me. I couldn't give her what she wanted.

"Have a lovely, lonely life, Max."

I couldn't bear to watch her walk away, so I turned back to the water. As I listened to her footsteps receding, a new doubt flared to life. Maybe I'd underestimated how much this would hurt.

All I could do was bury that doubt, ignore that hurt, and remind myself I was doing this for my son first and foremost.

Chapter Twenty-Six

Harper

I walked away from Max's house in a daze.

I didn't bother to check whether anyone saw me. What did it matter?

With my head down, I locked my gaze on my running shoes, watching each step, blocking out any emotions, feeling as if I was outside of my body.

Not going to break down. Left, right, left, right.

As usual, I'd worn running shorts and a tank. Tonight I'd put a thin hoodie on too. I pulled the sleeves down over my hands and crossed my arms over my chest, feeling chilled despite my swift pace.

I reached the square in no time, still filling my mind with surface things—the rhythm of my steps, my new mantra about not breaking down, the Saturday-night sounds in the heart of a small town.

The Fly was on my way home. I could hear the bar was crowded from down the block. Dakota was there with some of our friends, I knew. They'd invited me, but I'd said I was going to bed early because I worked tomorrow morning.

It was yet another fib I'd told to keep our secret. To protect Max. For no reason, it turned out.

Instead of leaning into the anger that was just below the surface, I decided to join my friends after all and stepped inside. Owen Engel was checking IDs. He greeted me warmly and let me pass, likely knowing how old I was to the month as we'd gone to school together and graduated the same year.

"Dakota's at the big table up front," he told me.

I made myself smile and got sucked into the crowd, thankful for the dark, noisy interior. I wasn't at all made up, wasn't dressed for a Saturday night out, but I didn't care. The thought of going home to an empty apartment, with only my thoughts to keep me company, sounded like torture.

The big table was indeed overflowing with my friends—Dakota, Piper, Jewel, Quincy, Shawna, Anna, and Olivia. Predictably, there was no shortage of people gathered around the table, lots of them guys. Piper was on the end and slid over enough on the booth to let me sit next to her.

"Dakota said you were staying in tonight," she said in my ear over the roar.

"Changed my mind," was all I told her.

Gideon Webb, another friend I'd graduated with, was hanging out in front of our three-sided booth. He leaned down and said, "I haven't seen you out much lately, Ellison. You too good for us?"

"I'm here now, aren't I?"

"You need a vodka cranberry?" he asked.

"God, yes. You know me well." Maybe I'd have ten of them.

Dakota was trapped in the middle of the booth but seemed happy to see me, as did everyone else. I attempted to soak in the good cheer and live in the moment, but there was a deep sadness in my chest just waiting to swoop in and take me under.

I made it through a dozen hugs, a handful of meaningless conversations, and half my vodka cranberry before the walls closed in on me and the noise became too much to handle. Without a word to anyone, I got up and left, knowing they'd assume I went to the restroom and wouldn't follow me.

The sidewalk was quieter but not private. I needed to be alone before the storm of emotions broke down my walls and made me sob like a baby.

I went around to the back of the buildings on my block and hurried for my door. I glanced at the back door to the shop space we were trying to make ours as I walked past. Normally it sparked optimism and hope in me, but now I couldn't summon anything besides sadness and defeat. I wasn't sure we could make our business a reality after all.

One more dream that was on the verge of shattering.

My eyes filled before I could get the apartment door unlocked, blinding me, making it that much harder to get the key in the hole. Finally I got it open and practically fell into the living room, then shut the door and locked it.

Without turning on lights, I went to my room and collapsed into bed on top of the blankets. I hugged my extra pillow, curling around it, inhaling, wishing for a hint of Max's scent like when I was in his bed.

Of course there was nothing of him on this bedding. He'd never been here except for the day I moved in. Our fling had been a one-sided effort.

I'd been stupid enough to make it easy for him to have his meaningless hookups without putting forth any effort. All the effort had been mine. The covering up where I was, acting like I was going to bed early, deceiving Dakota. Hiding it from everyone. All for no fucking reason.

Now that I was in the safety of my bed, alone, in the blessed dark, I gave in to the emotions, let them wash over me and try to drown me. They came out in ugly sobs. I couldn't have stopped them if I'd wanted to.

I cried for my stupidity. I cried for Max's stupidity. I cried in anger and regret and so much fucking sadness I thought it would suffocate me. My heart hurt so much I didn't know if I would ever get it all cried out.

I nearly jolted off the bed when I felt someone touch my leg.

Dakota.

Crap. I'd left the Fly a good two hours before closing, certain she'd stay until last call. I had no idea how much time had passed, but it definitely wasn't two hours.

"What are you"—sniff—"doing here?" I asked her, sitting up.

"You seemed off. Then I saw you leave. Sweetie, what's wrong?" Dakota moved in and pulled me into a hug.

That made me cry even harder.

She let me wail until my sobs quieted down. I held on to her, my face buried, my eyes drenching her shirt.

"S-sorry," I said, sniffling indelicately.

"Shh." She rubbed my back, soothing me as I hiccuped down from disaster-level crying. "What happened, Harper?"

Damn. I had to fess up to lying to her and

shacking up with her brother.

"I'm so...sorryyyy." Somehow my eyes leaked more tears.

"Shut up, you. Tell me."

"I've been a...bad friend." I took a shaky breath in, blew it out. "I've been sneaking out and spending nights with Max."

"I know that, Harper."

"What?"

"You're not very good at hiding it." She smiled sympathetically.

I frowned, trying to think back to a slip-up. "How long have you known?"

"I was suspicious since the gala. You stopped talking about him. Stopped going out as much. Then the day we moved in here, I knew."

"How did you know?" I was sure no one was here during our quickie.

"Body language. Secret glances. You two were so obvious it was funny."

"Why didn't you say something?" I asked.

"You clearly didn't want to talk about it. I was giving you time. I figured you'd tell me when you were ready."

My face scrunched up again, and the tears came back in full force. "We agreed not to tell anyone. I thought I was being respectful of his concerns about his job. My dad warned him off before the gala, so he was worried. Except then my dad apparently did a one-eighty and gave him his blessing weeks ago. Max never told me. He just let me go on believing we had to be secret. I'm such an idiot."

"Oh, my God." She cradled my cheeks and pressed her forehead to mine. "My brother is the idiot, Harper. I cannot believe him."

I couldn't argue with that. "I'm so mad. And hurt. And stupid. And sad. And messed up."

"Stop calling my friend stupid." Dakota crawled behind me and propped up the pillows against the headboard. "Come here. Tell me what happened."

I curled up next to her and spilled out everything, no holds barred. I'd kept all my Max stuff to myself for so long, even though I'd been dying to dish about him and my feelings the way girls did. I told her a lot of it now, poured it out as if that could make me feel better.

It didn't.

"I'm so sorry, Harper. Max is a fool. Completely, utterly. I could wring his thick football-player neck."

"I don't know why I thought there could be more," I said quietly. "He didn't lead me on."

"I knew our dad screwed him up, but I didn't realize he was still letting it run his life."

"He'd rather be alone than give someone a chance to leave."

Dakota scowled. I could *feel* her scowl in the dark. "Boys are stupid." She said it with so much feeling it made me crack a smile.

"Do you want to get up and drink?" she asked. "I only had a couple of beers earlier, but I'll do shots with you if you need to."

My smile grew. It was a bittersweet smile because my heart still felt like it was cracked open, but girlfriends were what got us through the hard times. "You're the best," I said. "I'm so tired and wrung out. I need to sleep."

"Are you going to call in to work tomorrow?"

I considered it. There was no way I'd feel even a spark of energy by my seven a.m. shift. I shook my head. "I'm going in. It's going to suck, but I'm not giving this the power to take me out. Not even for a day."

Dakota hugged me again. "I love you. You're going to be okay. I promise."

I nodded. "Yes."

"Go to sleep, pretty girl. But wake me up if you need to talk more."

I nodded, my lids heavy, my soul weary. My throat filled with sadness again.

I wasn't sure how, but I'd find a way to be okay.

Chapter Twenty-Seven

Max

"Max."

I jolted from a heavy, agitated sleep at the sound of my sister's voice and tried to figure out when and where the fuck I was.

In my house.

With Danny asleep beside me. On the sectional.

"What time is it?" I asked quietly. My eyes burned with grittiness and deep fatigue.

"Time for you to pull your head out," Dakota said from my kitchen.

Scowling, I raised my arm to check my watch,

being careful not to disturb my son. "Quarter after nine?"

A few more seconds passed while I racked my brain to recall what day it was. Sunday night. Dark outside.

I closed my eyes when I remembered my shit show of a day.

After Harper left, I'd sat on that dock for hours, trying not to think. I'd been reluctant to go inside to an empty house.

Levi had brought Danny home early this morning as we'd agreed. He'd taken one look at me, concluded the single dads had tied one on, shaken his head, and left. I hadn't corrected him. Because at least that would be a valid excuse for looking like shit.

Sleep-deprived and weighed down by a heavy sadness I couldn't kick, I'd switched into get-through-the-day mode for both Danny and myself.

We hadn't left the house, and I hadn't showered. We'd admittedly eaten like crap, but we'd eaten. For most of the day, football had been on the TV, toys had been strewn everywhere, and Danny was no worse for the wear. It would've been a chill day at home, just father and son and the NFL, except I was a fucking mess in my head.

I felt like shit for hurting Harper. She had every

right to be pissed at me, but I suspected she was beating herself up too. I hated that even more.

And fuck if I didn't miss her, which didn't even make sense. It was Sunday. We'd never spent daytime hours together, Sunday or otherwise, so the only time it made sense for me to miss her was in the dark of night. Check. I'd missed her so much last night I'd avoided my bedroom and dozed on the sectional.

Now I was over an hour late getting Danny to his crib. My sister was clanking around in the disaster that was my kitchen. And I felt like hell. We're talking bottle-of-tequila hell, but I'd only consumed two beers over the course of the day.

I summoned my last ounce of give-a-fuck and eased off the sectional. I could see from here my sister was on a mission in the kitchen, so I elected to get Danny to bed before I faced her.

She kept her mouth shut when she saw me with my son in my arms, heading toward his bedroom.

Danny wore a diaper and a Dragonfly Lake football jersey, which was as dressed as I'd gotten him today. Guys' day, I'd told him. He'd giggled and clapped his hands when I pulled out his favorite shirt.

He opened his eyes when I laid him in his crib, so I changed his diaper and put some clean pajamas on him. He was nearly back asleep by the time I snapped his pj's up. I leaned over and kissed him.

"Night, Danny boy."

"Nigh', Dada."

I tiptoed out, hoping like hell this was a sleep-through-the-night night. We made it about eighty percent of the time, but it'd serve my ass right if he woke me up. That's what I deserved for blowing off his routine today.

"What are you doing here?" I asked Dakota as I entered the kitchen.

"I could ask you the same." She was scrubbing off the pizza pan I'd left on the stove after lunch.

"I live here."

"But what are you *doing*, Max? Your kitchen is a wreck. You broke your no-sugar rule with Danny." She held up the empty animal cracker bag. "Pizza, popcorn, beef jerky? You ate like a couple of broke college students or hungover bachelors. You had him up past his sacred bedtime. Is this how it's going to be?"

"We had a guys' day," I snapped.

"You're father and son. Every day is guys' day in this house. This feels more like guy-who-knows-he-screwed-up-big-time-trying-to-cope day."

I narrowed my eyes at her, wondering if she knew about Harper. "What are you getting at, Dakota? You never said why you're here."

"I'm here because you need help seeing the light."

I raised my brows at her boldness. I was beginning to suspect Harper had talked to her, but I wasn't going to out myself.

She put away the pans then looked me straight in the eyes. "For being a pretty smart guy, you sure have some dumb-assery in you."

"I don't have the energy to stand here and listen to you insult me. If you have something useful to say, get on with it."

"Breaking up with Harper was a big mistake. Huge. Like, I can't figure out what the hell you were thinking, Max."

"That's between Harper and me. She knows what I was thinking because I told her. It doesn't concern you."

"Oh, I know what you told her."

"I thought she was keeping our business to herself," I muttered.

"She never breathed a word to me about the two of you before today. She went out of her way to protect you and your job even when you didn't need it. She held up her end of the bargain, but that deal disappeared the second you broke her heart."

"I didn't break her heart," I said automatically.

Had I?

"Keep telling yourself that."

I wanted to argue, but I couldn't get the look on Harper's face, that flash of hurt, out of my mind.

"If that's true, I'm deeply sorry," I said, feeling a hundred years old. "I assure you I didn't need you to come over to rant. I feel bad enough as it is."

My sister set aside the sponge and studied me. Her shoulders lowered, her expression gentling. "I didn't come here to rant, even though I am mad," she said, her voice softer.

"I don't see how it's any of your business."

"It's my business because two people I love are hurting."

"You can't fix this," I told her. I wanted to say I wasn't hurting, but I realized the scene she'd walked in on probably said otherwise. I did feel like utter fucking shit.

"No, but *you* can."

I didn't know where she was going, but I was sure I didn't have the energy for it. I sauntered back to the sectional and flopped down.

Dakota followed me and sat more sedately on the other side.

"Dad messed all of us up," she said. "Why else would none of us have any history with a single serious relationship?"

I nodded because she was spot on.

"I think you need to get over what Dad did and embrace what's right in front of you."

I raised a brow at her ridiculousness. "Just like that? Just snap my fingers?"

"Whatever it takes, Max."

"Your words don't hold a lot of weight seeing how you're in the same position."

"I'm not though. I've never fallen in love."

"I haven't either."

Dakota tilted her head and stared me down. Then she smiled indulgently, as if she were explaining the basics to a three-year-old. "You can deny it, but that doesn't mean it's not true."

I crossed one leg over the other knee. "Let me get this straight. You're advising me on relationships and love even though you've never had either one?"

"I guess I am, because I know you love Harper."

"I care about Harper, but we've only ever been a fling."

"Doesn't matter. You love her. I saw it the day we moved. You tried so hard to hide everything, but any time you looked at her, it was there in your eyes, in the look you got on your face."

"I thought you didn't know about Harper and me."

"I said she never told me. You gave yourselves away that day."

"We weren't serious, Dakota."

Even as I said the words, I heard Harper's declaration that she loved me. I'd spent hours last night questioning whether it was true. What I'd concluded was that she had no reason to say the words if she didn't believe them to be true. I knew her well enough to understand a part of her probably hated that she'd developed feelings. She'd basically said as much.

"You might not have set out to be serious. Hate to tell you, brother dearest, but if you didn't love her, you wouldn't be in this condition, with your house a shambles, your kid eating crap food all day, and yourself a smelly, disgusting mess."

I narrowed my eyes again, about to argue, but her words struck a chord. I'd had short-term, nonserious connections with plenty of women. There wasn't a single one that had made me do more than blink when it ended.

I lowered my leg and leaned forward, elbows on knees, running my hands over my face.

"I wouldn't know what love was if it smacked me upside the head and yelled at me," I said eventually.

A quiet chuckle came from my sister. "From where I'm sitting, it has." She pulled her legs up beneath her. "Tell me something. When was the last time you let a woman stay overnight at your place?"

I stared at her without answering. I didn't let

women stay overnight, not now that I had Danny, and not before he was in my life either.

"That's what I thought," my sister said. "Harper's different from everyone else. You're different with Harper."

"What if that doesn't matter?" I said, not fully convinced she was right.

"It matters, Max. If you love her, you shouldn't let her go. What if she could make you and Danny happy?"

I let myself think about that for maybe five seconds before shutting it down. "Danny's exactly why I can't take a chance. If I let her in and she leaves..."

"You would get through it, and so would Danny," she said. "But what if she doesn't leave?"

"Chances are good she'll leave."

"I understand that fear, but Harper is not Dad. With Dad, the surprise was he stayed as long as he did."

"Who told you that?" She'd been barely older than Danny when our dad took off.

"Mom. You should ask her about it sometime." Dakota shrugged and stood. "I need to go so you can get to bed. You look like hell."

"Gee, thanks." I walked her toward the door, my mind reeling with the crapload she'd put in my head.

"You know I'm not some big romantic in love

with love. I just have a feeling about you and Harper. I hope you don't screw yourself and my roomie and, most importantly, my nephew out of fear, Max." She rose to her toes and kissed my cheek. "Love you, big dummy."

"Get out of here, shorty. Thanks for caring. I think."

I shut the door as she walked toward her car, so bone-tired I wanted to ignore everything my baby sister had said. Unfortunately some of it hit too close to home.

What if she was right that I was in love with Harper?

I reminded myself that wasn't the point. Protecting Danny—and okay, I could admit it, protecting myself—was the point. I needed to figure out how to get over it all and move on.

Chapter Twenty-Eight

Max

I made it until Wednesday without asking my mom about my dad.

I wanted to ignore everything my sister had said Sunday night.

I wanted to get on with my fucking life and go back to how it was before, just Danny and me, fumbling our way through toddlerhood.

Yeah, and every time I tried to tell myself that, Harper popped into my head and made my chest hurt.

I tiredly made my way up the stairs to my mom's house to pick up Danny. Letting myself in like I always did, I registered my mom's and son's voices coming from the bedroom end of the house. Instead of joining them, I wandered to the dining room slider that looked out over the backyard.

My mom's yard was small but meticulously cared for, with her vegetable garden at the back, flower beds along the sides, and a meandering brick path. The deck was her haven, with potted mums everywhere and a maple tree shading it from the setting sun. The yard as a whole was like a miniature English garden.

This evening, I was compelled to go out the slider and sit on one of the chairs by the wrought-iron bistro table where my mom and Danny liked to eat their lunch. Normally picking up Danny was my favorite time of day, but tonight I was out of sorts. Tired in a soul-weary way.

Mills had been leaving school at the same time I left after football practice this evening. I'd kept my head down in the parking lot, acting as if I didn't see him angling toward his car, when he called out my name and jogged over to me.

Is everything okay with you, Coach? he'd asked, walking beside me despite my refusal to slow my pace for him.

Everything's fine, Mills. What's up?

You've been distant. Lisa noticed too. And I overheard four of your players in my sixth hour saying you've been weird at practice all week.

I haven't been weird.

Quiet, they said. Disengaged. Having Coach Castillo run most of practice.

I'd grunted. Oscar *had* been running things more this week, taking over drills, overseeing scrimmages. I'd been glad to let him because I was running on fumes from not sleeping.

You seem off-kilter, Mills had continued.

I'd merely grunted again and been over-fucking-joyed to reach my SUV. *Night, Mills*, I'd said, blowing all of it off in his presence.

I hadn't been able to blow it off as I drove to my mom's though.

I knew damn well I wasn't in top condition for anything. How could I be when I only got a couple of hours' sleep every night, and those hours were riddled with dreams of Harper?

The woman I loved.

I couldn't deny it anymore as much as I wanted to.

Dakota was right. I'd fallen in love with Harper Ellison. The last thing I'd ever set out to do.

My dreams of her were relentless, and surprisingly only a fraction of them were sexual. They were of her laughing at something I said, of us taking Danny out on the boat, of her eyes sparkling as she teased me. I'd had one dream of her behind the counter in the shop she and my sister and Cambria wanted to open, spreading her jewelry pieces across it proudly and confidently.

So much for our fling staying strictly physical.

I heard the door slide open behind me. Then my son's enthusiastic steps burst outside and crossed the deck to me.

"Dada!"

"What are you doing out here?" my mom asked as I picked up my boy.

I hugged him for an extra second, then kissed his nose, eliciting that giggle I loved.

"It's peaceful," I said, wishing that peace could penetrate the turmoil inside me.

She pulled out the other chair and sat, as if understanding I needed...something.

Danny climbed up on my lap, fiddling with my watch, talking about things I couldn't understand in his own language.

"Were you surprised when Dad left?" I asked my mom.

Her head whipped in my direction. "Where did that come from?"

"Dakota said you weren't surprised when it happened."

My mom didn't speak right away. Danny wiggled down and descended the two steps that led to the brick path. The yard was fenced in on all sides, so I let him go where he wanted, keeping an eye on him as he marched along.

"No, I wasn't surprised. Was there a reason you and your sister were talking about this?"

Danny trotted to one of the flower beds, chasing a butterfly. I didn't normally talk to my mom about personal stuff. I could shrug off her question now, or I could grow a pair and level with her.

As much as I didn't want to talk about my feelings, ignoring them hadn't gotten me anywhere.

"I've been seeing someone," I finally said.

"How did I not know this?"

"We kept it secret."

"Harper Ellison?"

I guess even when you managed to keep a secret in a small town, you still couldn't keep it from your mom. I expelled a breath. "Harper Ellison."

"Did she break up with you?"

"I ended it," I said. "Before anyone could get hurt."

I felt her look pointedly across the table at me even though I didn't take my gaze from my son.

"It doesn't take a master's in psychology to figure out you're hurting, Max."

"Why weren't you surprised when Dad left?"

She hesitated, letting nearly a minute tick by before she spoke. "Your dad and I got married because I got pregnant. I don't think he ever loved me."

That hit me like a linebacker from behind, the guy you never saw coming. I staggered, closed my eyes. Tried to get it to sink in. "Did you love him?"

"On some level I did. Or I loved the man I thought he was for all those years." Her voice pitched low, full of emotion. "I'm pretty sure he had other women the whole time we were married."

I didn't have a high opinion of my father, but that still stunned me. "I had no idea."

"I didn't either at first. As the years went by, he worked longer hours, came home later. He could've worked day shifts and had his employees cover nights at the bar, but he didn't. There were plenty of nights he claimed to fall asleep on the couch in his office, and I suspect he might have, but not alone."

Jesus.

My dad had managed Billy's, a small bar that closed about fifteen years ago. He'd been gone a lot of evenings; that was true. As far as I knew, that was what his job required. That's how it'd always been.

I guess now I knew why.

Looking back with a new perspective, it was so obvious.

"I'm sorry, Mom."

"I'm over it now," she said.

"Are you though? You haven't been involved with anyone since."

"That's something we do well in this family, isn't it? Avoid relationships?" She laughed, trying to lighten such an ugly truth. "Are you going to be the first to find the courage to change that, Max?"

I leaned my head back and closed my eyes, still reeling from everything she'd revealed, but the truth had never been clearer. My dad was a world-class self-centered asshole. Apparently he always had been.

Harper wasn't that.

She was caring and sexy and laughed easily and often. She made me laugh, made me look at life differently. Made me love her.

And she loved me.

She'd said she would never hurt Danny, and I knew she meant it. It was my job—mine and hers together—to make sure our relationship didn't get to the point where we hurt Danny.

If I could convince her to give me another chance.

"I believe I am," I said, a new determination burning in me. "I just need to figure out the best way to apologize and convince her."

Chapter Twenty-Nine

Harper

Friday morning at five after seven, I was giving myself a private pep talk as I headed toward the diner's coffeepot that had just finished brewing. My heart was heavy, but lamenting over my life wouldn't make me feel any better. All week I'd been forcing a smile at work and reminding myself about two hundred times a day I was going to be okay and this broken-heart bullshit would eventually get better.

I pivoted to take coffee to the two tables that were already occupied and nearly dropped the pot when Dakota walked into the diner.

Patrick, the other server on shift, met her inside the door to seat her. They small talked. Then she pointed to the counter and made her way toward it. After filling everyone up on caffeine, I beelined back to the counter.

"Is something wrong?" I asked Dakota, who'd settled on one of the middle stools at the otherwise empty counter. "Did we get another no on the shop?"

Dakota smiled sleepily. "Nothing's wrong. Can't a girl get some breakfast?"

When I'd left the apartment twenty minutes ago, she wasn't stirring yet. I'd thought nothing of it because she was never up before nine or ten. Her blond hair was thrown up in a messy bun on top of her head, her face unmade-up. I'd be more alarmed if she'd taken more time on herself.

"A girl can get some breakfast," I said, relaxing a notch. "I'm just used to you getting yours closer to lunchtime. Waffles and bacon?"

"You know it." She glanced over her shoulder toward the door as Luke Durham and Chance Cordova walked in.

I jotted down Dakota's order and poured coffee in her mug, not needing to ask her whether she wanted some, then pushed the creamers closer.

"Goddess. You guys need bigger mugs though."

"Talk to Monty."

"It didn't do any good the first twenty times," she said. Again, she checked the entrance behind her. "There she is."

Cambria entered, looking chipper and a lot more awake than my roomie. She spotted us and headed toward the counter.

"Hey, Cambria," I said. "So you two have a breakfast date?" I hadn't seen Dakota last night because she'd closed Henry's and I'd gone to bed early. She hadn't told me she was meeting Cambria.

"And you too," Dakota said. "While you work, so a sort-of breakfast date. Hi, partner." She directed the last to Cambria.

"Morning, ladies." Cambria side hugged Dakota, then settled onto the stool next to her. Reaching across the counter, she held out her hand, and I took it. "How are you doing, Harper?" she asked, concern in her eyes.

That was all it took to arouse my emotions that seemed to be perpetually bubbling right under the surface these days. I forced a smile and nodded as I waited for the tightness in my throat to ease. When I could answer without crying, I said, "Doing okay." I squeezed my lids shut on potential tears, refusing to go there at work. "Happy to see these two gorgeous faces so early in the morning."

"Bet I can make you even happier," Dakota said. "Ian decided to keep the property. The studio's safe."

I sucked in a gasp, my mouth popping open. "Really?"

"Really. He'll find someone to manage it and run it like a business."

"That's fantastic news," Cambria said.

"The best," I agreed. "Your wiles worked."

Dakota laughed. "I doubt that's it." She sobered. "He's got some weird stuff going on, I think. Like, regrets with Naomi if I had to guess."

"That wouldn't be surprising," I said. "We all owe you a big thanks anyway."

"That's not all," Dakota said, her eyes lighting up as she looked from Cambria to me. She leaned in closer. "He's considering financing us."

"What?" Cambria grabbed Dakota's arm.

I stared at my roomie, waiting for more.

"I don't know yet. It's too early to get our hopes up, but...my hopes are up."

I shook my head, trying to wrap it around the idea of the sullen, keep-to-himself guy I'd lived with for two weeks doing something so generous. "What does he want from us?"

"His percentage is reasonable, just like what we talked about."

Cambria and I looked at each other, our eyes wide.

"That's the best news we've had," Cambria said. "How can we convince him?"

Dakota laughed. "If I knew, I already would have. But we should get together to strategize."

"For sure," Cambria said.

"Order up," Monty called from the window, dragging me back to work before anything could really sink in.

When I turned around with the plates, I saw the diner was filling up faster than usual. Ben Holloway and West Aldridge and his three little girls had joined Luke and Chance. Dean Miller and Lisa Brimm, math teachers at the high school, were at a table close to the counter.

I delivered the food to Cash and Ava Henry. When I whirled around to greet the math teacher duo, I noticed my dad entering and sauntering toward the counter, so I greeted him.

"Hi, honey," he said, planting a kiss on top of my head as I passed.

"You know it's Friday, right?" I asked over my shoulder. He was a Monday regular, saying a good breakfast was the best way to start off a week.

"Sure do."

I'd just finished taking orders from Dean and Lisa when another group coming in the door caught my eye. I felt a pang in my chest at the sight of Max with Danny in his arms. Next to them were Max's mom and his brother, Levi.

I couldn't imagine why Max was here when he knew the odds of me working were high. Biting down on my lip, I turned my focus to another party to get their drink orders, fighting hard not to pay attention to Max's family as they walked behind me.

I heard Max greet Dakota and missed the drink orders I'd asked for. Had she known her whole family was coming?

"Getting busy early today," I told the customers, flashing them an overfriendly but distracted smile. "I'm sorry, can you repeat those?"

I wrote down their beverage requests and asked if they were ready to order food.

"We'll need a bit," the grandfatherly man said.

"Let me know if you have any questions," I said, hoping they'd give me an excuse to stay put for a bit longer.

When they merely nodded, I headed toward the pickup window behind the counter to see if any of my orders were up. I made a point of not looking in Max's direction—he was sitting on this side of Dakota, his family lined up on the stools between her and my dad, who sat on the end—and felt self-conscious and flustered instead of like the competent veteran server I was.

"I think that's mine," I told Patrick as he picked up the platters.

"I got it for you, sweets," he said, winking.

Which left me off-balance as I tried to avoid looking at the man behind me whose presence I found nearly impossible to ignore.

Orders. I'd just taken orders from two tables. *Put the food order in and get the flipping drinks, Harper.*

The Dawson family and Cambria were engaged in a lively conversation I did my best to tune out as I poured juices, coffees, and a hot water for tea, then scurried away to deliver them.

As I straightened from serving the last beverage, the little counter bell to get service during slow times obnoxiously rang repeatedly. I turned toward it, expecting to see an unsupervised kid. My mouth fell open when I realized it was Max, standing at the end of the counter, near my dad, staring right at me.

"Hey, everyone," he said loudly.

I froze where I was, unsure what was going on, not knowing what to do. I glanced to the kitchen window to gauge Monty's reaction. My boss had a smile on his face and gave Max a thumbs-up. What the...?

"Sorry to interrupt your breakfast," Max continued as the customers gave him their attention. "I've got something important to say."

I realized Dakota was staring at me, so I gave her a look that said, *What is going on?*

I couldn't read the smile she sent me, and then I couldn't think about it anymore because Max said, "Harper, would you mind coming over here?"

Beyond confused, I walked toward him, hoping to end the disruption before someone complained.

"Hi, Max," I said, acting as unbothered as possible as I came up next to him, my insides shaky.

Everyone at the counter had their gaze locked on me.

"I, um, have some tables who need to order," I told him.

"I'll handle your tables for a few," Patrick called out.

"What's going on?" I asked Max, darting a look at my expectant dad and starting to get the idea that everyone knew what was happening except me.

"I need to get some things off my chest," Max said, still at broadcast-to-the-whole-restaurant volume. "I screwed up and I want to rectify my mistake."

"I'm at work." I glanced toward the pickup window again, but Monty stood there watching us like everybody else.

"Hear him out," my boss said.

"As my sister so aptly told me," Max said, "I was a big dummy a few nights ago. I messed up." He let out a self-effacing chuckle. "I've been messing up for weeks, actually."

My heart raced, and I tried to catch my brain up.

He looked over the counter to the single dad group along the wall. "Chance, Luke, Ben, West? This is her. This is the *lady friend* I was so afraid of getting attached to. Just wanted to tell you the joke's on me. It's too late. I'm already attached."

My eyes widened. Then I looked to Dakota. She watched us with avid interest, her eyes less sleepy, more sparkling with expectation.

"I was lucky enough to have Harper in my life for several weeks," Max said.

An audible reaction filtered through the diner.

"I insisted on keeping it secret, and that wasn't fair to Harper. I realize now it probably seemed as if I was embarrassed or ashamed of her. I wasn't. I was being a big, dumb coward, hiding my feelings even from myself. I'm sorry, Harper. And I'm sorry I led you to believe your dad didn't approve."

I pressed my lips together and nodded, too confused, too overcome by this very public revelation to figure out what to say.

"Mills?" Max continued, his attention going to

his colleague. "You called it correctly. I've been a jerk all week at work. Thanks for bringing it to my attention."

"Anytime," Dean called out, then ducked his head as if he didn't like the spotlight.

I could relate but...what was Max doing? I hardly dared to get my hopes up, but it sounded like...

"Bob." Max addressed my dad now. "You gave me your blessing to date your daughter. Told me you thought I'd be good for her, but here's the thing. *She's* the one who's good for *me*." He took my hand, entwined our fingers. I held on to him, his strong hand so familiar it made me catch my breath. I stepped closer to him without thought.

Staring into my eyes, Max continued, "Harper keeps me on my toes and makes me laugh. She helps me take myself less seriously. She reminds me when I need to be easier on myself and go with the flow." He paused for a few seconds as if searching for the right words. "This woman has shown me what it looks like to have courage, to try new things, to take new risks that are uncomfortable and scary as you-know-what but have the potential to pay off thousandfold. Harper makes me a better person."

"That's my girl," my dad said quietly. I couldn't miss the pride in his voice. For me.

I slid my glance to my dad to acknowledge those

words I didn't remember him saying about me for years, if ever. Then I looked back to the gorgeous man who'd pulled me even closer.

I held my breath, no longer doubting what Max's purpose was but not wanting to miss a second of his memorable, swoon-worthy speech.

He entwined our other hands, putting us face-to-face, as if no one else in the place mattered anymore. "I love you, Harper. Will you give me another chance to show you how much?"

My eyes teared up and my insides melted to liquid. I nodded with zero hesitation. "I love you too, Max. I'm... You planned this, didn't you?" I laughed and waved a hand at the crowd, understanding he'd ensured certain people who were important to him or me or both had been here for this. "Like a formal unveiling."

He brushed his knuckles over my cheek in the most tender, loving way. My eyes fluttered closed momentarily as I reveled in it.

"It doesn't make up for my stupidity in the past," he said in a low, more private voice. "I need you to know that was solely about me. Never about you."

"What changed?"

With a sheepish chuckle, he said, "Well, to start with, there was an ass-kicking by your nosy roommate."

We both glanced over at Dakota, who was holding Danny now and said something in his ear. Max's adorable little boy pointed his index finger at us, grinned, then ducked his head into Dakota. I wiggled my fingers in a special wave just for him, making him giggle.

Max laughed, then sobered and turned his attention back to me. "I've missed you like crazy, Harper. Been miserable without you. I realized I need to be brave the way you've been brave these past few weeks if I want to be honest-to-God happy."

He leaned down and kissed me, a lingering, longing, but PG-rated kiss. We were in the middle of the diner, after all, with his son looking on. Even so, our friends and family applauded us, making me laugh again.

"I can make that a whole lot more tempting later if you'll let me," he whispered so only I could hear.

"After this?" I gestured to the crowd in the diner. "You know I will. I can't wait."

We kissed again, just a short promise of a lip-lock this time.

"One more thing," Max said when the kiss ended. He stepped toward the customer side of the counter, pulling me with him and attracting Dakota's attention again, then nodded toward Danny.

Dakota set Danny down, bending over him, pointing at Max, and saying something to the boy. Danny nodded. Then Max squatted, arms out for his son, who dashed over to us.

Max stood with Danny in his arms. "You remember Harper?"

The boy nodded shyly.

"Hey, favorite boy," I said to him. "I'm happy to see you."

"Hoppa," he said, attempting my name for the first time ever. I'd never guessed how one word from a child could grab my heart and squeeze. Beaming, I caressed his pudgy cheek.

"Harper, I'd be honored to have you be part of my son's life too. I'm sorry I ever tried to keep you away from him."

"It's okay," I said. "I know it's a big step."

"It is. I'm ready. I trust you."

Just when I thought I couldn't get any more emotional, I had to dab tears out of my eyes. Because that meant the universe to me.

"What do you say we take Harper out on a date tonight?" he asked Danny. "Maybe for a boat ride after work and dinner on the lake?"

"Boat!" Danny said with glee.

"That's the best idea ever. No football?" I asked.

"It's a bye week. We're all yours if you'll have us."

I kissed Danny's cheek. Then I ran my hand over Max's jaw, stood on my toes, and gave him another quick kiss. "I'll have you two handsome gents all day every day, for as long as you'll let me."

Epilogue

Four weeks later

Max

I'd been fighting all evening to keep my hands to myself—and my nervousness about later under wraps—as Harper shined her gorgeous heart out.

She looked like a million bucks and then some in a short teal dress with spaghetti straps and a lace-up open back that had my fingers itching to untie it. She wore her gorgeous dark hair down with alluring waves cascading over her sexy shoulders. Around her neck was a piece she'd made with a stone that matched her dress. She wore multiple bracelets and rings as well. Even as I stood off to the side, I couldn't help but track her every move with my eyes, counting down the minutes till we were alone.

I and dozens of other people were celebrating the grand opening of Earthly Charm with the three women who undoubtedly would make it a raging success and a fixture on the square for years to come.

I wholeheartedly believed that. I never would've invested half the startup costs if I didn't. Yes, I was crazy in love with one of them and the brother of another, but I'd gone into this financing deal with a mind to business.

The other half of their costs had shockingly come from Ian Finley, Naomi's billionaire brother, as it turned out. The guy apparently wasn't the aggressive bastard he'd presented himself as that fateful first night Harper and I had gone out.

The town had shown up for the evening open house in droves. For the past two-plus hours, the shop had been full of people filtering in and out, checking out the merchandise, congratulating the girls, and spending their money liberally.

Harper's dad was perched near the checkout counter like a proud peacock. My mom and brother had left a few minutes ago, taking Danny with them for a sleepover.

Harper, Dakota, and Cambria's friends had

shown up in force, as had my dad buddies, some of them with their kids. I couldn't count the number of my students and players, past and present, who'd greeted me, then gone on to check out the goods.

All of it made me so fucking proud of the woman I loved that I could barely contain it.

"You still haven't wiped that obnoxious grin off your face," Ben said.

The two of us stood close to the door to the back room, Ben holding his six-year-old daughter, Ruby, who'd tired of the crystals her older sister, Evelyn, was obsessed with. Emerson Estes, single mom of Skyler and Xavier, had assured Ben she'd keep an eye on Evelyn since her kids were enthralled by the rock display as well.

"It's a good night, with the potential to get even better." I shared a look with him, as he was one of about five people who knew my secret plans.

"Have you seen any sign of Piper?" he asked.

"She's still working away." I glanced around to see if she'd snuck in.

"And Cash?"

"Verified."

Emerson herded her two kids and Evelyn toward us, her phone pressed to her ear. She was involved in an animated discussion with whoever had called but broke off to say, "I need five minutes," to Ben.

"I got 'em." He took her daughter Skyler's hand.

From what I could gather, Evelyn and Xavier, her son, were involved in a discussion about rose quartz and obsidian. Then my attention was drawn to Emerson, who didn't move away as she continued her phone conversation.

"Kizzy, that's crazy talk. No way can you turn it down." Emerson paused to listen, laughed. "It's absolutely not a problem. We'll make it happen. For that kind of money? You can't say no. Nope, no more arguing." Another pause. "I don't know, but we'll figure something out. Yes, the chickens too. Call him back and tell him yes. The timing isn't a problem. Nothing's a problem, my dear."

I raised a brow at Ben to see if he knew what she was talking about since she wasn't hiding her end of the conversation. He shrugged.

"You're welcome. Congratulations, Kizzy," Emerson said, her face lit up. "Now hang up and call him back. We'll talk tomorrow. Love you."

She ended the call and looked at Ben, then me.

"Good news?" Ben asked. They were good friends, I knew. Ben had been close to Emerson's late husband, Blake, growing up. Some Saturday nights, Emerson watched Ben's kids during our single-dad get-togethers.

"My mother-in-law got a preemptive offer on

the house for significantly over the price she planned to ask."

"Your house?" Ben asked.

"Our house," Emerson confirmed. "She owns it. You know that."

Emerson and her two kids had moved in with Kizzy after Blake's death. Skyler had been an infant, if I remembered right. Just a few weeks ago, Kizzy had shocked the town with her elopement with an old friend who lived in Vegas.

"But you still live there," Ben said. "What are you going to do?"

"Find a place to live. ASAP," she said with a laugh that sounded nervous around the edges. "Somehow. But first, the chickens."

"I can house the chickens," Ben said before she could ask.

Emerson let out a breath. "Thanks. You're the best. One challenge down."

"How long do you have to find a new place?" I asked.

"Oh, you know, about three weeks." Her smile disappeared as she scrunched her face and squeezed her eyes shut.

"You've got your work cut out for you," I said.

"There's no way you'll find a place that fast," Ben said. "Not in this town. The market's tight."

I nodded, remembering what Harper had said before she'd lucked into her apartment.

"Something will turn up." Emerson's voice wasn't as sure as her words.

"Why don't you plan to stay with me for a couple of months. That'll give you a place to land and some time to look," Ben said.

"I can't impose like that. Not with these two." Emerson nodded toward her kids.

Ben grinned. "I hardly think two small humans plus you will make a dent with me, two kids, two llamas, a coop full of chickens, a rooster, three horses, two dogs, and a handful of cats."

"You, too, can move into the zoo," I joked.

"These two sometimes smell like a zoo," Emerson said. "Ben, I can't do that to you."

He shrugged. "I've got room. You know that. But if you need to be stubborn first and waste a couple of weeks looking for a place while packing an entire house, that's your right. My offer will be there."

I watched the back-and-forth, doing my best not to weigh in. It wasn't my business, but Ben made sense.

Emerson looked at me. "Happen to know of a long-term rental that'll take a dog and six chickens?"

I laughed. "I don't. It's November though. The

real estate market is probably deader than its usual dead. Is it the llamas holding you back?"

Instead of laughing at my joke, she frowned, as if the llamas were indeed an issue.

"Do you have a girlfriend you could move in with?" I asked, flipping to help mode. "One without llamas?"

"The llamas stay outside," Ben said as if we were idiots.

Emerson seemed to be thinking through options while Xavier pulled at her arm to ask if she'd buy him a crystal.

"The holidays are around the corner, your busiest time at the salon," Ben said. "You have two young children and a four-bedroom house to pack in three weeks. You're more than competent, Emerson, but you don't have superpowers." That seemed to get through to her as she closed her eyes, tilted her head back, and took in a tight breath. "You can stay with us until the end of the year, then find a place without all the pressure."

Emerson's eyes were still closed, but she was nodding. "Yes. You're right." Her eyes popped open, and she pegged him with an intense look. "Are you *sure*?"

"Of course," Ben said, his tone light. "It's what I do. Usually four-legged creatures, but we can do humans too."

"Bless you. Thank you. I accept. And now I need to get these two home." She put her hand on Ben's arm and squeezed in gratitude, then picked up Skyler, grabbed Xavier's hand, and rushed off with a "Bye, Max," over her shoulder.

I was on the verge of cracking a joke about Ben's tendency to rescue when a look flashed over his face that stopped me. It was gone before I could blink.

"Is there something going on between you two?" I asked quietly.

"What? No. Not at all. I'm just looking after her like Blake would want."

Before I could comment on that, Harper waltzed up to us, all grins. "You two look like the hired muscle over here."

I slid my hand around her, to her back, because damn if I could keep myself from touching her bare skin. Harper sidled up against me and kissed me soundly, her happy, joyful energy surging into me. "It's almost toast time. Then we're hitting Humble's afterward," she announced.

No, we weren't. But she didn't know that. "Who's we?"

"Dakota, Cambria, me, you, whoever else wants to. Ben, you're welcome."

He gestured to Ruby, who rested her head on his shoulder, as if to say, *no can do*, while I scanned for my sister across the crowded room. Dakota was behind the checkout counter, helping a customer, but she caught my gaze and gave me a subtle nod and a wink. She was my coconspirator, so she knew Harper wouldn't be there.

In the next five minutes, plastic champagne flutes were distributed and filled with bubbly or sparkling juice. Harper headed back to the counter and her business partners, then climbed on a chair so she towered above everyone. Someone in the crowd whistled to get people's attention.

"Thank you!" the breathtaking love of my life said as the crowd shut up. "Thanks to every one of you for coming out to support us. We appreciate you! This store was Cambria's baby originally, but she volun-told me to do the talking tonight," she said to a scattering of laughter.

She might pretend she wasn't good at speaking, but once again she was winging it, and once again I knew she'd have the crowd in her hands.

"First, I want to make sure everyone knows about that corner over there." She nodded toward the front corner opposite the door. "That's our Naomi Finley collection. Everything there was made by my dear friend Naomi before she died. Art was her life, and as you can see, she was gifted beyond compare." Harper stopped and swallowed hard, took a breath. Dakota squeezed her hand.

"Not only did Naomi's brother, Ian, help fund

our venture," Harper continued, keeping my name out of it as I'd requested, "but he also donated Naomi's artwork. Anytime you buy something from Naomi's corner, all the money will go toward her pet cause, bringing art supplies and instruction to schools. Naomi's love and giving spirit will live on in that little corner for as long as we have her work to sell."

The crowd applauded, with most of them craning their necks toward that section of the store as if giving it a closer look.

"It would make my heart happy if you'd drink a toast to dear, talented Naomi. I wouldn't be up here today if I'd never met her. Cheers, my friend." Harper raised her glass and her gaze toward heaven, her eyes sparkling with moisture.

The crowd hollered out a collection of "hear, hear" and "cheers."

"Second, I want to give all of you the biggest, most heartfelt thanks for showing up and supporting our shop. This..." She looked around from above, seeming to really take in the space and the people, then shook her head with a wide smile of disbelief, happiness, and gratitude. "This is beyond my wildest dreams, to be honest. I feel so lucky to be on this adventure with Cambria and Dakota, my partners and friends." She raised her glass and made eye contact with each of them below her. "So cheers to these two incredible women I get to work with every day, and cheers to every single one of you here tonight." She lifted her glass again. "I am *blessed*."

Again there was a collective "cheers" and "here's to you, ladies." Harper climbed down, and the three of them group hugged.

"I'm happy for them," Ben said after finishing his half glass of bubbly. "I need to get these two princesses home to bed. Best of luck to you." He gave me a knowing look.

"Thanks. Good night," I said, my nerves going taut because showtime was nearing. A line had formed at the register, with people ready to cash out and go home. I made my way over to the side of the counter, plotting my next move.

Harper's dad gave her a tight hug and told her how proud of her he was, said good night to me with an approving wink, and took his leave.

As Dakota rung up the last person in line a few minutes later and Cambria straightened the store, Harper hugged me again.

"Thank you. For everything from convincing me to *get more info* weeks ago to investing in us."

I kissed her. "You're welcome. You're going to do amazing things. The temperature's dropped outside, so why don't we go upstairs and get you something to put over your sexy dress."

Dakota caught my eye as I said it, telling me she understood the plan.

"I'll be right back, Dakota," Harper said, then took my hand and led me away.

I shook my head at my sister as if to say, *no, she won't*, grinning on my way out.

Piper had finally showed up at the shop, I noticed as we went to the back room. That was a good sign everything was ready.

As we went up the stairs, my heart raced. I'd been planning for so long, yet I had no idea how Harper would react. It was absolutely possible I was crazy in this.

Fuck, I hoped like hell I wasn't crazy in this.

At the door, we paused, and Harper unlocked it with one hand, her other still holding mine. She glanced up at me with a pretty, unsuspecting smile.

I held my breath as she pushed the door open. Before I could see inside, she gasped.

"Oh, my God." She stopped in the doorway, preventing me from seeing Piper's work. "Max. What the—"

She looked back at me and noted my grin.

"What did you do, Max?"

"I didn't do anything. I've been downstairs all evening."

Laughing, she burst into her apartment and spun around, taking in all the details.

There were candles, dozens of LED candles, all of them flickering, casting enough light to see the flower petals, which were everywhere, in every color. No monotone roses for my girl. I'd insisted Piper make sure every color in the rainbow was generously represented in the mix of thousands of petals she and her helpers had scattered throughout the room, leaving a distinct, bare path to the deck door.

"Are we supposed to go out there?" she asked.

"Looks that way," I said, laughing, loving every ounce of her reaction so far—and we hadn't even gotten to the good stuff.

Harper led me to the rooftop deck, where there were dozens more candles and petals, the bistro table set for two with multicolored tapers, handmade by Cambria, waiting to be lit, and two covered plates emanating a heavenly, savory aroma. Nearby was an outdoor heater, pumping away.

"Who..." Harper went over to the table and lifted one of the covers. "What...? Max, this is incredible. Did you do all this?"

"Let's just say I arranged it. Piper was in charge of decorating. Surf and turf dinner is compliments of Cash Henry."

She covered her mouth with both hands and took in the scene with a look of wonder. When I sidled up next to her, she threw her arms around my neck and kissed me. "This is to celebrate?"

"Of course," I said. "If you can handle more champagne." I pointed to the bottle chilling in an elegant bucket.

She was about to sit down when I went down to one knee beside her and said, "But first..."

Harper turned to look at me, first glancing up where my head would normally be, then realizing where I was. A heartbeat later, she gasped again, covered her mouth with both hands, and stared down at me, her eyes shining.

I reached deep into my pocket and took out the little velvet box. My hands were shaking. I popped it open to reveal the round-cut diamond with rubies on each side. I took one of her hands in mine and plunged ahead, thankful I'd rehearsed what I wanted to say until I was blue in the face.

"Harper," I said, peering into those beautiful brown eyes, "you're my first thought in the morning, my last thought before sleeping, and the reason I'm excited to wake up every day. You and Danny are the family I didn't dare to hope for. I thought he and I were doing pretty well, getting through the days. Then you came along, and boom! Our black-and-white lives suddenly turned into a vivid rainbow. You bring joy and lightness to me and remind me to take myself less seriously. I love you, Harper

Ellison, and I don't want to live without you." I swallowed, my heart thundering. "Will you marry me?"

She blinked, and two streams of tears ran down her cheeks. I stopped breathing. She was crying? Were they happy tears? Or was she about to crush me?

Then she nodded and laughed through the tears. "Yes!" She bounced up and down, one hand still over her mouth, her eyes sparkling.

That was all I needed to hear. I stood and wrapped my arms around her, ring box still in my hand, and lifted her off the ground. I'd never felt so overcome with emotions. I funneled all of them— joy, relief, love, devotion, hope—into a kiss, setting her down so I could cradle her head and get serious about it.

I poured all of it into her, and she gave me everything in return. When she broke contact, she lovingly ran her palms over my cheeks as she gazed into my eyes.

"You're the forever I didn't know I was ready for. You and Danny are everything to me, Max. I love you to the end of time and then some." She laughed, sheer elation bubbling out of her. "And that ring! Stop teasing, Max."

Hell, I'd forgotten to slide the ring on because I was so swept away by this woman that I couldn't

wait to get my lips on hers. I brought the box between us, plucked the ring out of its cushion, took
her left hand, and with my hands still shaking, slid
it onto her ring finger.

"It's stunning, Max," she said in a breathy voice.

"I hope you like it. You needed something with
color. If you'd prefer something besides rubies, we
can change them."

"It's perfect. I love it. I love you. I can't wait to
marry you."

"We should celebrate," I said with a glance at
the table, "before the food gets cold. We can join
your friends afterward if you want."

She shook her head. "Surf and turf, champagne,
then you naked. That's how I want to celebrate. All
night long."

"I'm yours, Harper. All night long, every night,
forever."

Bonus Epilogue

Max

"**A**re you ready for this?" Veronica Jones, our wedding photographer, asked as she and I walked to the west side of the Honeysuckle Inn.

"You better believe it," I said, unable to rein in the wide smile on my face.

I'd been ready for this day—the day I got to marry Harper—for seven months. Or maybe a lifetime.

Two years ago though, when my cousin Jamie and his wife died and I'd been granted full responsibility for Daniel, I hadn't been able to see it. Hadn't been able to imagine ever expanding Danny's and my world to include a third. I'd been paralyzed with that responsibility and determined to do whatever was best for my little boy.

I understood now Harper was not only what was best for *me,* but she was exactly what Danny needed too. The three of us together were the family of my dreams. Harper completed me and made me a better man, and she loved my son as much as I did and added a maternal touch we'd been lacking. She was the softness to my hard edges, the laughter to my seriousness, the well-rounded to my sports-minded self.

"You got a gorgeous day, Max." Veronica surveyed the honeysuckle garden as we reached it. "This is going to be perfect for your first look at your bride."

An honest-to-God giddiness bubbled up inside of me as I imagined the moment that was finally, *finally* drawing closer. Our lakefront ceremony was slated to begin at five, allowing time for aperitifs afterward on the sprawling patio that overlooked Dragonfly Lake and then a full dinner in the ballroom and dancing into the night. The timing made sense, but this had been one long day of anticipation.

"You'll stand over here, in the shade of the trees, so when you turn to see your bride, I can capture everything without the sun messing up my lighting.

Harper will come from this side," she said, using her whole body to demonstrate the setup one last time. "She'll stop right here in front of the bench and the honeysuckle backdrop."

The flowering bushes were stunning with their fuchsia blooms that would match the bridesmaids' dresses, but even if the shrubs were brown and dried out, it wouldn't take away from the moment when I laid eyes on the love of my life in her white gown.

I checked my watch. Three minutes till Harper would make her way out to me. I couldn't wait to see her, knew she'd be stunning and likely take my breath away, but I also couldn't wait to touch her, wrap my arms around her, feel her body against mine. I wasn't used to not seeing her for most of a day, particularly after not having her in my bed last night.

Though she stayed at my place frequently, last night she and her bridesmaids—Dakota, Cambria, and Harper's sister, Ashley—had rented rooms at the inn to prep for today. I was happy she was having the bridal experience she wanted. I wanted everything to be perfect for her, and I was sure they'd had a special girls' evening.

But honestly? I didn't at all care for waking up without her by my side.

"Okay," Veronica said after checking her

camera yet again and reading a message on her phone, "Dakota's about to send her out. Ready to take your place?"

In response, I went to the far side of the small stone terrace and stood with my back to the inn, my heart pounding in my chest as I noticed the scent of the honeysuckle. Sweet. Feminine. Like Harper.

My soon-to-be wife.

For the first time today, I was jittery with nervousness. I couldn't say why other than the anticipation was killing me.

"She's on her way," Veronica singsonged. I could hear the smile in her voice, discerned her last-minute movements as she disappeared into the background, as she'd promised.

All was quiet as seconds ticked by, with the only sound birdsong. Then I heard footsteps approaching, and my heart felt like it was lodged in my throat with all the anticipation of the past twelve hours, the past week, the past months as we planned this momentous occasion.

Harper, the woman I was going to marry, was nearly to the small, private garden terrace.

"Stunning," Veronica whispered behind me.

It was all I could do to not whip around to see.

"Don't move, Max," the photographer coached. "Almost time, I promise. And this beautiful girl will be worth every second of the wait."

I nodded, clenched my hand in my front pocket, nearly came out of my skin with eagerness.

Veronica's camera clicked repeatedly as she apparently shot Harper's approach. Then she came closer to me and took my profile.

I closed my eyes, worried I might turn too early and mess up our big moment.

"Almost, Max," Veronica said, seeming to flutter from one spot to another.

Then everything went silent again, but I felt Harper come closer, felt her presence like a crackle in the air.

The two of us stood there, a few feet apart, counting to ten like Veronica had coached us to do ahead of time. Every second was an eternity as my emotions built up and the significance of this moment settled into my blood.

"Turn around, Max," Harper said in a quiet, eternally familiar voice.

I swallowed and pivoted and...stopped breathing.

My gaze locked on hers, took in her beautiful, nervous smile.

A volcano of emotion erupted from me, and I couldn't immediately speak, couldn't do anything but reach for her hand, pull her to me, and rest my forehead against hers, knowing she was my heart, my soul mate. The reason for everything I'd been through in my life, both good and bad, was so that I would end up in this moment with this woman. With this future.

"Oh, my God, Max," she said in a shaky voice that told me she was as overcome as I was. "You're so handsome and hot."

We both laughed nervously, like a couple of preteens on a first date, which made me laugh harder. I sucked in a breath and tried to get a grip on myself, at least enough to speak.

"Harper," I finally managed. "You're stunning. Gorgeous."

I put enough space between us that I could fully drink in the sight of her.

Once again my lungs locked up. Love of God and all that was holy, this woman...

"What you do to me..." I managed.

Her dress was incredible. She in that dress was incredible.

It was lacy everywhere, with delicate straps and a neckline that dipped down nearly to her belly button, revealing her bronzed skin. White lace hugged her curves mermaid style to mid-thigh, where yards of sheer, gossamer fabric and lace billowed behind her.

Her hair was up, with braids and twists and tiny hot pink flowers adorning it. To me, she looked like a cover model, with flawless skin, a hint of pink in her cheeks, and gorgeous long-lashed brown eyes.

"Wow," I breathed out. "I love the dress. I love you. You take my breath away."

"Yeah?" she said, as if she didn't know what she did to me on any given day. Never mind in a fairy-tale white dress.

"How," I said in a low, nearly private voice as I traced my finger along her body from the delicate diamond dangling from her neck, down between her breasts, and dipping to where the plunging neckline ended on her abdomen, "am I supposed to focus on my vows when you look like my wildest fantasy come true?"

She trailed her hands up my chest and around my neck. "I have every bit of confidence in you."

I kissed her, the touch of her lips on mine as crucial as oxygen in that instant.

Harper pulled her mouth away just enough to grin and say, "I'm going to marry you today."

I closed my eyes, drew her in for another kiss, thanked my lucky stars for bringing this woman into my life.

Abruptly, Harper stiffened, ended the kiss, lowered her hands to my chest, and dipped her chin.

"What's wrong?" I asked, still dazed with love and joy.

She took a step away, then another, and the

message got through to me that something really was wrong.

"I..." She was breathing heavily, took in a slow breath through her nose, her eyes closed. "I'm gonna be sick." She rushed to the edge of the bushes, nearly tripping on her dress.

I hurried to her as understanding started to sink in. As she leaned over the greenery, I braced her with one hand on her middle and the other sweeping the piles of white fabric back out of the way.

My concern skyrocketed as Harper emptied her stomach, my mind spinning with thoughts of what could be wrong. Bad food? Flu? Nerves? Was she questioning getting married? She didn't seem to be five minutes ago but...

"Here," Veronica said, handing me an un-opened bottle of water as Harper straightened, her eyes still closed.

"Thanks." I held the bottle out for Harper, who looked paler, her face drawn, but she didn't take it. "What do you need?" I asked her. I tried to bite my tongue against firing a bunch of questions at her, but I couldn't hold them in. "Are you getting sick? Do you need a doctor? Is this nerves? Are you having second thoughts?"

Holy fuck. What if she was having second thoughts?

———

Harper

I was afraid to open my eyes, afraid I'd be dizzy again if I did.

I sucked in another deep, shaky breath, feeling a little better with each second that passed.

Max still held on to my arm, his grasp light but solid.

"My dress..." I said.

"You missed your dress. You missed everything but the plants. Impressive," he said in a low voice. "Let's sit you down. I've got water."

I nodded, then finally willed my lids up, relieved to have Max by my side even if I was mortified at the same time. I knew he wouldn't let me fall over if I had another spell.

I exhaled as I registered a lack of dizziness. Thank God. I was still shaky and weak, but I felt so much better. Turning my head slowly, I gauged the distance to the bench and glanced down at my dress. It wasn't far unless you were enrobed in miles of fabric.

"I'll get your train, sweetie," Veronica said in a

gentle voice as she bent down behind me and gathered and straightened at once.

"I've got you," Max said.

I made it to the bench, and Max swiped his fingers over it to ensure it was clean. At his nod, I lowered myself, with Veronica adjusting my dress out of the way as much as possible.

"Do you need me to get anything for you, Harper?" Veronica asked.

I shook my head as I took the water bottle from Max. "Just this for now. Thank you." I sipped it gratefully, carefully, not wanting to set my stomach off again.

"I'll give you two some time," Veronica said. "If I can get you anything, text me. I'll be over there." She nodded toward the side entrance then stepped away.

Max squatted in front of me and gazed up into my eyes, his concern twisting my heart.

This wasn't how this day was supposed to go.

It wasn't exactly how my life was supposed to go, but I knew we'd figure it out eventually.

First though...today. Right now. Poor Max.

"I'm okay," I said, managing to smile. "Well, super embarrassed that you had to hold my dress so I didn't yak all over it."

"Are you coming down with something? Do we

need to push back our start time? What can I do, Harper?"

Good questions, those. The only one I had an answer to was the first one.

"I'm not coming down with something." I glanced around to ensure we were still alone, thankful that the bushes mostly blocked us from view of anyone going in the main entrance. I patted the bench next to me. "Sit with me?"

"I swear to God if you're jilting me—"

That made me laugh. "Are you serious right now? I'm not jilting you."

Max sat next to me.

"I need breath mints," I said. "Or a tube of toothpaste. A toothbrush would be good."

"We'll get you all of them. First tell me what's going on."

Again I breathed in deeply, both to stave off nausea and gather my courage. I reached for his hand, took comfort in the strength of it as he entwined our fingers.

"I'm pregnant," I said quietly.

I dared a glance at Max's face, worried he'd be frowning. His mouth was gaping open, then his lips tilted toward a smile. A disbelieving, shellshocked smile.

I could so relate.

"Harper." He wrapped his arm around me,

pulled me into his side, tilted his head to mine, and just...held me.

I rested my head against his shoulder and grasped his other hand. "I know this isn't what we planned."

He laughed quietly, joyfully. "Not what we planned but I don't care. Harper," he said again, and I felt him shake his head. Then he stopped, straightened. "Are you okay with this?"

My throat clogged up with all the emotion and overwhelm I'd been wrangling with since first thing this morning when I'd found out, so I merely nodded and fought to keep the tears in check. It was definitely a cry-worthy moment, but I didn't want to ruin my makeup. Emerson had spent so much time getting it perfect, and it was almost time for photos.

Which meant we didn't have the luxury of sitting and talking about this for hours, not now. After today, we'd have the rest of our lives though.

"How long have you known?" Max asked.

"I just figured it out this morning. I've been super tired, but I figured that was normal with all the stress of planning and preparation. The last two days, I woke up feeling nauseated, and then I realized my period is late. Like, I can't remember when my last one was. Dakota went to Runner and picked up a test for me first thing."

"So she knows?"

I nodded. "She's the only one. I wanted you to be the first, but I couldn't just pop into the Country Market on my wedding day and buy pregnancy tests."

Max laughed, and God, I loved that sound. The familiarity of it, the security of it.

"I need to hug you properly but..." His voice trailed off as he gestured to my gown. "Your gorgeous getup doesn't make it easy."

"Plus I need breath mints."

"I'll text Dakota. If she doesn't have any, she can get some."

"We sell them at the store."

He typed into his phone, slid it back into his pocket, and stood. "I don't care about breath mints. Come here, my beautiful wife-to-be."

I let him help me up, feeling only a trace of dizziness, then fell intentionally into his arms.

"I love you," he said quietly. "Like, crazy love you, Harper."

"I love you too, Max." We held each other for a few seconds.

He trailed kisses along my jawline, then said in my ear, in the sexiest voice, "We're gonna have a baby."

I squeezed my eyes shut, smiling and yet again fighting off tears, merely nodding.

He ran his hand down to my belly, and we stood there, taking everything in.

This was hands down the best day of my life.

"Incoming," Dakota sang out, intruding on our moment.

I straightened, dabbed at my eyes, and held out my hand for the mints.

"You told him," she whispered knowingly as she handed me a tin. I popped one in my mouth.

Max nodded and wiped his eyes, and let me tell you, *that* got to me even more than everything else. This man...he was everything to me.

Dakota hugged her brother, told him congratulations, and sniffled herself. "You two are going to kill me with the feels today," she said as she stepped back.

"You haven't told anyone?" Max asked.

Dakota rolled her eyes. "No. I won't. Even if it *is* killing me." She held up a little bottle. "I brought you this."

"Peppermint. Amazing." I took it from her, unscrewed the lid, and sniffed the essential oil we carried in our store. "It helps with nausea," I told Max. "The trick will be stashing it on me somewhere. This dress doesn't have a lot of room in it."

"That dress hides nothing," Max said in a growl, "and I love it."

Dakota made a sound of disgust, then moved

closer to me. "Put a drop on your finger and dab it at the base of your nostrils. Ongoing peppermint action. I'll keep the bottle on me. Maybe I can stuff it in my flowers."

"You're the best." I did what she said and inhaled deeply, starting to feel a little steadier. "Thank you."

"It's time for pics. Let's go." Dakota headed off around the side of the building, toward the area on the shore set up for our ceremony.

Max caught my hand and pulled me into his arms again. I took another mint, then slipped the tin into his front pocket. Only then did I dare to stretch up and press a kiss to his lips.

Before he could react, I said, "Let's go get married, Max."

———

Max

Hours later, I barely remembered our wedding ceremony because I'd been so lost in Harper's beauty and thoughts of our future, our family, our life.

We'd made it through all the photos and the aperitifs with Harper going through mints like crazy, not so much to freshen her breath—she'd brushed her teeth—but because she swore on the power of peppermint, both in the mints and under her nose. It'd worked so far.

At dinner, she'd assuaged some of my concern by eating heartily, confessing quietly to me that she'd barely eaten all day before that, which might've contributed to her nausea earlier.

My brother, Levi, had the whole crowd in tears with laughter during his best-man speech. As everyone tried to recover, my sister had elicited even more sniffles, her maid-of-honor speech going sappy and emotional instead of funny. If I had to plan a wedding again with those two, I'd pass out tissues beforehand.

Harper had changed from her sexy long gown into a short, backless, sequined reception dress that did nothing to calm the fire inside of me and the need to get her alone so I could peel it off her. That was my wife—she could turn me on in a potato sack, but she loved to dress in clothing that showed as much as it hid. I fucking loved it.

Now, finally, we stood face-to-face, hands entwined, and I rested my forehead against hers as we waited for our song to start for the bridal dance. The first notes of "King of My Heart" played, and I pulled her body into mine.

"Wife," I said to her, still unable to believe there could be so much bliss in that one word.

"Husband," she replied with a musical laugh.

The song was faster than a lot I'd heard for the first dance, but it fit us perfectly, especially the part about our love being secret at first. She claimed the title fit, and I assured her she was also the queen of my heart.

I loved the way she moved, whether it was to music or not, to an upbeat song or our medium one, as she swayed those hips just so.

"You're good at dancing," I said as I smiled down at her.

"So are you, sexy husband."

"So much for it taking two to tango, huh? For us, it's three."

We shared a secret look as the song played on, the rest of the world fading away from my awareness.

"How much longer do we have to stay at our own wedding for the sake of propriety?" I asked her.

Harper's answer was slightly breathless. "I'm not sure, but I know it has to be longer than the first few dances." She feigned an innocent look. "Why do you ask? Are you in a hurry for some reason, Mr. Dawson?"

"You know exactly what I'm talking about, Mrs. Dawson," I growled.

My beautiful wife laughed, and I challenged myself to make her laugh every day.

"I'm pretty sure," I said as the song continued,

"that peppermint will be an aphrodisiac for me until the day I die."

"I'm pretty sure," she flipped right back, "I'll do everything in my power to ensure you don't need an aphrodisiac for the rest of your life."

I took in the mischievous sparkle in her eyes and pulled her body even closer. "It's working so far," I said, "and I'm feeling good about the next fifty years."

She looked up at me with so much love in her gaze. "So am I."

Note from the Author

Thanks for reading *Singled Out*! I hope you loved Max and Harper.

Next up is Single All the Way, Ben and Emerson's story. Watch for it in late 2024!

If you missed the Henry Brothers series, you can dive into book one, *Unraveled*! Find out how a marriage of convenience can test even the best of friends!

Find *Unraveled* in ebook, audiobook, and paperback in my author store at amyknuppbooks.com!

———

If you liked *Singled Out*, I hope you'll consider leaving a review for it. Reviews help other readers find books and can be as short (or long) as you feel comfortable with. Just a couple sentences is all it takes. I appreciate all honest reviews.

———

Singled Out is part of the Single Dads of Dragonfly Lake series, which includes:

- Singled Out
- Single All the Way

Also by Amy Knupp

<u>Single Dads of Dragonfly Lake</u>

Singled Out

Single All the Way

<u>Henry Brothers Series</u>

Untold (prequel)

Unraveled

Unsung

Undone

Unexpected

Or binge the Henry Brothers in audio:

Henry Brothers Audiobooks

<u>North Brothers Series</u>

True North

True Colors

True Blue

True Harmony

True Hero

North Brothers Box Sets:

North Brothers Books 1-3

North Brothers Books 4-5

North Brothers: The Complete Series

Or binge the North Brothers in audio:

North Brothers Audiobooks

Hale Street Series:

Sweet Spot

Sweet Dreams

Soft Spot

One and Only

Last First Kiss

Heartstrings

Hale Street Box Sets:

Meet Me at Clayborne's

Clayborne's After Hours

It Happened on Hale Street

Island Fire Series:

Playing with Fire

Heat of the Night

Fully Involved

Firestorm

Afterburn

Up in Flames

Flash Point

Fire Within

Impulse

Slow Burn

Island Fire Box Sets:

Sparked (books 1-3)

Ignited (books 4-6)

Enflamed (books 7-10)

OR

Island Fire: The Complete Series

<u>Themed Bundles</u>

Opposites Attract

Grumpy-Sunshine

Cinnamon Roll Heroes

Childhood Crush

Forbidden Love

Friends to Lovers

Coming Home

Musicians

Second Chance

Workplace Romance

North Brothers Audiobooks

About the Author

Amy Knupp is a *USA Today* Best-Selling author of contemporary romance. She loves words and grammar and meaty, engrossing stories with complex characters.

Amy lives in Wisconsin with her husband and has two adult children, two cats, and a box turtle. She graduated from the University of Kansas with degrees in French and journalism. In her spare time, she enjoys traveling, breaking up cat fights, watching college hoops, and annoying her family by correcting their grammar.

For more information:
https://www.amyknuppbooks.com